WITHDRAWN

BRUTE STRENGTH

The new 'Holly Winter' dog mystery

When *Dog's Life* columnist Holly Winter rejects applicants who want to adopt homeless dogs, she makes a lot of enemies. In dogs Holly trusts, and the dogs she trusts most are her beloved malamutes, Rowdy, Kimi and Sammy. But right now she could use a human friend. Lately, it seems wherever she turns, things go wrong: an anonymous call turns vicious, her husband is keeping secrets, and acquaintances die under mysterious circumstances. Then Holly's own life is threatened. Can the brute strength of Rowdy, Kimi, and Sammy protect her...

BRUTE STRENGTH

A Dog Lover's Mystery

Susan Conant

Severn House Large Print
London & New York

This first large print edition published 2012
in Great Britain and the USA by
SEVERN HOUSE PUBLISHERS LTD of
9-15 High Street, Sutton, Surrey, SM1 1DF.
First world regular print edition published 2011 by
Severn House Publishers Ltd., London and New York.

British Library Cataloguing in Publication Data

Conant, Susan, 1946-
  Brute strength.
  1. Winter, Holly (Fictitious character)--Fiction. 2. Dog
  trainers--United States--Fiction. 3. Detective and
  mystery stories. 4. Large type books.
  I. Title
  813.6-dc23

ISBN-13: 978-0-7278-7998-1

Severn House Publishers support The Forest Stewardship Council
[FSC], the leading international forest certification organisation. All
our titles that are printed on Greenpeace-approved FSC-certified paper
carry the FSC logo.

MIX
Paper from
responsible sources
FSC® C018575

Printed and bound in Great Britain by the
MPG Books Group, Bodmin, Cornwall.

To Jessica, Bill, and Nicholas in loving memory of Samantha (1993–2008), who was half Labrador retriever, half heaven knows what, and total perfection.

Acknowledgments

Many thanks to Rob Rabouin, Steve Rabouin, and Kenneth Clifton for technical advice. I am also grateful to Jean Berman, Roseann Mandell, Lillian Sober-Ain, Geoff Stern, Anya Wittenborg, and Corinne Zipps, and my editor, Anna Telfer.

ONE

One rainy Saturday morning in April, I was grooming dogs and making enemies when a fight broke out in the little hallway outside my kitchen door. If the combatants had been dogs, I'd have transformed myself into whatever larger-than-life figure the conflict demanded. Shazam! Billy Batson becomes Captain Marvel! Or in my case, Holly Winter, dog trainer and dog writer, turns into ... Gandhi! He's a useful alter ego, but strictly for resolving minor canine quibbles and tiffs. I haven't had to become General Patton in ages. When I do, I'm ferocious: *Listen, you dogs of war! This is Old Blood and Guts telling you to cut it out before the entire Third Army moves in and takes no prisoners!* But that's a lie. First of all, the closest I've ever come to serving in the military is attending dog-training classes at the Cambridge Armory. Second, I do take prisoners: miscreants get locked in their crates until I've metamorphosed back into Ms Sangfroid. The surest way to lose a dog's respect is to blow your cool.

So, over the years, I've learned to replace brute strength with a sneaky non-violence that owes more to Machiavelli than to the Mahatma.

9

I am, however, a dog trainer. I don't do people. Hence my hesitation.

'...not to be where I don't belong, Rita, and I don't—'

The voice belonged to Quinn Youngman, the man in the life of my friend and tenant Rita, who cut him off. 'Don't you Dylan me, Quinn! The only Bob Dylan you heard until you'd finished medical school was some easy-listening Muzak version of *Blowin' in the Wind*, if that, so don't play Dr Hip with me, because I know better. If Willie bit you – and it's a mega *if* – it was because *you* stepped on his paw.'

So, the fight was a dog fight after all. Rita's Scottish terrier, Willie, was a handsome, spunky, stylish fellow with flashing eyes and, on occasion, flashing teeth. The worst of Quinn's claim was thus its credibility. I'd cured Willie of flying at my ankles, but he hadn't necessarily generalized from my ankles to other people's. Never before, though, had Willie ever even nipped. Had he wanted to? Oh, yes. But he had superb self-control. Bite inhibition. He was a dog who understood never to put his teeth on flesh. Or so I'd believed, anyway. But as any dog expert will tell you, if the circumstances are perfectly wrong, any dog will bite. Lassie. Benji. Rin Tin Tin.

'With one of your big, heavy, affected, and totally unnecessary hiking boots! Here we are, a fifteen-minute walk from Harvard Square, which is the only place you're ever likely to hike to, and for that, you couldn't just wear ordinary shoes?'

'Suddenly you're a fitness expert, Rita? You? She of the bound feet?'

'I like high heels. So did you until five minutes ago.'

'When your goddamned dog bit me.'

That was when Rita really started hollering. *'You* stomped on Willie's foot. And he did *not* break the skin. In fact, I am far from sure that he *bit* you at all.'

'Rita, I am bleeding,' Quinn shouted back. 'Bleeding!'

As Rita had mentioned, Quinn was a doctor, but he was a psychiatrist whose specialty was psychopharmacology. According to Rita, Quinn was a clinical genius when it came to prescribing anti-anxiety agents, antidepressant medications, antipsychotic drugs, and anti-so-forth-and-so-ons, presumably including pills, capsules, liquids, and miscellaneous other elixirs that helped patients to become calm, cheery, or compos mentis enough to benefit from talking to Rita, who is a clinical psychologist. Still, Quinn presumably remembered enough from medical school to recognize blood when he saw it.

Rita, however, responded by lowering her voice and delivering a shrink's version of a low blow. 'Hysteria is not helping. And it's very unbecoming.'

'I am not hysterical!' he shrieked. 'I am never hysterical!'

My animals are unused to raised voices. My

11

cat, Tracker, was in my office, which is her abode. India and Lady, the two dogs who'd have reacted strongly, were with my husband, Steve, as was one of our three malamutes, Rowdy, who was having his teeth cleaned. Let me hasten to explain that Steve is not a dentist. He's a veterinarian. Anyway, when the ruckus started, I'd been in the kitchen grooming our other two malamutes, Kimi and Sammy. If India, our German shepherd dog, had been there, she'd have interpreted the shouting as a threat to our household. Lady, our timid pointer, would've been frightened silly. Our King of the Castle, Rowdy the Unflappable, would've assumed that no matter what the nature of the dispute, he'd have the brawn and brains to come out on top. In fact, Kimi is even more brilliant than Rowdy. Furthermore, she is fearless. As to Sammy, even I, a dog professional, am baffled by him. Rowdy's son, Sammy, too, is a dark gray and white intact male Alaskan malamute and a successful show dog. Furthermore, Sammy is immensely strong, ridiculously friendly, obsessed with food, and otherwise absolutely typical of his breed. There is, however, a naivety about Sammy's open-hearted innocence that always amazes me. If Sammy encounters a snarling dog, he looks at me with wide-eyed surprise, as if he can't believe that there's a creature on earth who doesn't love him. In some previous existence, perhaps he was a flower child.

All this is to say that Kimi needed no protection from the ugly sounds of Rita and Quinn's

12

fight, whereas Sammy, who was on the grooming table, leaned into me and trained those trusting brown eyes on my presumably all-knowing face. 'Nothing to worry about, Mr Handsome,' I said. Even so, I got him off the table and into the wire crate that lives in the kitchen, and I put Kimi in a down-stay.

Then I opened the back door. When Quinn was at his best, he wasn't the sort of person to whom you could say, 'Cut that out! You're upsetting my dog!' That's a damning comment on his character. But my opinion of Quinn didn't matter. Rita's did. So, instead of blurting out the raw truth, I said, 'I couldn't help overhearing. Quinn, if you've been bitten, you should wash the wound. I have first-aid stuff.'

I'll concede that Quinn was not bad looking. He was tall and had the kind of distinguished air that appeals to Rita. As she'd said, he had on heavy hiking boots. They hadn't left bloody tracks on the floor or on the stairs that run up to her third-floor apartment. Blood would've soaked right through the fabric of his khakis. I saw no sign of blood on him at all. The person who looked wounded was Rita: her pretty face was so bloodless that her careful make-up was identifiable as such, and her artfully streaked cap of dark hair was mussed, as if she'd been running her manicured hands through it. Although she was dressed in her New Yorker's idea of an informal outfit – a beige linen jacket and pants, a white shell, and relatively low-heeled leather shoes – her distress made her look almost childlike, especially by comparison with Quinn, who was twenty years her senior.

'I'm on my way to Mount Auburn,' he snapped.

The glorious red hair that runs in my family bypassed me, but I have traces of the quick temper. I said, 'Mount Auburn Hospital, I presume. Not Mount Auburn Cemetery.' Civility kicked in, as did loyalty to Rita, whose view of this pompous SOB was different from mine. 'Sorry,' I said. 'Do you want a ride to the ER?'

'I have my Lexus,' he said. Typical! Since Quinn owned only one vehicle, a simple 'I have my car' would've been unambiguous. If fate presented my husband, Steve, with a Rolls, he'd call it 'my car'. Actually, Steve would be so embarrassed by the evidence of conspicuous consumption that he'd get rid of the Rolls before he had time to call it anything.

Without saying goodbye to either Rita or me, Quinn left.

'Do we need to check Willie out?' I asked. 'His paw?'

'That was the first thing I did. Quinn felt slighted. But Willie is fine.'

'Steve can take a look later. Come in. If you don't mind...'

'...dog hair,' she said.

'Everyone's shedding. I'm not exactly grooming. I'm just doing preventive housework. Kimi and Sammy. The other dogs are with Steve.'

The kitchen was less hairy than you might expect, mainly because I'd been taking breaks to vacuum up undercoat. I shoved the grooming table out of the way, stowed the forced-air dryer and the Dyson canister vac under it, gave the dogs free run of the kitchen, and started making coffee.

'I keep reminding myself that Quinn is in good therapy,' said Rita, for whom psychotherapy is a religious vocation. From her priestly viewpoint, those fifty-minute hours are sacred rites. She believes in the power of her chosen form of prayer. For once, I refrained from saying anything about dog worship, the Sacred Animal, God's woofing, furry proof of celestial design and thus of boundless, bounding, leaping, panting love in this otherwise bleak universe; nor did I point out the mundane and obvious, namely that Quinn's accusation against a representative of the above mentioned Sacred Animal was a sign of bad character. And if the particular representative, Willie, had never liked Quinn? Well, Willie's dislike had been a premonitory sign of Quinn's deficiencies as a human being, hadn't it? But I was married, and Rita was once again without a human partner, or so I suspected. Consequently, I kept my beliefs and opinions to myself and let Kimi and Sammy minister to Rita. Kimi, who is preternaturally sensitive, licked Rita's hands as if they were ailing puppies, and Sammy put on a distracting show by dropping to the floor at Rita's feet, rolling onto his back, displaying his white tummy, and foolishly waving his big paws in the air.

As I made and served coffee, I kept hoping

15

that Rita wouldn't think of the possible consequences of a dog bite. Unfortunately, as I put her mug on the table in front of her, she asked, 'What happens now? The hospital is going to ask him about the bite.'

'If there was one,' I said. A puncture wound might not have bled, but Quinn hadn't just claimed to have been bitten; he'd said that he was bleeding.

'If there was,' Rita said, 'I honestly don't think that it requires medical attention. At worst, Willie nipped him. Or pinched him. I didn't see any blood. But who knows? Quinn could still report a bite.'

'If he does, all that'll happen is that you'll get a call from some Cambridge official, and you'll have to show Willie's rabies certificate. Steve can print you out Willie's whole history of immunizations. Don't worry about it.'

Rita fished dog hair out of her coffee. 'I don't think that Quinn would sue me.' There was doubt in her voice.

'Of course not. What would he sue you for? Besides, he wouldn't sue *you*. Look, his feelings were hurt. Willie was, uh, unfriendly to him.'

Rita crowed.

'Then instead of fussing over Quinn, you made sure that Willie's paw was OK. Quinn was jealous.' I added something that I didn't believe. 'He'll get over it.'

'Holly, what he'll do is spend hours in therapy figuring out how he happened to get involved with a woman who loves her dog more than she

16

loves him.'

'Rita, you wouldn't let a patient get away with that. You did say that Quinn's in *good* therapy.'

'He is,' she said. 'Or I hope so.'

TWO

After Rita left, I returned to the morning's tasks. In the short time since I'd stopped brushing and blowing out undercoat, Kimi and Sammy had managed to release yet more of the woolly stuff. It's not fair to blame the dogs, is it? I mean, they don't shed deliberately. They have no more control over their shedding than I do. No, the fault lies with dog hair itself, which has a perverse mind of its own. For the moment, I'd had enough of its evil ways. Once the rain stopped and the yard dried out, I'd take the dogs and the grooming equipment outside, where the neighborhood birds would do the clean-up for me. I folded the grooming table, put away the dryer, emptied the Dyson's canister, vacuumed, emptied the canister again, vacuumed yet again, and eventually returned to the task of making enemies, by which I mean turning down the applications of people who had applied to adopt dogs from our local Alaskan malamute rescue group.

17

I exaggerate. Screening applications can be fun. I outright love making the perfect match between a homeless dog and a wonderful applicant, and I don't mind helping people to decide that my challenging breed would be a poor match. It's no fun to disappoint people, but I'm just never going to find the right rescue malamute for the family with three Chihuahuas, five cats, two parrots, eight hamsters, six pygmy goats, thirty-five chickens, and a flock of exotic geese, especially if the resident species all get along beautifully, and the proposed dog is expected to do the same. Introduce an Alaskan malamute into the peaceable kingdom, and what you get is warfare. When I turn down an application like that one, I always think of the dogs awaiting homes and feel guilty. From the malamute viewpoint, it's a delectable home. It's hors d'oeuvres, a poultry course, a meat course ... and here am I depriving a big, hungry dog of a week-long feast!

But the applicants I absolutely hate dealing with are the people who are going to give me a hard time, and our other volunteers feel the same way. Almost all of our applications are submitted online. There's a special section of our website where volunteers claim applications from a database. We then reply by email or by phone. The alpha figure of our organization, Betty Burley, has decreed that every applicant gets a polite response – no one disagrees – and that applications are to be claimed in the order in which they were submitted, first come, first

18

served. In reality, troublesome-looking applications sometimes sit unclaimed for weeks. I handle them only when it's obvious that no one else is going to or when I feel like a bad human being who needs to make recompense. Good Catholics go to confession and say Hail Marys. My act of contrition consists of telling people that they won't be allowed to adopt malamutes.

'Mrs Di Bartolomeo,' I said, having verified her identity, 'this is Holly Winter from Malamute Rescue. Thank you for your application.'

'Well, it's really my husband who wants one,' she said.

Question on the application: *Do all members of your household know that you plan to adopt a malamute?* At least Mr Di Bartolomeo had told his wife. Men don't always. More commonly, teenage boys don't tell their parents.

'The application is in both names,' I said. 'Are you familiar with malamutes? Did you read the material on our website?' The website is packed with warnings about food stealing, predatory behavior, shedding, and the notorious malamute wild streak.

'Oh, Don did,' she said. 'He's been after me for a dog for years, ever since his last one got killed by a car. I finally gave in.'

The husband had written that his last dog had died of cancer at the age of fifteen. If I'd checked the mandatory vet reference, I'd have uncovered the truth, but when I suspect that I'll have to reject an applicant, I don't bother to check the vet reference.

Lying to us is grounds for rejection. Besides, it offends me. In a token act of revenge, I asked, 'Mrs Di Bartolomeo, who does the vacuuming in your house?'

'I do.'

'And you've been told about the shedding.'

'Oh, that's why I gave in.'

'Pardon me?'

'Don says that they don't shed. A medium-sized dog that doesn't shed. That's what I told him he could get.'

I broke the news. Our conversation ended.

I made two more calls and left voice messages. Then I reached a man named Irving Jensen, who lived in Lynn, an industrial city on the coast about ten miles north of Boston that's best known as the subject of the following piece of folkloric doggerel:

Lynn, Lynn,
City of sin,
You never come out
The way you went in.

So far as I knew, Lynn was, in reality, no more sinful than dozens of other Massachusetts communities, and I'd known excellent dog owners who lived there. What made Jensen's application one of my Hail Marys was that he'd stated that he didn't believe in fences. Also, he was equally opposed to neutering dogs. Jensen and I spoke briefly.

'All of our dogs are spayed or neutered,' I

informed him.

'I want one that ain't,' he said.

'That's your privilege, but you can't get one from us.'

'Why not?'

'It's the policy of my organization.' I'd learned long ago that it was a waste of time to elaborate: breeding should be done selectively and seldom; we almost never knew the genetic history of our rescue dogs; we didn't need to create business for ourselves; and so on. The valid points never convinced an applicant like Irving Jensen; on the contrary, they fueled arguments. I added, 'Every other reputable rescue group has the same policy.'

'You're telling me you're going to kill these dogs before you give one to me?'

'We almost never have to euthanize dogs unless they're sick and in pain.'

'Bullshit,' he said.

Swear at a volunteer, and you don't get a dog. I said goodbye and hung up. Jensen had been impossible, anyway. Among other things, although he'd stated on his application that he'd owned a lot of dogs over the years, he'd provided no vet reference. Instead, he'd written: 'Dogs were healthy. Never needed a vet.'

Before Rita and Quinn's fight, in between grooming Sammy and Kimi, I'd replied to applications from a man named Hollis, a woman named Jenna, and a couple called Blatherwicke. The last of my Hail Mary calls was to Eldon Flood, whose application stated that he and his

21

wife, Lucinda, wanted a dog to tag along with them on their farm the way their last dog, a Border collie mix, had done. According to the application, the Floods had no fenced yard, no kennel, and no dog crate. No vet reference was given. Calling the Floods might not even qualify as doing penance. Once they'd talked with me for a few minutes, they'd probably decide on their own to look for a different breed.

As it turned out, when I reached Eldon Flood, he immediately asked, 'How much you want for them?'

'There are a few things we need to discuss,' I said. 'I see that you want a dog who'll stay right with you.'

'Yeah.'

I gave a detailed explanation of the need to keep malamutes on leash except in fully-fenced areas, the same explanation that appears on the web.

'That's just if you don't train 'em right,' said Eldon Flood.

Kudos to me! I was patient. I said that I'd been training dogs and showing in obedience since childhood; that two of my malamutes had advanced obedience titles; and that malamutes were radically different from the golden re-trievers I'd had previously.

'You gotta understand,' he said. 'I got a special knack with dogs. Like a gift, you know? I like the look of this one called Thunder. How much you want for him?'

'I can't approve your application,' I said. 'This

is just not the right breed for you. If you want to read up on malamutes and reconsider, you're welcome to get back to me.' I gave him my home phone number. 'But at the moment, I can't approve your application.' The phone went dead. At least he hadn't sworn at me or accused me of murdering dogs.

As if Rita and Quinn's fight, the Di Bartolomeos, Irving Jensen, and Eldon Flood weren't enough, I'd no sooner hung up than that damned Pippy Neff called me. Pippy was a somewhat disreputable malamute breeder who showed her dogs all the time, much to the irritation of those of us who also showed and who did so in the hope of having fun, a hope more easily realized in Pippy's absence than in her presence. The second I heard her distinctive voice on the phone, I knew what she wanted. Her demands for Rowdy's stud services had started at a show when she'd pointed at the gorgeous boy and announced, 'I'm using him.' As if I had no choice! When Pippy had followed up by calling and emailing me, I'd put her off by saying, truthfully, that I'd need information about Rowdy's proposed mate: health clearances, hip and eye certifications, the results of a recent thyroid test, and so forth. While failing to send any such thing, Pippy had continued to plague me.

'Pippy,' I said, 'I've told you that no one uses Rowdy until I've seen clearances. Send them, and we'll talk.'

'Goddamn it, there's nothing wrong with

Nifty's hips,' she said. Some people sing off-key. Pippy somehow managed to speak off-key. 'You've seen Nifty.' Tundrabilt's Pretty Nifty. Pippy Neff used an egotistical system of nomenclature: Tundrabilt's Perfectly Neat, Power Now, Pretty Nifty, and so on. Indeed, Positively Narcissistic. I had, in fact, seen Nifty in the show ring. I'd also tried to look her up in the online database maintained by the Orthopedic Foundation for Animals. The database, available at http://www.offa.org, has information about eye exam results and other health matters, but OFA is principally known for its ratings of hip X-rays. Nifty's absence didn't necessarily mean that she had hip dysplasia. My guess was that Pippy had been too cheap to send hip X-rays to OFA or hadn't had X-rays done at all. I'd have bet anything that she hadn't paid for PennHip, which is an alternative system for evaluating hips. It's excellent and costly.

'Pippy, we've been through this,' I said. 'My mother was a breeder, and one thing she drilled into me is that any stud dog I own is unavailable unless I see those clearances. This has nothing to do with Nifty. She's beautiful. She looks sound, but I don't have X-ray vision. It's just a policy I have. No exceptions. It's nothing personal.'

Pippy was obnoxious, but she wasn't stupid. 'Well, I take it personally. It's an insult to Nifty, and it's an insult to me.'

'I'm sorry if you take it that way. That's not how it's meant.'

'You entered on Saturday?' she asked.

'No. Rowdy and Sammy are both out of coat. But I might go anyway.'

'If you do, we'll talk,' she said.

Threat or promise?

THREE

In case any of my rejected applicants decided to call back and argue with me, I got out of the house. The rain had stopped, and the dogs and I needed exercise. My cousin Leah was supposed to take Kimi running, so Sammy and I set out by ourselves. We live at the corner of Concord Avenue and Appleton Street. At big-dog pace, we're about twenty minutes from Harvard Square, Fresh Pond, or the Charles River. The square is the dogs' favorite destination. It offers the delectable combination of a big potential audience and an ample supply of discarded food, but I felt like stretching my legs without having Sammy draw a crowd and try to wolf down trash. On a Saturday afternoon, the trail around Fresh Pond would be thick with off-leash dogs, including dog-aggressive dogs presumably turned loose on the theory that after repeatedly attacking innocent dogs like mine, the miscreants would mull over the folly of their behavior and spontaneously decide to reform: *Geez, now that I've devoured two Yorkshire terriers, the left ear of a Lab, and miscellaneous body parts of six or eight other breeds, I've come to realize that other dogs are, after all, my dearest friends, and I have vowed henceforth to be Mr Socialization!*

So, Sammy and I headed up Appleton Street toward the river. Our block of Appleton was once part of a pleasant working-class and middle-class neighborhood, but the area has been glorified by proximity to the ivy-choked league-of-its-own institution from which my cousin Leah was about to graduate. Once you cross Huron and head uphill toward Brattle Street, however, you soon come to big, grand houses that beg to be gawked at. If I'm feeling powerless in real life, I imagine that any house of my choosing will be mine and that my task is to select and reject as I please: the mauve place with twenty or thirty rooms is tempting, but its yard is too small. The creamy-yellow colonial might make my cut if it were set farther from the street. My dogs certainly do not share this fantasy. Rather, being dogs, they pay closer attention to scent than to sight. What they smell in the vicinity of Brattle Street just has to be money.

So, Sammy was sniffing a utility pole, and I was making up my mind about selecting or rejecting a hotel-sized brick Victorian when a woman's voice hailed me. 'You! With the malamute! Wait up!'

Caught! Spotted by the owner of the brick house just as I was about to accept it as a gift! Embarrassment practically sent me flying into the air. Sammy, however, rapidly returned me to earth by transferring his attention from the fascinating odors at the base of the utility pole to the tantalizing sight of a somewhat overweight black-and-white female malamute approaching from the direction of Brattle Street. At the human end of the leash was a fit-looking fiftyish woman who broke into a run and called out, 'Another malamute! Wait!'

Being half malamute myself, I disobeyed the order. Instead of standing still, I headed toward her and asked, 'How is yours with other dogs?'

'Fine with males. Yours?' The woman had shoulder-length brown hair attractively shot with gray. She wore running shoes, tan cords, and a black sweatshirt with red letters across the front that spelled out *Dog is my co-pilot.* I owned the T-shirt version, which I'd ordered from *Bark*, a publication accurately self-described as 'the modern dog culture magazine'. Because I was afraid that the co-pilot slogan would give offense, I was selective about where I wore the T-shirt. The precaution was ridiculous in the sense that anyone offended by the sentiment would be even more offended by *me*, unless, of course, I took the time to explain the genuineness of my reverence for all creatures great, hairy, and woofy, but the time required would have been days or possibly even weeks, and besides, the average person who hates your T-

27

shirt isn't going to be interested in listening anyway. There's a lot of religious intolerance in this world, isn't there?

Sammy answered the woman's question about how he was with other dogs by giving a preparatory head-to-tail wiggle before puffing himself up and issuing a prolonged series of *woo-woo-woo-woo-woo*s. In response, the object of his affection wagged her plump hind end and threw Sammy a lusty come-hither look.

'OK if we walk with you?' the woman asked. 'Or do you live...?' She gestured to the brick house.

'I was afraid it was yours,' I blurted out, 'and that I'd been caught gaping. Or maybe it is yours?'

'Ours isn't anything so grand,' she said.

'Neither is ours,' I said. 'We're at the wrong end of Appleton.'

'So are we. As of last week.'

'The humble end. Not that I'm complaining,' I said. 'Welcome to the neighborhood. Sammy and I are heading toward the river. Or maybe Brattle Street. If you—'

'Oh, I love Brattle Street,' she exclaimed. 'I've been walking Ulla there and pretending I've won a contest and get to pick any house I want. I'm Vanessa Jones, by the way.'

'Holly Winter. And this is Sammy.'

By then we were moving at malamute speed with the dogs side by side in front of us. Everything was still damp from the rain, and the dogs were investigating the scent that clung to the moisture on the grass and shrubs we passed. Vanessa and I also explored shared interests. When I mentioned *Bark*, she complimented me on a short essay I'd published there and went on to say that she read my column in *Dog's Life* magazine.

'I knew you lived in Cambridge,' she said. 'I was hoping to meet you. You don't mind?'

'Why would I mind?' I didn't. On the contrary, I had the happy sense of encountering a kindred spirit. Before long, Vanessa and I had established that she lived only a half block from me. I'd known that the house had sold, but I'd been out of town on the day she and her family had moved in. She'd already met the McNamaras, who were her next-door neighbors. They had a charming puli named Persimmon. I knew them from Appleton Street and also from the Cambridge Dog Training Club. Vanessa had spent most of her life in Vermont, but her husband, Jim, had died of a heart attack during the winter, and she'd wanted to be near her son, Hatch, who was a resident in internal medicine at Brigham and Women's Hospital, as was Hatch's fiancée, Fiona. Vanessa's father, Tom, and her daughter, Avery, lived with her.

'We'll have to see how that works out,' she said. 'My father's been with me since my mother died, but in Vermont, he had his own little apartment. And then there's Avery. Oh, my. I sometimes think that life would be easier if my relatives would all turn into dogs, preferably malamutes. Speaking of which, it's as if these

29

two have been friends for years.'

After that, we talked malamutes and malamute rescue. Vanessa had always had dogs, but Ulla was her first malamute. 'She's sort of a rescue dog,' Vanessa said. 'I got her when her original owner died.'

'Do you know anything about her background?' I asked.

'Everything! Ulla's owner, Olympia, lived near us. Ulla was bred by a woman named Pippy Neff.'

I limited myself to saying, 'Pippy.' Then I added, 'I thought Ulla had a familiar look.'

Vanessa laughed. 'Aren't you the soul of tact!'

'Rarely,' I said.

For the remainder of what turned into a long walk up and down the side streets off Brattle, we continued to talk about Alaskan malamutes and then drifted to our shared admiration for Jane Austen. In retrospect, I realize that we could hardly have chanced on a more jarring juxtaposition of topics: the most prominent feature of the malamute character, the wild streak, is singularly absent from the civilized society of Jane Austen's novels. As we were returning home by retracing our route down Appleton Street, we ran into my cousin Leah and Kimi, who were finishing their run. The humidity had turned Leah's ponytail into red-gold corkscrew curls. Loose tendrils framed her face. Her cobalt spandex clung so tightly to her curves that she was safe running on her own only because she was accompanied by a big dog. When she

30

stopped to say hello, Kimi came to a neat sit at her left side. Ulla had the good manners not to stare at Kimi; the two glanced at each other, and that was that.

Meanwhile, I introduced Vanessa and Leah. 'Leah is a senior,' I said without specifying where. Just as traditional Jews avoid speaking God's name, so do Cambridge types refrain from uttering the word *Harvard* aloud. Not that I'm a pure type. I'm just struggling to adapt. 'Leah is going to Tufts Veterinary School in the fall. Leah, Vanessa and her family have just moved to our block of Appleton Street.'

For all Leah's considerable academic accomplishments, she has remained as friendly as ever. Her tendency toward high-handedness is also undiminished. After she and Vanessa had exchanged chit-chat and had admired each other's dogs, Leah invited Vanessa and her family to have dinner with us the next evening. 'Holly's father and stepmother will be there,' Leah said. 'You can meet the family.'

'What a lovely invitation,' said Vanessa. 'But I'm afraid that I'm committed to making dinner for my own family. My father, my daughter, my son, and his fiancée, Fiona. You don't want the whole crew.'

'Oh, yes we do!' insisted Leah, who knew how unpredictable my father was.

Still, I seconded the invitation. Vanessa accepted but insisted on contributing a salad and dessert. For all I knew, my father, Buck, might act charming. He and my stepmother, Gabrielle,

31

would be stopping on their way home to Maine from Connecticut, where they were attending the memorial service of an ancient personage in the world of golden retrievers, a woman who had been a friend of my late mother's and whom Buck was scheduled to eulogize. It was possible that whereas other people attending the service would be left with sad thoughts of loss and finality, Buck would emerge energized and cheered, especially because he'd have had a starring role. He tends to be at his most obnoxious when he's happy. Gabrielle, I reminded myself, was reliably delightful. Fool that I am, I looked forward to the dinner.

FOUR

My father's favorite food is aged venison. By 'aged' he means so rotten that cooking it pollutes the house for a week. He also likes game birds peppered with lead, but he'll settle for non-toxic shot. Fortunately, he and Gabrielle often arrive from Maine with lobster and clams. This time, they were returning from Connecticut, so Steve and I were providing the food, which would have to suit Vanessa's family and Leah as well. Around here, it's become increasingly impossible to plan a meal because almost everyone has a major food restriction. At the moment, Leah was a pesco-ovo-lacto vegetarian: fish, eggs, and milk, but no meat. Some member of Vanessa's family was bound to be lactose intolerant or allergic to shellfish or committed to consuming no white foods or nothing but local produce. It often seems as if the only universally acceptable menu would consist of one course after another of distilled water, but there are probably people who'd object on grounds of health, ethics, or politics. Thank God for the Arctic heritage of Alaskan malamutes. If the entire US population shared the malamute's genetically programmed determination to ward off starvation, it would be a lot easier than it is now to have friends in to dinner. You'd just throw any kind of old garbage at your guests, and they'd gulp it down and love you forever.

In the hope of pleasing everyone, I had bought a leg of lamb and had made a trip to Watertown for Armenian goodies, including hummus, taramasalata, and lamejuns – Armenian pizzas – with and without meat. At about six o'clock on Sunday evening, Leah had just put a big rectangular spinach and cheese pie – spanakopita – into the oven and was cleaning up her work area. It was typical of her to invite dinner guests and then redeem herself by laboring over a work-intensive dish.

'Now Leah, remember,' I said. 'Do not mention Steve's fishing trip to my father!'

Steve mimicked me in a voice two octaves

33

higher than his normal bass: 'Do not mention Steve's fishing trip!'

In pure-bred dogdom, when your dog has a big win, or even a small one, or earns a title or otherwise accomplishes something, you're expected to brag. Otherwise, people feel that you're disrespecting your dog by failing to show proper pride in his achievements. In that spirit, let me say that although Steve hasn't had a win or earned a title beyond his DVM, his existence merits a boast. He is tall, lean, and muscular, with curly brown hair and eyes that change from green to blue and back again. Also, he's a great vet. As if all that weren't enough, he goes out of his way not to create housework and sometimes even helps with it. At the moment, he was unloading the dishwasher.

'They're here,' I said. 'So if you don't want Buck joining you or feeling left out, don't mention it yourself. Don't mention Grant's Camps. Don't even mention the Rangeley area.'

My father's moose-like bellow from the back hallway heralded his arrival. Although I've seen moose hundreds of times, they are always bigger than I expect, and thus it is with Buck, who didn't just enter the kitchen but expanded as if to fill it and squeeze the rest of us out. 'Where are your dogs?' Buck demanded. He knows perfectly well that malamutes steal food. He then compensated a little by getting India and Lady to offer their paws. Even Steve admits that Buck has a gift with dogs.

'Crated,' I said. Then I hugged Gabrielle. She

usually rebounds quickly from the trying experience of being incarcerated in a vehicle with my father, but her recuperative powers evidently weren't yet asserting themselves. She is a remarkably pretty woman, plumper than she would like to be, but in my father's eyes, deliciously voluptuous. The incredible bone structure of her face usually diverts attention from the damage the sun has done to her skin, but she now looked pale and tired, and the ash blonde of her hair cast grayish shadows on her eyes. For once, she wasn't carrying her bichon, the fluffy little white Molly, who scampered across the floor to greet India and Lady.

'Are you OK?' I whispered to Gabrielle.

'Later,' she murmured. Her rich, throaty voice sounds beautiful even when it's barely audible.

Meanwhile, my father was belatedly greeting Leah and Steve, which is to say that he was booming at them. Although he sounded jovial, within minutes he was going to get after Leah for having chosen Tufts over Cornell and Penn, and either before or after that, he'd irritate me by voicing his unsolicited opinion that Sammy was a better show dog than Rowdy. As I was mulling over the question of how Buck would irk Steve, the phone rang. Instead of letting the machine pick up, I took advantage of the welcome interruption. Without bothering to check caller ID, I answered.

'Is Vinnie there?' a man's voice asked. Or so I thought. Although Buck had lowered his volume, there was still some background noise.

'Sorry, I'm having trouble hearing you,' I said. 'Who?'

'Is Vinnie there?' he repeated.

Vinnie was my last golden retriever. She was the most wonderful competition obedience dog who ever lived, and she was as cooperative, intuitive, and close to flawless in daily life as she was in the ring. If Rowdy hadn't healed the pain of her loss, I'd be crying for her still. But the man obviously wasn't asking to speak to my dead dog.

'You must have the wrong number,' I said.

'Holly?' he asked.

'Yes,' I said.

What followed were torrents of maniacal laughter that alternated with the demand to talk to Vinnie. Suddenly, with no warning, the call became hideously obscene, so graphic and ugly that I spent a few foolish seconds struggling to believe what I was hearing. Then I hung up. Belatedly, I checked caller ID, which uselessly read: Unknown name, Unknown number. In spite of the presence of my protective, reactive father, I might have tried to trace the call and told everyone about it, but the doorbell rang, Vanessa and her family poured in, and the house was filled with happy activity that drove the nasty little incident to the back of my mind.

Although Vanessa had been living in Cambridge for only a week, I'd learned on our walk that she'd graduated from that place down the street. In any case, she had the local look: simple hair, minimal make-up, ethnic beads, and a

36

flowing jersey outfit with inadequate foundation garments. As promised, she'd brought a salad, a big one in a wooden bowl swathed in aluminum foil. Since the dessert was in individual serving dishes, her daughter, her son, and his fiancée all carried portions of it in baskets and boxes. Only Vanessa's father was empty-handed.

'Cherry crisp,' Avery said listlessly. 'We'll need to nuke it for a minute or pop it in the oven.'

Even for a New Englander in a rainy April, Vanessa's daughter was pale. Indeed, everything about Avery was pallid. Her eyes were a grayish blue, her hair was a dingy blonde, she had a wan expression, and she wore faded jeans and an almost colorless chambray shirt. Hatch, the son, looked like a tall, male version of his mother. He had Vanessa's regular features, and like her, he radiated fitness. His mother had told me that he was an internist, but his vigor suggested sports medicine. When I tried to remember what Vanessa had said about Avery, all that came to mind was the subsequent statement that she wished that her relatives would turn into dogs. Had the two children been thus transfigured, Avery would clearly have been the runt of Vanessa's litter. The young woman suffered by comparison not only with her brother, Hatch, but also by comparison with my vibrant cousin, Leah, and with Hatch's fiancée, Fiona, whose name had led me to expect a Scot, but whose ancestry was Asian. In heart-wrenching contrast to Avery, Fiona was strikingly beautiful. Her

37

shiny dark hair fell to the shoulders of a shimmery red shirt that somehow managed not to be too formal for the occasion. Within minutes of Fiona's arrival, Steve had supplied her with a glass of wine, and my father was ushering her into the living room, offering her a choice of appetizers, and hearing about her training at Brigham and Women's. When she sneezed, Buck pulled a gigantic white handkerchief out of his pocket, and Hatch and Steve both proffered tissues. Aren't men wonderful? Here was Fiona, an MD completing her training at one of the nation's top hospitals, yet Buck, Hatch, and Steve leaped to act on the assumption that she couldn't wipe her own nose without male assistance.

'Allergies,' Hatch explained.

He and I were lingering between the kitchen, where Avery was fussing with the bowls of dessert, and the living room, where Leah was chatting with Vanessa and her father, Tom Oakley. Leah was helping Steve to supply drinks and making sure that people had little plates for the food arrayed on the coffee table.

'Is Fiona allergic to dogs?' I asked. Lady, India, and Molly were wandering around. 'Because we can—'

'No, thank God,' Hatch said. 'Plants, trees, pollen. Spring is rough for her.'

Overhearing, Fiona said, 'Oh, I love dogs. Hatch and I both do. We're getting one as soon as we're settled in San Francisco.'

The casual remark provided the opportunity

for everyone to ask about Hatch and Fiona's plans. They were getting married in California in June and moving there in the fall. Their wedding would be held just outside San Francisco, where Fiona's family lived. Her father was also a doctor, and she'd be joining his practice. Hatch was going to be part of a research team at UCSF Medical Center. In our household, the mention of getting a dog naturally triggered an intense discussion of precisely what breeds Hatch and Fiona were considering. When mention was made of Ulla, they said that they were crazy about malamutes but that as a child, Fiona had had a golden retriever and was longing for another. Buck was ecstatic. My parents raised goldens, and Buck has one, Mandy. He had to hear everything about Fiona's childhood dog and everything about Ulla as well.

When the time came to move to the dining room, everyone except Tom Oakley pitched in to help transfer the food to serving dishes and carry everything to the table. The pale Avery, who'd kept herself out of the conversation, had what I saw as a sad tendency to cast herself in the role of kitchen help. Instead of socializing, she spontaneously began to scrub the roasting pan, wipe the counters, and load the dishwasher with the plates we'd used for appetizers.

'That can wait,' I told her. 'Just leave all this. Steve and I will do it later.'

As I look back at the ten of us who gathered around the table that Sunday evening, I remember being filled with love for my family and feeling happy to have made new friends. As Leah filled our glasses with red wine, she spoke warmly to everyone. We toasted to new friends. Fiona, who had switched to water because she'd be driving, raised only her empty hand; she said that toasting with water was bad luck. At the head of the table, Steve was carving the lamb with surgical precision. I can recall feeling oddly pleased to watch my husband perform the traditional male task with skill and flair. In spite of my father's idiosyncrasies, I felt grateful to him not only for marrying Gabrielle but for bequeathing me his love of dogs and, with it, the comfort and security of belonging to an amiable pack. When Gabrielle turned her charm on Tom Oakley and drew him out, I also felt increasingly thankful that for all Buck's faults, he was not in the least bit given to imaginary ailments.

'Gabrielle tells me that you're a writer,' Tom said to me. 'Carpal tunnel syndrome?'

'Nothing wrong with Holly,' my father answered. 'Sound as a bell. Always was.'

Before Buck had the chance to compare me point by point to a healthy puppy, I said, 'Steve's the superhealthy one. He never even gets a cold.'

Tom looked disappointed. 'Even after all your contact with animals?' he asked. To Leah, who was passing the salad, he said, 'Thank you, but no. My poor beleaguered stomach won't tolerate roughage.' Tom did not, by the way, look sickly. He was a dapper man with bright blue eyes, short white hair, and good color.

'Haven't caught anything yet,' Steve said.

'Really,' said Leah, 'getting a dog or cat or any other animal is the best thing you can do for your health. But dogs are the best because you have to get out and exercise them.'

Buck looked up from Lady, who was at his side, and beamed at Leah, as did Steve and I. To compensate for the negativity I've expressed about my father, let me point out that he is no dog snob. You can tell at a glance that the three malamutes, Rowdy, Kimi, and Sammy, and India, the German shepherd dog, are the products of careful breeding. The same quick look will tell you that Lady is what's called 'pet quality'. Although my father combines a vast knowledge of American Kennel Club breed standards with a great eye for a dog, he fully appreciated our nervous little Lady as the valuable individual that she was.

'Walking Ulla is beyond me,' Tom said. 'I don't know how Vanessa keeps up with her.'

'Easily,' Vanessa muttered.

'With her mitral valve prolapse,' Tom said.

'Ulla has mitral valve prolapse?' I asked.

'I do,' Vanessa said. 'It's nothing. A normal variant.'

Hatch and Fiona nodded, but Tom said, 'What Ulla has is hypothyroidism. She has to take two pills a day.'

'I'm mildly hypothyroid myself,' Gabrielle said.

'It's very common in dogs,' I said. 'Especially in northern breeds. But if you—'

41

Before I could say that if you didn't intend to breed a dog, hypothyroidism was no big deal, Tom said, 'And then there's Avery. She's at dangerously high risk for osteoporosis. Thin white women, you know.'

Vanessa sighed. 'Avery broke her wrist two years ago. He's been on this kick ever since. It was an accident. Avery's the picture of health.'

To my mind, Avery looked bloodless and depressed, but I didn't say so, of course. What I did was cast a pleading glance at Gabrielle, who read my wish and smoothly changed the topic by saying, 'Speaking of accidents, Holly, I wondered about the ladder that's outside. You and Steve aren't using that, are you?'

'I am,' I admitted. 'But I'm being careful.'

'Climbs like a monkey,' said my father. 'Agile as a cat.' He has always had trouble reconciling himself to my membership in the species *Homo sapiens*.

'I'm a do-it-yourself type,' I admitted. 'The north side of the house doesn't want to hold paint, and it galls me to pay to have it done and redone all the time, and gutters and downspouts need some work.'

'That we should hire someone to do,' Steve said.

'With all this rain,' I countered, 'I haven't even been up on the ladder, but I don't believe in hiring people to do work that I can do myself.'

'Yankee self-reliance,' my father said with approval. Miraculously, he did not go on to

42

compare me favorably to a lodge-building beaver or any other sort of animal.

Fortunately, the subject of home maintenance diverted Tom from his interest in disease and Buck from his pride in me. Steve and I offered the names of reliable plumbers and electricians, Leah said that Elizabeth and Isaac McNamara would be great neighbors, and I encouraged Vanessa's interest in taking Ulla to classes at the Cambridge Dog Training Club. Vanessa said that she regretted having already found a local vet for Ulla; Steve, she said, would've been perfect. Leah discovered that Hatch and Fiona had gone to medical school at the University of Vermont, where one of her close friends would be starting in the fall. Gabrielle did her valiant best to befriend Avery and eventually elicited at least a tiny spark of interest in food. As Gabrielle recommended our local shops on Concord Avenue and got Avery to utter a few words about Loaves and Fishes, the big natural-foods emporium at the Fresh Pond traffic circle, it occurred to me that the person who'd adore the aisles of vitamin supplements and alternative remedies at Loaves and Fishes was Tom, who, as if on cue, asked whether liquid supplements were available there.

'I have an exceptionally small throat,' he explained. 'I'm forced to have prescription medicine specially compounded because I can't swallow anything except the tiniest pills and capsules.' He then questioned Gabrielle about exactly what type of hypothyroidism she had.

43

Hashimoto's? Or something else?

It struck me that Tom's excessive interest in illness must be hard on Steve, who spent a good part of his work life listening to owners report on the symptoms of their pets, and even worse for Hatch and Fiona, who had to hear their patients complain about sickness and were then deluged with ailment talk whenever they saw Hatch's grandfather. At the moment, all three medical types were escaping the all-too-familiar subject. Steve and Hatch talked about fly fishing. When Buck joined in, he came dangerously close to mentioning Rangeley and asking Steve whether he was going to get any fishing in this spring. Leah and Fiona tried to draw Avery into a discussion of novels they both liked, but even when their efforts led to movies based on Jane Austen's books, Avery was sadly unresponsive.

'I hate to rush off,' Fiona said when everyone had finished dinner, 'but I'm on my way to Vermont tonight, and it's a long drive.'

'All the way to Burlington,' Vanessa said. 'But do stay for dessert. It won't take a second to heat up. Holly, no! Stay put. Avery and I will do it.'

'How about if we all carry in our own dishes,' Gabrielle said, 'and then we'll leave the dessert to you.'

Gabrielle is a natural leader with a gift for eliciting social cooperation. People always seem to end up feeling glad to participate in doing what she wants. As soon as she spoke, all of us, even Tom, rose, and in almost no time, the table was clear. I made caffeinated coffee for Steve,

44

who is impervious to its effect, and for Fiona, who had a long drive ahead, and decaf for everyone else except Tom, who had a delicate stomach. I'd like to be able to give a detailed report of who was where when, and who did what, but I was busy with coffee cups, teaspoons, dessert forks, sugar, and cream. The time? It must have been about nine o'clock. I know that I gave Avery a hand-held electric mixer to whip cream for the cherry crisp. At some point, Vanessa urged Fiona to spend the night at her house and to leave for Vermont in the morning. Fiona refused. Her cadaver partner from medical school was about to have a baby. Labor was to be induced the next morning. Fiona had promised to be there. I also remember that Fiona swallowed a pill from a prescription bottle that she retrieved from her purse. She said that she was taking an antihistamine that didn't cause drowsiness. I had the passing thought that the medication might actually be a stimulant meant to keep her awake during the drive to Vermont. If so, so what? As a young doctor who was just finishing her training, Fiona must have up-to-date knowledge of drugs and doses. Besides, what she swallowed was none of my business.

'I really should hit the road,' she said as we returned to our seats in the dining room, 'but Avery will be hurt if I miss dessert. Besides, it's rude to eat and run.'

'Please don't worry about us,' I said. 'Being with a friend in labor? That has priority. And

45

you don't want to be exhausted. Really, if you want to go now, that's fine.'

She smiled. 'Thank you.' In a whisper she added, 'I don't want in-law trouble before we're even married.'

For all the to-do about transporting the dessert in individual bowls and heating it up at the last minute, the cherry crisp was nothing but an old-fashioned cobbler made with canned sour cherries instead of apples. Buck likes that plain Yankee cooking, so he raved about it, and who doesn't like whipped cream? The specialness turned out to be a family tradition. Cherry crisp had been a childhood favorite of Hatch's.

'I need the recipe,' Fiona said. 'Not now! I really have to go.' She thanked everyone, and when she said what a pleasure it had been to meet us, she sounded genuine. In fact, Fiona had an openness and authenticity that I liked. Before she left, she and Leah exchanged email addresses, and Buck and Gabrielle gave her their phone number so that she and Hatch could call them if they needed help in finding a responsible breeder of goldens or in raising their puppy. As people were exchanging contact information with Fiona, Avery and Vanessa cleared the table and rinsed out the salad bowl and dessert bowls they'd brought.

'We'll go, too,' Vanessa said. 'You know, I'm sorry we haven't had a chance to see your malamutes tonight. Soon?'

'Absolutely,' I said. 'You haven't even met Rowdy.'

'And I wonder if we could make a play date for Sammy and Ulla. One of the reasons I bought the house is that it has a big yard, at least for Cambridge. Fenced.'

'Ours is fenced,' I said, 'but it's not very big. Yes, let's get them together.'

We agreed to talk the next day and to set a time. Then all our guests left at once. Steve and I accompanied them out to the sidewalk. Leah got on her bicycle and rode off with everyone waving to her. Avery, I remember, was clinging to her brother almost as if she rather than Fiona were his fiancée, and Tom was issuing alarmist cautions to Fiona, who said, 'Really, I've done this drive dozens of times. With no traffic, it'll be under four hours, and it's highway all the way.'

Tom put his arm around her shoulder, hugged her, and said, 'You're very dear to us, you know.'

'You're very dear to me, too,' Fiona said.

FIVE

When the phone rang at nine o'clock on Monday morning, my father was living dangerously: he was cooking with a malamute loose in the kitchen. For once, Buck wasn't burning food in grease. He'd put two slices of bread in the toaster and was at the stove scrambling eggs. Rowdy was in perfect heel position at Buck's left side, his almost-black eyes fixed adoringly on Buck's face. Speaking of adoration, I'm just going to blurt out the full, raw truth about Rowdy, which is that he's the most beautiful dog who ever lived. Period. As it happens, he is the incarnation of the American Kennel Club standard for the Alaskan malamute – the ideal made manifest – but even if you could barely tell a show dog from a river rat or if you mistook Rowdy for a Siberian husky or a mix of muscular Arctic breeds, you'd take in his powerful build, his handsome gray-and-white stand-off coat, his gorgeous broad head, the sweeping white plume of his tail, and all the rest, including his warm, gentle expression and his air of owning the universe, and you'd say to yourself, Now that's a magnificent animal! I make that very remark to myself all the time.

48

AKC judges have said exactly the same thing. Increasingly, they say it about Rowdy's son, Sammy, too.

For all his splendor, Rowdy is not without fault: he steals food. And for all his knowledge of dogs, my father can be tricked. Thus it was that at the very second the phone rang, Buck foolishly took his eyes off Rowdy to glance at his eggs, and the Alaskan malamute standard incarnate, who'd been awaiting his moment of opportunity, vanished from Buck's side and, in a flash, had his massive white paws on the counter and the fresh toast in his jaws. Does Rowdy watch bread descend into the toaster and start counting? Maybe. He definitely knows to the nanosecond how long the toaster takes to release its contents. Kimi also filches toast right out of the toaster. She's world class. Rowdy is merely fast. Kimi is canine lightning.

'And at the end of the first inning,' I said, 'the score is one to nothing. Malamutes lead.' When I picked up the phone, I was laughing. To my relief, caller ID read: Jones, Vanessa. I felt relieved that I wouldn't have to deal with another nasty anonymous call in my father's presence. When I'd told Steve about the call as we were getting ready for bed, I'd promised him that if another such incident occurred, I'd immediately hang up. Still, I was glad to see Vanessa's name. She was, I assumed, calling to thank me for dinner and to set up a play date for Sammy and Ulla.

'Hello?' I said.

I heard what sounded like a muffled gasp. 'Holly? Oh, Holly, the most awful thing has happened. Horrible!'

'Vanessa, what is it?'

'Fiona. Holly, Fiona is dead. She fell asleep at the wheel. Her car went off the highway. Why did I ever let her leave so late?'

'Vanessa, you did everything you could. You told her to stay with you and leave in the morning. Your father warned her, too.'

'Oh, who listens to him? I should have made her stay. I should have insisted. Hatch should have. All of us.'

'I don't think she'd have listened. And she didn't seem exhausted. Or even sleepy. She hadn't been drinking. She had a small glass of wine before dinner, but after that, she drank water. I'm positive. And then coffee. Real. Not decaf. I should have made her take a Thermos. Oh, Vanessa, I am so sorry. I can hardly believe it!' I made the inevitable and useless offers. 'If you need help with Ulla, Steve and I could walk her. Feed her. Anything that either of us can do. Anything at all.'

'I don't even know what's going on yet,' Vanessa said. 'But thank you. There'll have to be a funeral, presumably in California. Her parents are devastated.'

'And Hatch.'

'I don't know what he'll do,' his mother said. 'There's that research team to deal with. That'll obviously have to be rearranged. I've told him to come and stay here, but ... And there'll be

50

something at the hospital, too, I assume, some sort of memorial service. I have no idea yet.'

As the call ended, Gabrielle appeared in the kitchen. When she and my father heard the terrible news, they were, of course, shaken and saddened. Reluctant though I was to do it, I called Leah and then Steve. For once, I managed to reach both of them directly. They echoed the useless offer I'd made to Vanessa, certainly with my own unspoken sense that the only truly useful thing that anyone could do would be to raise the dead.

Although it was still raining, Buck wanted to walk one of my dogs. In Rowdy's opinion, water belongs in dog bowls and nowhere else. If you try to walk him in the rain, he balks and glares at you. The attitude represents an admirable defense against hypothermia. Kimi, however, doesn't share Rowdy's Arctic-dog determination not to freeze to death, and neither does Sammy. I expected Buck to take both of them, but he picked only Sammy, probably because Kimi is a serious being, whereas Sammy's heart is forever light. In Buck's absence, Gabrielle and I settled ourselves at the kitchen table, each of us with one hand on a mug of coffee and the other on a dog. Molly sat in Gabrielle's lap, and Kimi rested her lovely dark head in mine. At first, we talked about Fiona.

Then, with some hesitation, I asked, 'Gabrielle, is something wrong? When you got here yesterday, I had the feeling ... but maybe...?'

As if she were uttering a complete sentence,

51

she said with great deliberation, 'Your father.'

Instead of asking what the hell Buck had done now, I waited.

'I do know,' Gabrielle said, 'that your mother was a fine woman.'

I understand Buck all too well. 'He didn't! Damn it! At the memorial service, instead of delivering his eulogy the way he was supposed to—'

'Oh, he delivered a eulogy! A very touching one.'

'To my mother.'

'Well, to give Buck credit, it wasn't exclusively about your mother. And I'm afraid that I reacted very childishly. Not that I let my feelings show. But the truth is that I felt hurt and jealous.'

'Of course you did! Anyone would have. If I could apologize for him, I would. Well, I will anyway. I am so sorry. He has all the sensitivity of a hunk of granite. He is an idiot. He should fall at your feet and grovel. Gabrielle, he adores you! And he did *this*!'

'Well, I do have to admit that Buck may have ... it's possible that ... well, let me spit it out. I do have to tell you a little secret.'

I nearly wept. Buck's marriage to Gabrielle had been as wonderful for me as it had been for him.

Gabrielle said, 'I have taken up dog training.'

'What?'

'I have been training Molly. And I do *not* want your father to know.'

'It's nothing to be ashamed of,' I said. 'It's great! So, why...' I stopped myself. 'He'd move in and take over. He'd intend to help you by offering advice. He'd say that he was sharing his observations, and he'd make you feel like the most incompetent person who ever told a dog to heel. I absolutely hate showing a dog in obedience when he's within a hundred miles of the ring. Are you using a book? A video?'

Gabrielle's eyes sparkled. 'Oh, no, Molly and I take private lessons.' She gently clucked the little white dog under the chin. 'It all has to be very hush-hush, so we couldn't go a class, or Buck would find out. We go once a week to the nicest woman. We sneak off! She's in Ellsworth. Theodora, her name is.'

'She has Border collies,' I said. 'You could not have a better instructor. And she's lovely.'

My late mother, I must mention, was a dog-obedience fanatic. As an instructor, she was not lovely. She was a martinet. I should know. But as Buck had probably mentioned in his inappropriate eulogy the previous day, she and her dogs got very high scores.

'We are practicing for the Canine Good Citizenship test,' Gabrielle said. 'Now, I know that to you, that's nothing. But Theodora believes in setting a goal.'

'She's right. And the CGC test is the perfect place to start. When are you thinking about taking it?'

'Well, there's the problem. Theodora says that we're ready. Molly is such a good girl! But it's one thing to scoot off to Ellsworth for lessons and swear Theodora to secrecy and practice when Buck's not around. But—'

'He knows everyone in dogs,' I said. 'Everyone in Maine anyway. If he didn't turn up at the test, he'd hear about it.' I thought for a moment. 'I have a solution. All you need to do is come here for a visit. There's a little obedience match a week from Saturday, and there'll be CGC testing, too. Steve and I are judging obedience, so we'll be going, anyway. Besides, it will be good to have you here.'

Gabrielle looked delighted. 'We'll think up some excuse,' she said. 'We'll plan something girly so Buck will stay home. Actually, there is something ... Holly, thank you.'

'My pleasure. It really is.'

My father and Sammy burst into the kitchen. Buck shook off more water than my dog did. 'Your pleasure what?'

'To have Gabrielle in my life,' I said.

SIX

To create the opportunity to firm up plans for Gabrielle's visit without having Buck listen in and invite himself to accompany her, I carried her suitcase to the car. She followed with a tote bag of Molly's gear in one hand. In the other hand, she held Molly's leash. Miracle of miracles, Molly was trotting along at the other end of the leash. From the time I'd first met Gabrielle, she'd been in the habit of carrying the little dog. The AKC standard describes the bichon frise as 'a small, sturdy white powder puff of a dog'. Molly was, indeed, small and sturdy, but she must have weighed twelve pounds or so and was consequently a bit of an armful. Even so, Gabrielle had often clutched Molly as if the dog were a fluffy white muff.

'Theodora is drumming it into my head,' Gabrielle remarked, 'that small dogs are dogs, too, and that Molly needs to learn to stand on her own four feet.'

Molly showed no sign of objecting to the new policy, but she almost never objected to anything. I'd wondered off and on whether her almost marsupial existence had contributed to her evident sense of contentment and security.

For whatever reason, she was an altogether cheerful creature.

'You're both doing beautifully,' I said. 'So, a week from Friday? Sooner? You're always welcome.'

'I have ... well, let me arrange things.' Gabrielle looked vaguely mysterious or even secretive, but I didn't want to pry.

After Molly had been settled in her crate, Buck barreled down the back steps and said, 'There was a call for you, but I handled it.'

'Who was it?'

'Rescue call. Some young guy who wanted to dump his dog.'

'I hope you got his name and number.'

'I told him to call the breeder. This is one of those guys who never should've gotten a dog to begin with. He's a kid. Works twelve hours a day, and with the commute, he's gone fourteen hours at a stretch.'

'You know, you really should've just taken his name and number, and told him I'd call right back. Look, I'm the one who does malamute rescue. You are not. Did you get the name of the breeder?'

'Pippy Neff.'

'Buck, this situation could be delicate. You know as well as I do who Pippy Neff is, and in case you don't know, I'll tell you that she does not always take responsibility for her dogs. How old is the dog?'

'Six months. A puppy. Expected to hold it for fourteen hours. I asked him how he'd like it.'

'Buck, what else did you say?'

'That he never should've gotten a dog.'

'You didn't! Buck, get this straight! If someone wants to surrender a dog, you do not alienate the owner until the dog is safe, damn it all! For all we know, the next thing that'll happen is that this puppy will end up in a shelter, and God knows which one. And if you answer my phone and the call is for me, then it's for me! In the future, please don't answer my phone. Let the machine pick up. Or limit yourself to taking messages. Please do not handle *my* calls.'

Although Buck did not apologize, our parting was fairly amicable, mainly because I remembered caller ID. With luck, I'd be able to return the call that had been mine to begin with.

I also consoled myself with the thought that the puppy's owner might have found a list of Malamute Rescue volunteers and was getting in touch with all of us, as happens fairly often. If so, he'd reach Betty Burley or some other legitimate representative of our organization, as opposed, for example, to my father. As it turned out, that's exactly what had happened. Throughout Monday, I played phone tag with the owner, whose number did, in fact, show up on caller ID, but Betty Burley phoned me on Tuesday afternoon to say that she'd talked with him and persuaded him to call Pippy Neff.

'And,' Betty added, 'I told him to tell Pippy that according to Malamute Rescue, responsible breeders take permanent lifetime responsibility for the lives they bring into this world. Is she

57

still pestering you about Rowdy?' Betty reminds me so vividly of my Kimi that I understand what she means even when she doesn't say it outright. Now, what she actually meant was that I was at fault for allowing Pippy to get away with plaguing me.

'Now and then,' I said. 'If she doesn't take back this puppy, at least I'll have the perfect excuse to turn her down. And I know that you don't think I need an excuse! But Pippy is someone I don't want as an enemy.'

'Hah! I'd send her away with a flea in her ear,' Betty said. 'Now, there's one other thing. Have you had any peculiar phone calls?'

'Yes. On Sunday. Why? Have you?'

'No.' Betty sounded offended, possibly at the notion that a crank caller would dare to target her. 'Katrina had one. She is very upset.' Katrina was a quiet young woman who'd begun to do foster care after she and her husband had adopted a dog from us three years earlier. 'She is very sensitive, you know. She takes things to heart.' Betty sounded as if the concept of sensitivity were so foreign to me that I required a translation.

'Was her call about rescue? Mine was ... I think it was personal. It was some man who asked for Vinnie. Vinnie was my last golden. At first, I thought the name was a coincidence. I just thought he had a wrong number. But he knew my name, and then he started laughing and laughing. And it turned into an obscene phone call. I hung up.'

'Oh, dear. It does sound like the same sick man. But how did he know about your dog?'

'Dog's Life. Or the web. I've written a lot about her.'

'Oh,' said Betty, who venerated the Alaskan malamute and couldn't understand why I'd ever bother to write about another breed.

I said, 'Maybe the thing to do is to hope that he's made his calls, and that's that. No, you know what? It's possible that other people have had calls that we don't know about. And if it's someone with a grudge against all of us, the whole organization, then there might be people he hasn't called yet. We ought to warn them. I'll post to the list.'

As soon as I hung up, I went to my office and sent a message to the little email list maintained for active volunteers in our organization:

From: HollyWinter@amrone.org
To: Rescuelist@amrone.org
Subject: Strange Calls
Two of us have had obscene calls from a man who laughs like a maniac. Has anyone else had weird calls? If so, please let all of us know.

Holly

After sending the message, I worked on an article about preventing pet poisoning in the home. The topic is a staple for dog writers. It's up there with such all-too-familiar subjects as treating flea infestations and teaching your dog to like vet visits. As I would obviously never admit in print, I was thoroughly tired of warning people about the toxicity of almost all common house plants and shrubs, but my editor at *Dog's Life* had insisted, so I was once again hammering out cautionary words about aloe, pothos, oleander, tulips, ferns, foxglove, and so forth. When I took a break to check my email, I found only one reply to the message I'd sent earlier:

From: BettyB@amrone.org
To: Rescuelist@amrone.org
Subject: Re: Strange Calls

This laughing fool has now targeted me. That makes at least three of us to hear from Mr Unknown Name, Unknown Number. I assume he is finding our names on the web and looking up our phone numbers there, too. Some people will do anything for attention. If he calls you, hang up.
Betty
PS. The number doesn't show up on caller ID.

The obscene calls angered me but didn't scare me. Our next-door neighbor, Kevin Dennehy, is a Cambridge cop, and Rita is, of course, a shrink. On previous occasions, I'd heard both of them express professional opinions about anonymous callers. Kevin and Rita had agreed that the people who made these calls were afraid of direct confrontation. Calling was what they did; in almost all instances, they stopped there. As I saw it, cowards stayed cowardly.

At three o'clock, I finished the article, emailed

it to my editor, and checked Google News in the hope of finding answers to my questions about Fiona's death. What I knew was almost nothing: she'd fallen asleep at the wheel and had a fatal accident. The stories I found provided a few details but no real explanation. The following is typical:

Crash in Nashua under Investigation
Nashua, N.H. Nashua police are investigating a fatal one-car rollover that happened near Exit 4 from Route 3/ F.E. Everett Turnpike around 10 p.m. on Sunday. Police said that a Toyota driven by Fiona Frazer, 29, swerved off the exit ramp and collided with a tree. Frazer was killed in the crash. Police had little to say about the cause of the accident except that alcohol was not a factor.

The damn thing about the web – and especially about Google – is that it tantalizes you with the prospect of being able to find out everything and then, just when you think that omni-science is within your grasp, reminds you that even Google can't make you God. So, even if the police had discovered more than was reported in the news, God only knew why Fiona had taken that exit from the highway and why she had smashed her car into a tree and died. Had she felt sick? Or sensed that she was in danger of falling asleep at the wheel? Or been in search of a ladies' room? In any case, although Google had failed to tell me everything, the stories it provided left me with a sharp, painful awareness of the reality of Fiona's death. Furthermore, for the first time, I was hit with the realization that the accident victim could easily have been a member of my own family rather than a member of Vanessa's. Leah, Steve, Buck, Gabrielle, and I all drove back and forth between Cambridge and Maine all the time, and we weren't always careful to do long drives only when we were well rested. Feeling ridiculously vulnerable, I called Leah, listened to her voicemail message, and then called Rita at work and invited her to dinner. I was hoping for her sake that Quinn had apologized and that she'd refuse my invitation because he was taking her out. In fact, she hadn't heard from him since Saturday's fight and sounded happy to accept. When I made lasagne for the three of us, I made a second pan for Vanessa's family. Since lasagne is perishable, you can't leave it on a doorstep, so I called to make sure that someone was home.

Avery answered. When I'd explained the reason for my call, she said, 'What?'

'I have a lasagne for you,' I repeated. 'I wanted to see whether I could drop it off.'

'Why?'

Although taking food to the bereaved is a little old-fashioned, it isn't freakish. Furthermore, as I reminded myself, when Avery's father had died the previous winter, she must have become familiar with customary responses to a death in the family. Even so, I said, 'I thought that after Fiona's death, it might help to have food in the house.'

'We already have food.' Belatedly, she added, 'But it was nice of you to offer.'

I'd also intended to ask about writing to Hatch and to Fiona's parents, but I didn't feel like listening to Avery's response to a request for addresses. For all I knew, she'd never heard of sympathy notes and would find my intention incomprehensible. I settled for asking to speak to Vanessa, but Avery said that her mother wasn't home. I was heartily glad to have the call end.

'A barbarian!' I said to Rowdy. 'And to think that her mother reads Jane Austen.'

SEVEN

On Wednesday morning over breakfast, Steve and I talked about Rita, but neither of us could think of a way to help her. At dinner the previous night, she'd done her best to be sociable, but she'd seemed like someone in mourning. All we could do, we decided, was to be with her. Two hours later, when I met Max Crocker, I changed my mind.

As is perhaps needless to say, Max Crocker had not submitted an online application to become the new man in Rita's life. Rather, he had adopted a malamute from a shelter and wanted another as a companion for himself and as a

63

playmate for his dog, a male named Mukluk. I'd claimed his application for two reasons. First, I was the Malamute Rescue volunteer closest to his house, which was in Cambridge. Second, having performed the unpleasant task of turning down the Di Bartolomeos, Irving Jensen, Eldon Flood, and so on, I deserved a reward. Screening Max Crocker's application would constitute what dog trainers call a 'jackpot', a fantastic treat given for first-rate performance, usually when the dog has completed a whole series of desired behaviors one right after the other. Animal behaviorists will tell you that in dog training, jackpots don't work. Among volunteers for breed-rescue groups, we take positive reinforcement where we find it or where we dole it out to ourselves.

I loved Max's application the minute I read it online, and I continued to love it when I'd printed it out and studied it in detail. Among other things, not only was his yard fenced, but he was concerned that the fence might be insufficiently secure to contain the new malamute he wanted to adopt. Mukluk, he wrote, respected the fence and showed no desire to escape. Would someone from Malamute Rescue be able to take a look at the fence and advise him about its adequacy for a more typical malamute? Would she ever! With few exceptions, the dreadful applicants go on and on about what great dog owners they are and what perfect homes they'll provide; and the perfect applicants express doubts about themselves and ask for advice. Anyway, Max had provided a detailed list of the dogs he'd owned, including a Scottish terrier his family had had when he was a child. The veterinary clinic he gave as reference was in New Haven, Connecticut. I called the number.

'This is Holly Winter from Malamute Rescue,' I said. 'One of your clients has applied to adopt a dog, and I'm calling to check the reference.'

'The client's name?' the woman asked.

'Max Crocker. The dog is Mukluk. Max also has a cat.'

'Oh, Mukluk! He's a great dog. We're going to miss him. Max is a wonderful owner. He was in here all the time. He does everything. He goes above and beyond.'

So, to skip ahead, ten o'clock on Wednesday morning found me ringing the bell of Max Crocker's house, which was on a quiet street a few blocks from Fresh Pond Parkway, not far from Huron Avenue and thus not far from where Steve and I live. Like our house, which is the barn-red one at 256 Concord Avenue, Max's had three stories and was made of wood, but his had experienced greater upward social mobility than ours had. Both had started out as unabashedly plebeian. The improvements we'd made on ours, including work I'd done with my own hands, had gentrified it a bit, but Max's showed unmistakable signs of having been transformed by a Henry Higgins of an architect. In place of a plain porch, it had a little deck with natural wood partitions and planter boxes, and the creamy yellow of its facade had jazzy but tasteful details, including wide frames around obviously new windows. The front door was made of a rich, dark wood so exotic that I didn't recognize it. The hardware looked like solid brass.

Mukluk may have been atypical of his breed in respecting the boundary of an iffy fence, but in greeting me by dropping to the floor and rolling over for a tummy rub, he was pure malamute. I was almost certain that he'd originally come from a pet shop, which is to say that he'd been whelped at one of the thousands of puppy mills that breed dogs with less care and compassion than amateur gardeners lavish on their tomato plants. Alternatively, he'd come from a back-yard breeder who'd bred one pet-shop dog to another. Like my own three malamutes, he was dark gray and white, but he was tremendously tall and rangy, with long, fine-boned legs, a narrow chest, a head that belonged on a collie, and ears that suggested Dumbo in flight. When I'd finished rubbing his white chest, he rose to his feet and greeted me with peals of *woo-woo-woo* so familiar and so heartfelt that I couldn't help laughing.

'Holly,' the man said. 'Thank you for coming. Max Crocker. And Mukluk.' Max was a handsome, rugged-looking man who could've modeled for the Orvis catalog. In fact, his charcoal sweater might well have come from Orvis. His short brown hair was shot with gray. He was about five ten, with broad shoulders, and when we shook hands, his grip was firm. He'd said on

66

his application that there was only one member of his household. Even so, with Rita in mind, I checked out the third finger of his left hand and was happy to find it bare. Rita appreciates a clean-shaven, well-dressed man with skilfully trimmed hair and neatly cut nails. Max Crocker was just such a man.

After I'd said the usual things about being glad to meet both of them, I voiced my admiration for Max's house and managed to do so without referring to Rita, who would love the place as much as I did – and would, I vowed, do so at the earliest possible moment, that is, as soon as I could contrive to introduce her to Max. The interior of the house had obviously been gutted and totally redone. The design was simple and open, with floors made of hardwood in the living room and dining room, and smooth stone in the foyer and kitchen. The couches and chairs were leather, a material that stands up well to dogs. Artwork was everywhere: bold paintings and striking photographs on the walls, pieces of stone sculpture in the backyard, the fence that had, alas, been chosen for aesthetics rather than for canine containment.

'Well, you're right,' I told Max. 'The typical malamute is going to get under and out of this in seconds.' To Mukluk, who was trailing along with us, I said, 'You are an exceptionally good boy.'

'He really is,' Max said. 'Of course, he's never out here alone. In New Haven, I had a six-foot fence – we just moved here a month ago – and I still didn't leave him out by himself. But from what I understand, he's an exceptionally easy malamute. We've never had a problem with other dogs, including males. And he and the cat are great friends. They both sleep on the bed with me.'

Naturally, I didn't respond by asking, 'And does someone sleep *in* the bed with you?' When we screen homes for rescue dogs, we feel entitled to grill people. Because many rescue dogs have been repeatedly passed along from owner to owner, booted out, neglected, or worse, we try to make sure that our adopters will offer permanent, loving, responsible homes. Still, there are limits to the kinds of questions you can get away with asking. For example, after one young couple complained about having been interrogated about what kind of birth control they used, Betty banned the topic.

'The cat,' I said. 'That's the only potential problem with your application. We just don't get a lot of dogs we can trust with cats. Also, you need a female, and the dogs coming into rescue tend to be males. Mukluk might be fine with another male, but it's the other one I'd worry about. So, you need a female who'd be good with Mukluk and your cat. We don't have one right now.'

'I can wait,' he said. 'That'll give me time to do something about the fence.'

'Think of me as your matchmaker,' I said. 'Or your adoption social worker. Your advocate. I will do my best to find you the right dog. We're

68

getting a young female from Maine, but I don't know much about her yet. She'll need to be evaluated and vetted. I have no idea how she is with other dogs. Or with cats. But I'll find out.'

Max offered me coffee. I accepted. As we sat at the granite island in his kitchen, he made the same French roast that Rita buys, and I learned that he was a professor of psychology. A psychologist! Just like Rita! So, of course, I immediately said that I had a dear friend and tenant who was also a psychologist, and when I mentioned Rita's name, Max sat up a little straighter and, if I may slip into the Boston vernacular, looked wicked impressed and said that Rita had an excellent reputation. He went on to explain that he was not a clinician but an academic psychologist, a researcher. Close enough for me! I didn't say so, nor did I mention that he and Rita were both from New York City, and instead of telling Max that Rita had a Scottie, the breed of his childhood, I decided to let him make that discovery for himself. Furthermore, on inspiration, I created the occasion for him to do it.

'I don't know if you'd be interested,' I said, 'but my dog-training club is having an event in a few weeks. On May eleventh. It's a Saturday. It's part of National Pet Week. The idea is to help educate the public about responsible dog ownership. There'll be what's called a Meet the Breed part, so people learn about different breeds, and we'll have booths run by rescue groups, including ours. I'd love to have Mukluk there. He'd be perfect. It's at the Cambridge

Armory, which is on Concord Ave., right near the Fresh Pond traffic circle. It's no distance from here. You could walk.'

Max agreed to be there with Mukluk. All that remained was to persuade Rita to show up, too. Well, almost all. There was also the matter of Willie's less than ideal temperament. If I muzzled Willie, Rita would protest, and a muzzle would, in any case, create a poor and misleading impression of the breed. Could Steve be persuaded to drug Willie for the occasion? Probably not. Besides, a sedative might have the paradoxical effect of making Willie agitated instead of peaceful. There was also the matter of Willie and Max's cat, a gorgeous and gigantic male red tabby Maine coon cat who strolled in while we were having coffee. Anyway, the problem of Willie was one I'd solve later. If need be, I'd drag Rita there without her dog. The crucial thing was to get Max and Rita together. I felt absolutely confident that they were made for each other.

EIGHT

Sweeping her eyes over the dogs and handlers, Avery said softly, 'Hardly any men. I don't know why Mom bothered dragging me here. She should've brought Hatch instead.'

Although Steve was standing a good two feet away from me, I could feel every muscle in his body stiffen. The remark jolted me, too. Fiona had crashed her car and died on Sunday night. It was now Thursday evening, far too soon for Hatch or anyone else to be on the lookout for a replacement. At least for now, decency required everyone to think of Fiona as irreplaceable.

To backtrack. On Wednesday, when I'd called Vanessa to get the information I needed to write sympathy notes to Hatch and to Fiona's parents, she'd asked about dog training. 'That must sound heartless, but I believe in getting back to normal life as quickly as possible,' she'd explained. 'No matter how hard it is. When Jim, my husband, died, that's what I did, and that's what I made the children do. Life simply has to go on. Different people deal with loss in different ways, but that's ours. So, dog training?'

The armory where the Cambridge Dog Training Club holds its classes is less than a half mile down Concord Avenue from our house, so Steve

71

and the dogs and I often go on foot. I'd invited Vanessa to walk with us, but she'd said that her father would be with her and that he might insist on going by car. 'Or worse, once it was time to go home, he'd decide that it was too dark and dangerous in the big, bad city, and we'd be stuck begging a ride or trying to find a cab that would take Ulla. No, we'll see you there.'

So, when Steve and I were checking in at the desk in the front hallway, Vanessa appeared with Ulla and also with Tom and Avery; why, I couldn't imagine until Avery glanced into the big hall where we train and made the unfortunate remark about the shortage of men and, of course, about Hatch. I chose to ignore Avery's tactlessness. After all, I knew nothing about her relationship with Fiona. They'd seemed to be on good terms, but I couldn't remember having noticed any particular affection or closeness between the two. For all I knew, Avery had hated Fiona and was relieved to have her dead and thus out of Hatch's life.

'I'm afraid you'll be very bored,' I told Avery. 'We don't even have a spare dog for you to train.' We'd brought only two, Lady and Sammy. Neither Steve nor I had any great ambitions for Lady as a competition obedience dog. Rather, I was convinced that the structure and clarity of formal obedience work would help to build the timid little pointer's self-confidence. As it was, she trusted Steve completely. She also trusted his shepherd, India, and she'd made gratifying progress in trusting Rowdy, Kimi,

Sammy, and me. She continued, however, always to look outside herself for strength. Corny though it may sound, I hoped that in mastering the exercises, she'd discover her inner resources and thus her own strength. In contrast, full-of-himself Sammy was convinced that the point of obedience training was the point of life itself: fun, fun, and more fun! At the moment, as we waited for our classes to begin, he was fooling around with Ulla, who was preening and *woo-woo*ing and otherwise flirting with him so outrageously that one of our instructors said as she passed by, 'Oh-oh! Sammy's got a girl-friend!' And he did, too.

'These two were made for each other,' Vanessa said.

The Cambridge Armory, however dear to me, is not one of those funky Richardsonian Romanesque fortresses. Rather, from the outside, it looks like an unprepossessing elementary school, and the big interior space we use for dog training is the kind of gymnasium you find in high schools and YMCAs everywhere. The bleachers that line one of the long sides can be folded up to create extra floor space, but we extend them for classes so we have seating for people who aren't working with their dogs and a place to leave our jackets, coats, and training gear. Seated at the near end of the bleachers was Elizabeth McNamara, who always accompanied her husband, Isaac, to dog training, but who never handled their young puli, Persimmon. A tall, lanky man of about seventy-five who dressed in khakis and plaid flannel shirts, Isaac liked to imagine that people mistook his wife for his daughter. The error probably did occur now and then. Elizabeth was ten or fifteen years his junior, and the two differed radically in size and style. Elizabeth was a tiny little woman with delicate bones and small feet and hands, and she carried to the extreme the Cantabrigian preference for ethnic and artisanal clothing and accessories. Almost everything she wore had been spun, woven, embroidered, or crafted by hand in Third World countries or in economically disadvantaged regions of the United States: Peruvian vests, African paper beads, hand-knitted Appalachian shawls, and loose peasant shirts made of unbleached muslin. Their house was full of museum-quality quilts. Elizabeth's full, curly, shoulder-length white hair framed her pretty face. She made no perceptible effort to look younger than she was, but she had an appealing agelessness. I suspected that her diminutive build and her husband's affection for her made him see her as she had looked when they'd first met. She had a high-pitched voice, and her laughter was like tinkling bells.

Spotting Elizabeth, Tom headed straight for her and in no time was settled next to her on the bleachers. The sullen Avery sat with them. The classes that had been meeting when we'd arrived came to an end, and Vanessa and I, with Ulla and Lady, joined the big drop-in class that served a variety of functions. Some of the dogs and handlers in the group had just completed the basic beginners' class and were there to keep training and to have fun, and others were preparing for the Canine Good Citizen test. Lady and I were there to work on the nit-picking details of the obedience exercises in a relaxed, cheerful context; in other words, I expected the low-pressure atmosphere to counterbalance my insufferable perfectionism, as I'm glad to say that it did. When I tell a dog to sit, I'm not just telling him to put his rear end down. What I'm after is a fast, perfectly straight sit in which the dog is close to my left side but not leaning into me. Furthermore, in my estimation, a dog whose eyes are fixed on anything except my face is a dog whose mind is wandering and who is thus not sitting at all. In case I sound like a tyrant, I must mention that by way of compensation, I train with first-rate treats: bits of steak, roast beef, liver, and Cheddar cheese. Also, when I expect a dog's total attention, I give exactly the same complete concentration in return. Because the class had about twenty dog-handler teams, the instructor had two assistants, so Lady had lots of opportunity to practice letting people put their hands on her during the stand-for-examination exercise. The combination of hard work, high standards, great tidbits, and lavish praise did wonders for Lady, who was too busy to be nervous, and before we knew it, the hour was up, and the class ended.

I'd left my gear on the bleachers near Tom, Elizabeth, and Avery, and when Lady and I approached them, I realized that Tom and Elizabeth had used their time together to discover and pursue the passionate interest they had in common: illnesses, diseases, ailments, and remedies of every possible kind. Instead of greeting me and saying something encouraging about Lady, Tom immediately conveyed the fascinating news that Elizabeth had celiac disease. 'No gluten whatsoever!' he announced. 'She can't tolerate even an iota of it. She tells me that she has been instructed to think of it as rat poison, can you imagine?'

'Dogs can be gluten intolerant, too,' I said. 'Actually, it's quite common in people of Irish ancestry and in Irish setters. It's pretty easy to manage in dogs. You buy food that contains rice or whatever instead of wheat.'

'Just as easy to manage in people,' Elizabeth said, 'once you educate yourself and adapt to it. If only arthritis were that easy!'

'Elizabeth suffers terribly,' Tom said with satisfaction.

'So do you!' she exclaimed, as if Tom had given her unfair credit.

'And neither of us can tolerate anything but Tylenol,' he said. 'Acetaminophen. We both buy the generic.'

Overdoses of acetaminophen occur fairly often in dogs, and the drug shouldn't be given to cats at all. Steve won't even let me keep it in the house. But I didn't say so. Far be it from me to spoil this cozily shared valetudinarianism. In any case, Isaac and Persimmon appeared, as did Vanessa and Ulla, and all of us began to gather our belongings together and get ready to go home.

'How did it go?' I asked Vanessa.

'Great!' she said. 'The instructor – what's his name? – says that we should take the CGC test and then start getting ready for a show. A trial, I should say.'

'Ron,' I said. 'He's a terrific plumber, by the way, if you ever need one. There's a CGC test a week from Saturday. Gabrielle is coming down from Maine, and she'll be taking Molly. It's at a park in Newton. There'll an obedience match, too. Steve and I are judging. You could put Ulla in Prenovice obedience, too, if you want. Prenovice is all on leash, so nothing too embarrassing can happen. It's fun.'

'But watch out for us,' Steve said. 'We're what the old-timers call hard markers.'

'We are not,' I said. 'Don't listen to him! We're not even licensed obedience judges. We just do matches once in a while. This is a fun match. It's supposed to be fun.'

'Is Leah going?' Vanessa asked.

'I don't think so,' I said. 'That's when Reading Period starts, and she needs to finish her term papers and study for finals.'

Harvard students, I should explain, have about ten days after classes end and before finals begin to do all the work they were supposed to have been doing from the beginning of the semester. Harvard being Harvard, this opportunity to cram and thus to pass courses in spite of never previously having cracked open a book is not

77

called something appropriate such as Procrastinators' Interval or Sluggards' Last Chance. Rather, it is known as Reading Period and, Leah tells me, is officially billed as a time of reflection and contemplation. About what? The consequences of flunking out?

'Reading Period,' Vanessa said with a nostalgic sigh. 'When all the feeble-minded white male legacy admissions used to borrow my notes. Too bad about Leah. I hope we'll have a chance to see her again soon.'

'She'll be around all summer,' I said. 'She'll be working for Steve. And she'll be at this National Pet Week event the club is doing, too. It's in a couple of weeks. May eleventh. Saturday afternoon. Her exams don't start until after that.'

'Don't bother asking Vanessa to help,' said Isaac, who was the principal organizer of the event. 'She's already signed up. I recruited her before she'd even been here! She's contributing food, and she's already doing publicity. We're on all these events calendars on the Internet. And Holly, you promised me some books.' The club's major public-education effort took place every September, when AKC-affiliated clubs were encouraged to hold Responsible Dog Ownership Day events. Isaac and a few other exceptionally competitive members had decided, however, that if our club were to be in the running for one of the American Kennel Club's Community Achievement Awards, we'd have to do a lot more than our usual RDO day; rather, we were supposed to make the club an integral part of the community in dozens of ways. It seemed to me that our small obedience club stood almost no chance against big kennel clubs with large memberships, but I kept my opinion to myself.

'Isaac, I have not forgotten.' Steve and I had co-authored a dog diet book with a blunt title: *No More Fat Dogs.* I had also promised copies of my solo effort, *101 Ways to Cook Liver*, which was purportedly a dog-treat cookbook but was actually about training with food. 'If you don't trust me, I can drop the books off at your house, but I'll be there. I promise.' I was on the verge of telling Isaac about having recruited Max Crocker and Mukluk, but I stopped myself. If Vanessa heard about Max, she'd do her best to match him up with Avery. I had no intention of letting her do any such thing. With all my experience in pairing rescue dogs with just the right adopters, I was the veteran matchmaker. Furthermore, I'd already met Max, whereas Vanessa didn't even know that he existed. Besides, he was too old for Avery. And ideal for Rita.

When Vanessa spoke, I must've leaped two feet in the air. 'We'll have to get the two love-birds together soon,' she said.

In a second, I realized that she meant Sammy and Ulla rather than Max and Rita or possibly Max and Avery.

'Absolutely,' I said with the enthusiasm of relief. 'Absolutely! Whenever you like.'

NINE

On Friday morning over breakfast, Steve said, 'I don't like the way Fiona's just disappeared. It's like she never existed. You did write to her parents, didn't you?'

'Yes. Of course! And to Hatch. Leah did, too. And I sent the addresses to Gabrielle and my father, not that he'll do anything, but Gabrielle will.'

'There's no funeral around here? Memorial service?'

'I looked online. Her parents are having a memorial service, but that's in California. There just has to be something at the hospital, Brigham and Women's, but maybe it's private. I couldn't find it listed anywhere.'

'We could make a donation. Do that, would you? Sorry to dump it on you.'

I refilled our coffee cups. 'It's OK. It's better than OK. It's a good idea. I'll send something to the hospital in her memory.'

'You know, Holly, if it'd been one of our dogs...'

'Don't say that! But you're right. We'd be flooded with calls and cards and email. Maybe her parents are getting that kind of support, and we don't know about it. I hope they are. And

Hatch, too.'

'Not from his own family.'

'Steve, we don't know that, either. This could be the face they show to the world. Some people believe in a brave front.'

He turned his attention to what was left of his scrambled eggs and toast. Eventually, he said, 'It bothers me that Fiona left from here. From our house.'

'Steve, I don't like it, either. And I especially don't like it that she had that accident so soon after she left. Nashua is ... maybe it's an hour away. Less? That's practically no time! But I've been over it again and again in my mind, and Fiona had almost nothing to drink. She had one small glass of wine when she first got here, and after that, she had a big dinner. With no more wine. And what I found online said that alcohol was *not* involved. She did take an antihistamine, but she was a doctor. She had to have known what she was taking. And she wasn't just any doctor. She was a young doctor finishing a residency at Brigham and Women's. It's one of the best hospitals in the country. In the world! She of all people would've known not to take something that would make her drowsy.'

'A moose, maybe. Or a deer.'

Collisions with moose and deer are fairly common in northern New England. But Fiona had hit a tree. I said so. 'Of course,' I added, 'she could've swerved to avoid wildlife. But that doesn't account for why she'd left the highway. What I read on the web was that the

81

accident took place on an exit ramp. Or maybe just off the ramp. I wondered whether she was afraid that she was falling asleep. Or maybe she felt sick.'

'It couldn't have been the food. The rest of us were fine.'

'And if she'd felt dangerously ill, you'd think she'd have called for help. She must've had a cell phone.'

'For all we know, she did call.'

'The news report didn't mention that.'

'If it's not on Google, it didn't happen?'

I laughed. 'Exactly. And it's also possible that she was just looking for a ladies' room. But I may know more later. Sammy has a play date with Ulla at three o'clock. I'm not going to ask for details, but Vanessa may say something.' I thought for a moment and said, 'Something such as, "Thanks for offering the lasagne that my unmannerly daughter was rude enough to refuse".'

Weirdly enough, as it turned out, at three o'clock that afternoon when Vanessa opened the gate to her yard and welcomed Sammy and me, one of the first things she said was, 'Thank you for offering food. I hope that Avery told you how gracious it was of you.'

'Of course.' I mean, what else could I say? That besides training her dog in the rudiments of good citizenship, Vanessa should have been instilling those fundamentals in her daughter? Not that any self-respecting malamute would've refused a pan of lasagne. 'Sometimes in these situations, people are overwhelmed with food.

And offers.'

'We're not, really. It's not as if Fiona had really been part of the family.' She paused. 'Even so. Well, distraction is the best medicine, isn't it? Ulla, look who's come to play with you!'

Ulla hardly needed to have her attention directed to Sammy, who was wiggling and waggling all over and straining at his leash in response to her adorable play bow. Is that the cutest posture in dogdom? Front down, rear up, tail swishing back and forth? And that let's-play gleam in the eye?

Correctly reading my hesitation, Vanessa said, 'Fully fenced. Gates closed. You *are* paranoid, aren't you?'

I smiled. 'I'm very careful.' Then I admitted the truth: 'Careful to the point of paranoia.' With that, I let Sammy loose. And the chase was on! Ulla zoomed away with Sammy after her, and when she veered around, he streaked ahead, doubled back, and ran a little circle around her. By city standards, Vanessa's yard was big, more than twice the size of mine, long and narrow, so the dogs had the space they needed to run full tilt, and a beautiful sight they were, speeding down and back, around and around in great ovals. Vah-vah-vah-voom!

Vanessa and I had the sense to stay out of the dogs' way. At first, we stood with our backs almost pressed against the fence near the gate, but when the dogs had slowed down a bit, we moved to a patio at the back of the house, an area paved with bluestone where we took seats on wrought-iron chairs that matched a long rectangular table. Overhead was an iron structure, a trellis or pergola, I suppose, with vines that hadn't yet leafed out. Just in back of us were glass doors to an expensive-looking kitchen, the kind that's all granite and glass and stainless steel. The day was mild and sunny, so we were comfortable outdoors.

'I've always liked this house,' I said. 'I didn't know the people who were here before you, but I've walked by it hundreds of times.' Like Max Crocker's house, Vanessa's was gentrified working class, but it blended more smoothly than his did with the surrounding neighborhood. Like his, it was painted in a warm shade of pale yellow, but it retained its original porch and hadn't gained the kinds of window frames and outdoor partitions that architects love to add.

'You've never been in it? We'll have to give you the tour. It was all redone about ten years ago, and the kitchen was done all over again maybe five years ago. The third floor has apartment possibilities. I may do something about that. For my father. Or maybe Avery or Hatch. We'll have to see what develops.'

'Ulla is going to ruin your yard,' I said.

'Fair enough. It's hers. But she's not a big digger, and if she starts, I intervene. The yard is one of the reasons I bought this house. The fence is high enough, and it's sort of a bonus that everything's lawn and mulch with shrubs and trees by the fence. There aren't any flower beds to ex-

84

cavate. Just look at the two them! Bats out of hell!' My yard isn't heaven, but it's hardly hell. Vanessa must have seen my expression. 'No offense meant! I just meant...'

'I know. And this chance to run hell for leather is exactly what Sammy needs. Leah takes Kimi running, and Steve usually takes a dog or two to work, where there's an exercise area. My neighbor Kevin is a runner – you'll have to meet him – and sometimes I take Rowdy or Sammy and tag along with him. But all of our dogs need this kind of chance to just fly around and let off steam. Sammy most of all. They tear around in our yard, but we just don't have this kind of space.'

'You're more than welcome here! Just show up!'

As I was about thank her, one of the glass doors to the kitchen opened, and Avery stuck her head out. Although it must have been three fifteen or so, she was dressed in blue-striped pajamas and a white terry cloth robe. 'Mom, are we out of sugar?'

'Of course not. If the bowl is empty, look in the cupboard. There's a bag there. And for heaven's sake, Avery, get dressed! Holly will think that you just got out of bed. And if you're making coffee, make some for us, please.'

When Avery had closed the door, Vanessa said quietly, 'She refuses to go back to Bennington. I've signed her up for Harvard Summer School. She needs to start getting out. It was one thing right after her father's death, but this has gone

85

on way too long. It's just not practical to hang around doing nothing until you find yourself. Well, thank God for dogs! These two were made for each other!'

'They really do play well together,' I said. 'They know all the right moves.'

'If only the same could be said for all of us! Coffee?'

I accepted. For some unknown reason, instead of just filling up two mugs, Vanessa insisted on bringing out cups, saucers, spoons, a sugar bowl, a creamer, and an insulated carafe of coffee. Worse, she also carried out a small plate of cookies. Coffee alone would've worked, but the food attracted the attention of the dogs, who were determined to have their share. I managed to get Sammy in a reasonably solid down-stay on the bluestone, but Ulla refused to be deterred and kept flinging herself in the air. Vanessa eventually settled for holding the little plate well above her head while she and I each took a cookie. I ate mine as fast as possible. As Vanessa was lowering the plate, when it was at about shoulder height, Ulla sprang, and all the cookies slid as one mass off the plate and into her mouth.

'Oh, well,' said Vanessa. 'At least they were lemon wafers and not chocolate. They won't do her any harm. Life with malamutes! But look how good Sammy is! He really is the perfect dog.'

Sammy's eyes were gleaming, and his tail was sailing back and forth, but his belly was still on the bluestone, and he'd refrained from crawling

86

forward.

'If Ulla hadn't caught all the cookies, he'd've lost it,' I said. 'But he is a good boy, aren't you, Sammy? You are a good, good dog.' After checking to make sure that there were no crumbs to trigger a dog fight, I released him from his down. 'OK!'

The food having vanished into Ulla's stomach, the dogs resumed their zooming around, and Vanessa and I were left to drink our coffee. The opportunity to ask about Fiona was almost palpably absent. Furthermore, I couldn't think of a way to inquire about Avery's difficulties. Rita, being a psychotherapist, was always asking outrageously nosy questions with such calm self-confidence that people tended to supply answers without taking offense. If anything, they seemed to find her interest flattering. In my place, she'd have drawn Vanessa into a discussion of what anyone would have seen as Avery's prolonged mourning and depression, and Rita'd have gone on to find out whether Avery was seeing a therapist or taking antidepressants. My stepmother, Gabrielle, would've been as effective as Rita. I comforted myself with the thought that both Rita and Gabrielle lacked my absolute self-assurance about investigating canine causes for concern. If I'd been worried about Ulla, I wouldn't have hesitated to interrogate Vanessa. What's more, with not a trace of embarrassment, I could've checked Ulla for mammary tumors or stuck my nose in her ears in search of the nasty scent of infection. Yet here I was, unable to formulate a simple statement of concern about Vanessa's daughter! Of course, I had yet to raise the matter of Ulla's weight, but I'd eventually find the opportunity, and Avery was far more depressed than Ulla was plump.

So, we drifted into talking about Jane Austen and, in particular, about *Emma*. Vanessa turned out to share my dissatisfaction with the ending. Because Cambridge is filled with people who study literature, whereas I merely devour it, I was usually reluctant to voice my view that Emma's marriage to Mr Knightley was a gigantic mistake.

'She marries an old man!' I exclaimed. 'And a bossy, critical, controlling old man, too. Not that Knightley is a terrible person. In a lot of ways, he's a good friend to Emma, but the point is that he should stay that way. He's a paternal friend who compensates for the inadequacies of her father. And she marries him?'

'And what about twenty years later?' Vanessa demanded. 'When Emma is still a vigorous woman, Knightley is going to be in his dotage. What happens to all those country walks then?'

'Emma gets a dog,' I said. 'That's my only other complaint about the book, really. I mean, Emma *needs* a dog. A papillon, I think. I see her with a toy breed, something she could pick up and carry on a long walk. Of course, in Jane Austen's time, the whole phenomenon of pet ownership wasn't what it is now. Still. But there's no such excuse for Knightley. The age difference is just too great.'

'Like our dear neighbors,' Vanessa said. 'Isaac can't keep up with Elizabeth. Not that he's condescending or moralistic the way Knightley is. Not at all. But the age difference!'

'I don't think that Elizabeth minds,' I said. 'And it's only recently that the age difference matters. Even now, Isaac isn't in his dotage. He's as sharp as ever, and he's active.'

'But for how long? He has terrible arthritis. He lives on anti-inflammatories. And he has some kind of heart problem. Oh, God! I sound like my father. Leave it to Tom to know everything about everyone's infirmities. And remedies.'

'It's just his way of getting to know people,' I said charitably.

Sounding grateful, Vanessa said, 'Tom can be a dreadful old bore, but he is a dear man. He's generous to a fault. He overindulges all of us. He truly does want us to have whatever we want. We really cherish him. All of us do. And there's nothing actually wrong with him, you know. He'll be with us for a long time.'

Not ten seconds later, Tom Oakley appeared at one of the glass doors to the kitchen. Easing it open he said, 'The two of you! You'll get pneumonia sitting out there.'

Vanessa rolled her eyes. 'We're perfectly comfortable. Did you and Elizabeth have a nice walk?'

'Very pleasant. I'm getting to know the neighborhood. Now if you'll excuse me, I'm getting out of this draft. And I'd advise the two of you to do the same.'

When Tom had shut the door to the kitchen, Vanessa said, 'He's been keeping Elizabeth company when she walks Persimmon. As I said, Isaac can't keep up with her.'

'Oh, that's just their usual division of labor. Isaac trains their dogs, and Elizabeth walks them. *Dog*, I should say. Singular. Persimmon is the only one they have now. Sammy, here! I should get going. We'll have to do this again soon.'

'Absolutely! Tomorrow? Or are you going to a dog show?'

'We're not entered,' I said as I snapped Sammy's leash to his collar. 'Rowdy and Sammy are out of coat, Rowdy more than Sammy. I'm not crazy about the judge, anyway.'

Looking hesitant, Vanessa said, 'Well, if I wouldn't be in your way, I'd love to tag along sometime. I've never been to a dog show.'

'You've ... you've never been to a show?' I stammered. 'Never? No, you've been in Vermont, but there are...' Barely knowing where to begin, I broke off and thought fast. For good reason! Indeed, there I was confronted with a heathen who was telling me that she'd never so much as set foot in a church. 'We'll go tomorrow.' I had intended to devote Saturday to scraping the flaking paint off our house, but this was an emergency. Vanessa's immortal soul was in danger! There was no time to be lost.

'Lovely!' she said. 'What fun!'

TEN

'Is there anyone here you *don't* know?' Vanessa demanded with a laugh. 'Or I should say, is there anyone here who doesn't know you?'

'More people know Tom Fool than Tom Fool knows,' I said, remembering only a second too late that her father's name was Tom. Happily, she showed no sign of noticing my faux pas.

A big outdoor show with splendid tents and sunny skies would've offered the ideal setting in which to introduce Vanessa to the pageantry of dog shows. I'd never much liked the site of Saturday's show, a trade center with all the festive allure of a failing carpet factory, but if you're hell-bent on baptizing someone by immersion, it doesn't make sense to whine about the inadequacies of the local creek or to delay the rite until the water rises. We'd been wandering from ring to ring and now, at about one o'clock, had just finished watching the judging of Italian greyhounds. In the course of our meandering, I'd stopped to chat with a few people. By my standards, there hadn't been all that many. Malamutes had been judged early, before we'd arrived. Besides, the judge had been as unpopular with others as he'd been with me, so the total malamute entry had been a

pitiful three. The show was just that, a conformation show – a beauty contest, but don't tell
anyone I said that – with no obedience, agility,
or other performance events, so we'd run into
only a few people I knew from those little sub-
kingdoms of Greater Dogdom. Still, the crucial,
defining elements of a show were there in rich
abundance: the sights and the sounds, the beauty
of the breeds both great and small, the woofing
and yipping, and the thick, complex, delicious
scent of grooming spray, liver bait, freshly
bathed dog, stale sandwiches, and all the rest, in
my case, mother's milk. No exaggeration! It's a
miracle that I was born in a hospital instead of
being whelped at a show in a dog crate or on a
grooming table, and it's entirely likely that at
some point in my infancy, one of my parents
mistook a bottle of coat conditioner for a baby
bottle and pacified me with some sort of lanolin
concoction in place of formula.

Have I digressed? Sorry.

'Besides,' I said to Vanessa, 'I've been showing dogs my whole life. So, I do know—'

'Holly! Hey, I didn't know you'd be here. I
need to talk to you.' The speaker was Katrina,
the rescue volunteer Betty had mentioned, the
one who'd been upset by a strange phone call. A
soft-spoken, unassuming young woman, Katrina
had a round face, fair skin, and white-blonde
hair styled in a Dutch clip. When Katrina and
her husband had applied to adopt a dog, I'd
wondered whether she had the force of character
needed to manage a malamute. As it turned out,

she was as persistent as she was gentle, and she'd worked wonders with the shy Kaya, who'd spent the first two years of her life alone in a chain-link kennel. So far as we could tell, the first time Kaya left her owner's property was the day I picked her up and drove her to Steve's clinic, which was apparently the first building she'd ever entered. She'd had no socialization, no training, and no vet care. The sound of her own name meant nothing to her, and she had no idea what to do with dog toys. Now, three years later, because of Katrina and her husband, John, Kaya was happy and astonishingly self-confident.

So, when I introduced Vanessa and Katrina, I naturally had to tell Vanessa about Kaya, and Katrina about Ulla. Dog people being dog people, both of the women sped through the business of being happy to meet each other, and each dwelt at great length and with marked enthusiasm on how absolutely thrilled she'd be to make the acquaintance of the other's dog.

'Kaya isn't here, of course,' Katrina said. 'I'm helping a friend who shows Dobies. All I'm doing is lugging gear and keeping an eye on her dogs. She doesn't like to leave them unattended.'

'Good for her,' I said.

Speaking even more softly than usual, Katrina then asked me whether I'd heard the details of her phone call.

'Betty told me,' I said. 'You must've seen on the list that I had one, too. Horrible laughing.

93

Something about the dog I had before Rowdy, a golden. My Vinnie. And then obscenities. It was ugly.'

'What a horrible thing!' Vanessa exclaimed.

'Same man,' Katrina said. 'At first, I was very upset, but I'm OK now. Misery loves company!'

'I'm not exactly miserable,' I said, 'but I know what you mean. It's less personal.'

'John was furious,' Katrina said. 'And when he heard that this joker called you, too, and then Betty, he decided that the guy had something against rescue. You know, somebody who got our names from the website and took it from there. The days of privacy are long gone.'

'Not everyone realizes that,' I said.

'It's true,' Vanessa agreed.

'Yes, it is,' I said. 'Speaking of which, did you try to trace the call?'

'All I got was the area code, seven eight one, and that's hundreds of places. It's like a circle, well, a three-quarters circle outside Boston. But, Holly, the worst is that John is threatening that if anything else happens, we're going to quit doing rescue.'

I nearly wept. The greatest need of every breed-rescue group in the country was foster care, and foster care was just what Katrina and John had been providing.

'But if I get another call,' Katrina continued, 'I'm just not going to tell him about it.'

'Well, if he's the one who answers—'

What drowned me out and cut me off was the sound of Pippy Neff's off-key voice speaking my name. Possibly in response to the irritating tone, Katrina excused herself and took off, but if I'd sprinted away, Pippy'd have been on my tail. I did, however, make an effort to divert her from the topic of Rowdy.

'Pippy,' I said, 'this is Vanessa Jones. Vanessa, Pippy Neff. Vanessa has a bitch of your breeding. Ulla.' *Bitch:* the dog fancy's good, clean word for female. By defining the term in the context of introducing Pippy, I don't mean to suggest ... well, Pippy was, admittedly, female, in fact, decidedly so. She was a short, wide woman of maybe fifty-five with curly hair colored a vivid shade of coppery flamingo, but her most distinctive physical feature was her bosom, a tremendous outcropping of flesh that simply had to have been encased in wide bands of industrial-strength elastic. It's entirely possible that the constriction caused by this massive support affected her voice and that when she was naked, she no longer spoke in sour notes.

To Vanessa, Pippy said, 'It was a shame about Olympia. A tragedy.'

'Ulla's first owner,' Vanessa explained to me. 'A neighbor of mine. And a friend.'

'Such a nice girl,' Pippy said. 'I was sick about what happened. In the midst of life, we are in ... Holly, about Rowdy. I—'

'Has your puppy buyer reached you?' I asked. 'He talked to my father and to Betty Burley. He was—'

'Good news!' Pippy said. 'He's going to be able to keep his beautiful puppy. That's the best outcome, isn't it? He loves his puppy, and he's going to be able to keep him.'

I slowly inhaled and exhaled. 'As I understand it, the owner is away fourteen hours a day.'

'Oh, it's all going to work out,' Pippy said. 'He's looking into a dog walker. Or doggy day care.'

I held my tongue.

'So,' Pippy continued, 'you tell Betty that it's all taken care of.'

Vanessa and I exchanged glances, and as if acting on an unspoken plan, Vanessa looked at her watch and said, 'We'd better get going!'

'Yes, we should,' I agreed.

When we'd made our escape and were wandering from vendor to vendor, Vanessa said, 'I feel sorry for her dogs. Dogs have such sensitive ears! How do they stand her?'

'I've wondered.'

'And she never asked a thing about Ulla. She never even asked whether Ulla was all right.'

'Yes, I noticed.'

'Olympia didn't think much of Pippy.'

I shrugged.

'Does anyone?'

'Oh, yes,' I said. 'Pippy has a very high opinion of herself.'

ELEVEN

When I got home at three or so, our yard presented the kind of scene that always compels my father to bellow about the lilies of the field: 'They toil not, neither do they spin: And yet I say unto you, that even Solomon in all his glory was not arrayed like one of these.' Buck wouldn't have meant Steve, who was on the high ladder scraping paint while the gloriously arrayed Rita and Willie were keeping him company. As to their array, Rita, who was seated at the picnic table with the *Times* spread out in front of her, wore a cream-colored sweater, cropped black linen pants, and black leather shoes with wedge heels. Her hair was a neat brown cap of lightly streaked waves. Willie was, as always, groomed like a show dog – not by Rita, who'd be as likely to clip a dog's coat as she would be to cut her own hair, and who, in any case, had found a skilled terrier groomer to whom she paid a fortune to have Willie's coat hand-stripped. Pulling out the dead hair instead of cutting it produces great results, but pet owners almost never want to spend the money that hand-stripping costs, and few of them know how to do it themselves. As was also typical, Willie wore yet another brand-new collar, this one black and red, and he and Rita together could've been posing for a photo for the style section of a voguish publication, maybe even the *Times* itself. When I said hello to everyone, Willie's dark eyes flashed, and he cocked his head, but he remained at Rita's side and didn't bark or fly at me.

So, let me say now what I couldn't say to Rita. Let me shout it! What the hell was wrong with Quinn Youngman? Here was Rita, sensitive, perceptive, intelligent, witty, a loyal friend, a brilliant psychotherapist, looking not simply as pretty as a picture but actually looking like a picture, indeed, a picture of perfection; and complementing her was her equally stylish Scottie, Willie, groomed to match her and behaving flawlessly. And special credit to Willie, who worked so hard to control his naughty impulses. Here he was, the very model of the handsome canine gentleman! Separately and together, they deserved the best, as Quinn Youngman certainly was not, at least in my opinion. Steve, for God's sake, who liked almost everyone, had to struggle to get beyond Quinn's affectations and pretensions! Out of gratitude to Rita, who had been a wise counselor to both of us, Steve and I had knocked ourselves out to put aside our own feelings about Quinn and to think only of Rita's. And what were Rita's feelings about Quinn? God help her! As the saying goes, if love lights on a manure pile, there it will stay.

'Rita's refusing to have dinner with us,' Steve called down from the top of the ladder. 'Legal.'

Translation: Legal Sea Foods, which originated as a humble fish store in Inman Square in Cambridge but now has restaurants all over Boston and in some other lucky cities. Our destination was the one in Harvard Square.

'Steve just can't stand to see me stuck at home,' Rita said, 'even if I'm a little too old to mind not having a date on Saturday night.'

Treat in hand, I edged toward Willie without making eye contact, slipped the food into his mouth, gently touched his shoulder, moved slowly away, and took a seat at the picnic table.

'Good dog,' Rita told him. 'I must've asked you this before, but did you see any blood on Quinn?'

'No, I didn't. And I looked. Why? Have you heard from him?'

'No. Not from him and not from the dog catcher.'

'The Cambridge Animal Commission,' I corrected. 'Animal control.'

'Nor have I received a bill from Mount Auburn Hospital.'

I shrugged. 'Rita, I don't know what to say.'

'To hell with him,' Steve said. 'How about that?'

'Would you get down from that ladder?' I said. 'That's my job, you know. I'm the one who volunteered for it.'

'These gutters are bad,' he said. 'They need to be replaced.'

'I want you to get down. Remember the rule? Your rule? No working on the high ladder when there's a dog loose in the yard.'

Steve laughed. 'The rule doesn't apply to Willie. Or India or Lady.'

'Hah! Anti-malamute legislation,' I said. 'From you of all people. Rita, come to dinner with us! It has nothing to do with having a date or not having a date.'

'I have plans for the evening,' Rita said. 'In fact, I am spending Saturday night with Mr Darcy.'

'You're staying home to read *Pride and Prejudice*?'

'I've read it. More than once. Tonight, I'm watching it. *We* are watching it. Willie and I. In other words, I do have a date.'

'Mr Darcy!' I sighed deeply. 'I've been in love with him since I was about fifteen. But you could have dinner with us and then watch *Pride and Prejudice*.'

'I appreciate the offer, but I am fine on my own.'

'We know that! This is not a charity invitation, Rita.'

'Jane Austen never married, you know,' Rita said.

'Yes, but she had dinner with people.'

'Thank you, anyway,' Rita said, 'but I already have a date. A big date.'

'A date with your dog,' I said. 'You didn't get that idea from Jane Austen.'

'No, I didn't,' Rita said. 'I got it from you.'

TWELVE

When I opened the envelope late that same afternoon, Kimi was meandering around the kitchen and sniffing the floor in her usual hope of finding delicious morsels that the other dogs had overlooked. 'Damn it! Damn it all! Who sent me this?'

I addressed Kimi, but the question was rhetorical. Although I considered Kimi to be the most brilliant of our five dogs, I didn't actually expect her to reply in English. Also, if the anonymous message had been hers instead of mine, she wouldn't have minded at all. For one thing, not much bothers Kimi. For another, as applied to a female malamute, the word *bitch* is so ordinary that it doesn't pack a lot of punch.

Steve walked in. 'Sent you what?'

I handed him the sheet of plain white paper with the single word 'bitch' spelled out in glued-on letters that had been cut from a newspaper.

'Where'd this come from?' he asked.

'Mixed in with the mail. The envelope has a stamp, but there's no postmark and no return address.'

'I didn't notice.'

Because this was my house before Steve and I got married, the bulk of our mail is mine, so

101

Steve usually just scans for his own name, puts glaringly obvious junk with the recycling, and leaves everything else for me.

'There's no reason you would have.'

'Let me see the envelope.'

As Steve examined it, I took a second look and once again found nothing remarkable. It was the kind of cheap business-size white envelope sold by the million at office-supply stores, supermarkets, drugstores, and discount department stores. The flap was the kind that you have to moisten, not the pull-and-seal type that's becoming increasingly popular. My name and address were neatly and evenly printed on the front in blue ink. The printing was in the style that everyone is supposed to learn in first grade. The stamp showed the Liberty Bell.

'That's a Forever stamp,' I said. 'It's good even if the postage goes up.'

'Looks like a teacher's printing.'

'Why would a teacher have something against me? But you're right. There's nothing sloppy about any of it. The stamp is in the exact corner, and the printing is perfect. The lines are straight. The letters are evenly spaced. That's true about the glued-on letters, too. So, a neat person thinks I'm a bitch. You know what? I think I should forget about it. Let's feed the dogs and get going.'

And that's what we did. Because we both took showers and because Gabrielle called as we were about to leave, it was seven before we were settled in a cozy booth at Legal, where we ordered drinks, heard about the specials, studied the menu, and began to catch up with each other.

'I'm tempted to order lobster,' I said, 'so you won't think I'm a cheap date, but I think I'm going to have fried oysters and fried clams. Or maybe fish and chips. And you're having cherrystones and...?'

He shook his head. 'No, I'm having clam chowder and that scallop special. You know, I've been thinking about that letter.'

'It's hardly a letter.'

'Hate mail.'

'It isn't even that. Steve, it's not worth thinking about. If it were, I'd show it to Kevin. But if I do, he'll either tell me that it's not threatening—'

'True enough.'

'Or he'll overreact and deliver his usual cop lecture about the need to be on red alert about everything. He's hardly going to turn it into an official police matter. You've heard Kevin on the subject of people who watch crime-scene shows on TV and then expect the Cambridge police to do DNA tests for every trivial little—'

'He probably didn't lick the envelope, anyway. But that reminds me. I was thinking—'

The server appeared and took our orders. When he'd left, I said, 'You were thinking?'

'If you were going to send ... or especially if, let's say, Leah wanted to send an anonymous message, not that either of you would, but if you did, how would you go about it?'

'Email? Except that I'd have to figure out how

103

to stay anonymous. But yes, a lot of people our age or younger would use a computer, at least to address the envelope and print the word "bitch". Those glued-on letters from the newspaper are *old*, aren't they? You and I get most of our news online and from NPR, but a lot of people Leah's age practically don't know that newspapers exist. So, we're dealing with someone who's technologically illiterate, maybe, or who thinks of paper first, let's say. And that fits with the envelope – the kind you lick, which is becoming sort of old-fashioned. So, someone who's not at the forefront of technology.'

'That call you had—'

'The call! I meant to tell you. I saw Katrina today at the show. Damn it! I hope ... if this were just me, OK. I can deal with nasty phone calls, and so can Betty Burley, better than I can. If someone thinks I'm a bitch, well, so are Kimi and Lady and India, and I believe in the First Amendment, but it just infuriates me to have this ... this son of a bitch jeopardize our ability to help these poor dogs. Katrina is OK, but her husband John is turning protective and saying that maybe they should stop doing rescue.'

'I can't say that I like—'

'Of course not, Steve. But Katrina and John are young, and their relationship is different from ours. I just hope ... damn it all! Let this idiot target me and leave the other volunteers alone! Or target Betty and me. Betty is even tougher than I am.'

Steve smiled. 'The human Kimi.'

The server appeared with Steve's clam chowder and my fried oysters, and we began eating.

'You want one?' I offered.

'No, thanks.' Steve managed to keep the smile off his mouth, but his eyes crinkled up. 'Redeeming yourself by offering to share?'

'No redemption is necessary. Yes, as you have astutely observed, I do tend to read a menu and then order whatever has the most grease, but as fried food goes, Legal's isn't greasy, and I love fried oysters and fried clams, and if I ordered both, so what? It's what I happen to be hungry for.'

He shrugged. 'How sure are you that Betty is any tougher than you are?'

'Very. But by the time I'm her age, who knows? In the meantime, I have to keep my strength up.' I ate one of the oysters and said, 'Speaking of age and ... Steve, I'm worried about Gabrielle.'

'Gabrielle is ageless.' He smiled. Everyone loves Gabrielle. Steve is no exception. 'When's she getting here?'

'Thursday. She's going to dog training with us that night and then to the match on Saturday, but she's staying for a week after that, and she's being sort of mysterious about why.'

'Gabrielle?'

'I know. She's usually ... well, what she says is that she's seeing a doctor about quote a little female problem unquote, which could mean ... well, I don't know. That's what's scary. And what really worries me is, why is she coming to

Boston? There are perfectly good doctors in Maine. So, if she needs to see someone here, does that mean that she needs some famous specialist?'

'Getting away from your father,' Steve said. 'Look, if she has a lump or unexplained bleeding and your father knows about it, he'll drive her crazy. What's she telling him?'

'Don't ask me! But she did say that she'll tell me all about it when she gets here, and you're probably right. She knows what Buck is like in panic mode.'

When our main courses arrived, I happened to glance around the restaurant and saw a sight that made me want to holler and swear. Happily, I had the self-control to wait until the server had left before I said, 'What is this? National Damn It All Day? Steve, I can't believe it! Look over ... no, don't look. Damn it! Quinn Youngman, the skunk, is sitting at a table to your right, near the window, with Avery Jones. Avery! I mean, Quinn is practically old enough to be her grandfather. What is she thinking, going out with him?'

'Quinn likes younger women,' Steve said.

'Rita, that was pushing it. But Avery? Avery isn't even an adult, really. She's as adolescent as she can be, and she's a very depressed adolescent. Steve, she needs a psychiatrist, but not as a date. Quinn must know that.'

'Good thing Rita didn't come with us after all.'

'Absolutely!'

'She's well rid of him,' Steve said.

'Agreed. Especially after this. Steve, we have to find Rita another man. She is so lonely! And you know how wonderful she is. It's just a damn shame. Among other things, it's too bad that she's not lesbian, but she isn't, and I'm not even sure that there are all that many available women who deserve her. Where are all the eligible men? Well, in malamute rescue! We get a lot more males than females, which reminds me, there *is* Max Crocker. I still don't have a rescue dog for him. There's a female in Maine, and I was hoping that she'd be a good match, but she's terrible with cats, and Max has a Maine coon. Anyway, Max is a psychologist who lives in Cambridge. He grew up with a Scottie, and he and Rita would be the perfect match. All I have to do is maneuver Rita into taking Willie to the National Pet Week event, and at least I'll have the chance to introduce her to Max.' After a pause to chew and swallow, I said, 'You can have all the fried clams you want. They're really good. And French fries. Help yourself.'

Steve accepted the offer and insisted on giving me some of his delectable scallop dish. It's easy to imagine Steve as he must have been in kindergarten or first grade. I know how cute he was – I've seen pictures – and I'm sure that his personality was the same then as it is now. At five and six, he went about his lessons in a thorough, systematic way, and every school report undoubtedly read, 'Steve plays well with others.'

'You play well with others,' I said. 'You share your toys. I love you.'

For dessert, we had a big plate of profiteroles, cream-puff shells filled with ice cream and topped with chocolate sauce, served with two spoons, and we stopped talking about other people. On our way out, we passed by the table where Quinn Youngman and Avery Jones were sitting. As we approached, I heard Quinn saying something about Bob Dylan and wondered whether Avery had any idea who Dylan was. If so, she probably thought of Dylan as someone her mother had listened to in her distant youth. Catching sight of us, Avery said a polite hello. Quinn just nodded, but his face flushed crimson. When we were out of his hearing, I said, 'Child molester. You're right. Rita is well rid of him.'

THIRTEEN

Steve and I spent a peaceful Sunday together listening to country music, working on our house, and playing with our dogs. By unspoken agreement, we said nothing about Quinn Youngman, Avery Jones, Rita's love life, obscene phone calls, or anonymous letters, and we avoided the topic of Fiona's death. I was tempted to call Gabrielle in the hope of allaying my fears about her need to consult a Boston doctor, but I restrained the impulse: Gabrielle was usually so forthcoming about everything that if she wanted to remain silent, she had a good reason. Furthermore, one secret that she was keeping from my father – dog training – was entirely innocuous. The other might be equally so.

On Monday morning, after a day of escape from worry, having settled myself at the kitchen table with my notebook computer and cup of coffee in front of me and with Rowdy and Kimi at my feet, I turned to the mystery of the nasty phone calls and the anonymous message. After an uninterrupted day with Steve, I felt comfortably imbued with his calm, systematic rationality. My own approach to the problem would've been to try to find out everything all at once and as quickly as possible. So, I compromised by taking a calm, systematic approach to trying to find out everything all at once and as quickly as possible. In other words, I stopped to make a list of names before I hit the web.

First on the list was Pippy Neff, even though I didn't seriously suspect her. For one thing, she lived in the central part of the state, west of the communities with a 781 area code. For another thing, her hideous voice would've been impossible to disguise; even if she'd tried to sound like a man, that grackle-like squawk of hers would've remained identifiable. She could've had a man make the calls – she had two sons – but the maniacal laughter had seemed grotesquely heartfelt. Besides, Pippy still imagined that she'd succeed in persuading me to let her use Rowdy; and having assured me that her puppy buyer was going to keep his dog, she'd seemed to believe that Malamute Rescue now viewed her as a model breeder.

The applicants whose names I listed were Diane and Don Di Bartolomeo, Irving Jensen, and Eldon Flood. The Di Bartolomeos lived in Quincy. Their area code was the same as ours, 617, but I had no idea whether the calls had come from the laughing man's home number. Because I'd spoken only to Diane, I'd never heard Don's voice. All he had against me and against Malamute Rescue was that I'd disabused his wife of the notion that the Alaskan malamute was a medium-sized, non-shedding breed, as she'd eventually have discovered for herself, probably before her husband actually got a dog. Big deal! Irving Jensen, the man who didn't believe in fences or neutering, was by far the most unpleasant person on my list. Among other things, he'd sworn at me. Worse, to my way of thinking, he'd explained his failure to give a vet reference by stating that his previous dogs had been healthy. As if those dogs hadn't needed exams, immunizations, heartworm testing, and preventive medication! Furthermore, he lived in Lynn, Lynn, city of sin, and his number had the right area code, 781. So, Irving Jensen wasn't just on the list; his name belonged at the top. Eldon Flood, whose name was last, had subscribed to the common conceit that he had a

110

special gift for training dogs. He'd had a particular rescue dog in mind: Thunder. I'd politely told him that I couldn't approve his application. Still, he'd probably felt insulted and angry that I'd been unimpressed by his self-proclaimed power over dogs and that I'd refused him the dog he wanted. Also, hadn't I informed him that the Alaskan malamute was the wrong breed for him? He'd hung up on me. By my standards, I'd been more than civil and respectful. I'd avoided ordering Eldon Flood never to get another dog again as long as he lived; I hadn't even said, as I'd done more than once when speaking to applicants with magical gifts, 'And don't imagine that you're going to succeed where the rest of us have failed!' So, I'd been a good, good girl. Still, Eldon Flood might not have thought so. Besides, his phone number had an area code of 781.

What about the voices? Could my caller have been Irving Jensen? Eldon Flood? I just did not know. Neither Jensen nor Flood had spoken in memorably deep or high tones, neither had sounded notably old or young, and neither had had a marked regional accent. And the caller? I'd answered when Buck, Gabrielle, and Molly had just arrived. Even though my father had lowered the volume of his bellow, the background noise had made it hard to hear perfectly. What's more, at first, I'd been distracted by everything that was going on in the kitchen, and I'd subsequently been too startled and offended by the content of the call to focus on the

111

speaker's voice. Still, I'd remember deep bass or falsetto tones, a foreign accent, or some other distinctive characteristic. I'd had no impression of extreme youth or age.

Moving to the web – we're wireless – I learned disappointingly little. The website of Pippy Neff's Tundrabilt Kennels was under construction. Its amateurish pages showed little except photos of dogs of hers I'd seen at shows. Google confirmed what I already knew: she showed a lot and advertised puppies everywhere. Irving Jensen, the Di Bartolomeos, and Eldon Flood were listed at the addresses they'd given on their applications. Jensen was a total nonpresence in cyberspace; Googling his name, address, phone number, and email address, I found nothing. There was nothing about Don Di Bartolomeo, either, but his wife, Diane, was mentioned in a lot of places because she was an avid scrapbooker who gave talks and lessons about scrapbooking all over eastern Massachusetts. Eldon Flood had told me that he had a farm. As it turned out, he and his wife, Lucinda, actually had a farm stand west of Boston that was open year round. The website was less amateurish than Pippy's, but not by much. In addition to a photo of the stand, the site was mainly devoted to giving directions and to listing items that the Floods sold, including jams, jellies, home-made pies, and dried-flower wreaths, as well as seasonal produce that included vegetables and apples.

As I was reading about the jams and wreaths and apples, I came to my senses. What had I expected to discover? A news story with the headline 'Jensen Confesses to Placing Obscene Phone Calls'? Or posts from Don Di Bartolomeo to an online forum with tips and tricks for sick individuals who enjoy snail-mailing anonymous letters? What had I actually found? Trivia! Jellies and pies. My list, I realized, was ridiculous. Among other things, the 781 area code told me almost nothing. Dozens of places had that area code, and without additional information, there was no way to know whether a call came from someone's home phone, work phone, or cell phone or even from a phone listed to someone else. Furthermore, over the years, I'd turned down hundreds of applicants for rescue dogs, as had the sharp-tongued Betty Burley. For all I knew, my bitch message, as I thought of it, had no connection with the phone calls or with Malamute Rescue. *For all I knew?* All I knew was almost nothing. Unless – until – one of us got another phone call or letter, I was wasting my time.

FOURTEEN

'Where do you suppose Quinn met her?' Rita asked.

It was six thirty on Wednesday, and I'd just broken the news about seeing Quinn Youngman with Avery Jones at Legal Sea Foods. Steve was due home from work any minute, and our next-door neighbor, Kevin Dennehy, together with his obnoxious girlfriend, Jennifer, as well as Rita, would be joining us for dinner. Rowdy and Kimi were in their crates, but Sammy was loose in the kitchen. When I opened the oven door and put in two chickens to roast, he hovered around but failed to execute a Kimi-style strike.

'Good boy!' I said. 'I have no idea where they met. I didn't ask.'

Rita took an all-too-casual sip from her glass of white wine. 'What's she like?'

'Young and depressed.'

'How young?'

'Twenty? About that. She hasn't finished college. Her father died this past winter. I think that's why she's taking this semester off. Or maybe she's dropping out. Vanessa, her mother, has signed her up for Harvard Summer School. But I don't know much about Avery. She's not very communicative. When the whole family was here for dinner on Saturday, people tried to draw her out. Leah tried, and so did Gabrielle, and they're both good at it, but neither of them had any luck. Avery just *looks* depressed, too. And what's she doing going out with a man who's so much older than she is?'

Rita rolled her eyes. 'Not to mention what Quinn's doing. Let's just hope that he didn't meet her—'

I'd had the same thought. 'He could've met her anywhere, Rita. At a bookstore. At Loaves and Fishes. She has some interest in cooking. And food. For all we know, they met at the sushi bar at Loaves and Fishes. Anyway, I have no reason to believe that Avery was even thinking about seeing a psychiatrist. They could've met in some perfectly innocent place.'

'As opposed to some guilty place, such as Quinn's office. I hate to think that he's descended to *that*.'

The phone rang. 'Sorry,' I said as I hurried to answer it. The realization that I had insufficient information about my horrible phone call had transformed my attitude toward the possibility of once again hearing the lunatic laughter. Instead of dreading the harassment, including the cruel reminder of my Vinnie's death, I was eager for the chance to learn something – anything – about the caller. I'd resolved that the next time, I wouldn't be caught off guard. Toward that end, I'd dug out the manual for our phone system and read the instructions on how to record calls. Now, caller ID again displayed 'Unknown

Name, Unknown Number'. But when I answered, the caller hung up. Furthermore, dialing the code that was supposed to reveal the caller's number got me nothing except the area code, 781, which included a zillion places north, west, and south of Greater Boston.

As I was on the verge of telling Rita about the call, the phone rang again, and at the same time, Steve, Lady, and India came in through the back door. Although no one was issuing my father's kind of moose-like bellow, the noise level rose as Steve and Rita greeted each other and as Sammy let out a joyous, welcoming series of *woo-woo-woo*s. Damn it! For a second, it seemed to me that fate was contriving to make sure that the nasty calls came only when I'd be unable to listen carefully to the caller's voice. But as I was heading for the quiet of the dining room with the phone in hand, I checked caller ID, and was half relieved and half disappointed to see a local cell number. In fact, the call was from Elizabeth McNamara.

'Holly? Oh, I'm so ... I have to ask you a favor. You or Steve. Could one of you run down the street and let Persimmon out in the yard? And feed her? But ... this is such an imposition! The key! I'm at Mount Auburn – Isaac is in intensive care – and I can get a taxi to drive the key—'

'Whatever you need,' I said. 'There's no one in the neighborhood with a key? Vanessa? Tom? Or Kevin Dennehy?'

'No. Stupid, stupid of me. I never expected...'

'Elizabeth, Steve is here, and one of us will

116

run over to the hospital and get the key and take care of Persimmon.'

'She's been locked in the house since noon! I should've ... I'm just not thinking straight.'

'Of course not,' I said.

When we'd arranged to meet in the main lobby, I hung up, explained the crisis to Steve and Rita, and took off. According to a report that had recently been featured in the news, the presence of a husband typically creates seven extra hours of housework for a wife each week. I felt thankful that my marriage was atypical. In particular, Steve was more than capable of getting dinner on the table and playing host to Rita, Kevin, and Jennifer.

During the five-minute drive to the hospital, I wondered what had landed Isaac in intensive care. Vanessa had mentioned something about his arthritis and some sort of heart condition. Although she'd remarked that he couldn't keep up with Elizabeth, I hadn't noticed any change in him. Elizabeth had always been the one who'd exercised Persimmon and their previous dogs; Isaac had seldom accompanied her. As far as I could remember, Isaac looked the same as ever: he was neither pale nor red-faced, and he hadn't gained or lost weight. In planning the club's upcoming event, he'd given the appearance of having his usual energy. My guess was a sudden heart attack or possibly a stroke.

When I drove up the ramp to the multilevel parking area attached to the hospital, I decided for the sake of time to use valet parking instead of hunting for a free space. The doors from the parking area open into the main lobby, and I'd barely entered when Elizabeth rose from a seat and, to my surprise, ran to me and almost threw herself into my arms. I knew Elizabeth and Isaac from the club and from our neighborhood, but we'd always been on friendly rather than affectionate or intimate terms. Still, as dog people, we shared the kind of bond that exists among members of an extended family; indeed, it *is* the same bond because we really are members of a great big family. Consequently, Elizabeth's relief in seeing me and her freedom to seek comfort from me sprang, I knew, from her sense of being with one of her own.

Her need for comfort was clear: her soft white curls were in disarray, and although the lobby was comfortably warm, she was wearing a thick handwoven yellow shawl and trembling with cold in spite of it. Releasing her grip on me, she said, 'You are an angel.' Her high-pitched voice almost seemed to fade away.

'Steve and I will do anything you want. I hope you know that.'

'Oh, Holly, this is a nightmare!'

'A heart attack?' I asked.

'No. Worse! And out of the blue. On Saturday, he had some little stomach bug, not so little, really, but all he did was tell me to stop fussing. I tried to get him here, to the emergency room, but he wouldn't listen to me, and I wanted to try to reach his doctor at home, but Isaac was having none of it. You know how stubborn he can

118

be! And then, well, I thought he was right, because he got over it. He was fine! Until this morning. And all of a sudden, he collapsed. I called an ambulance, and we've been here ever since. The doctors are talking about liver and kidney failure.'

Example number 5,365,188 of the superiority of dogs to human beings: when confronted with a person in great distress, a dog never offers advice or makes suggestions. Had Rowdy, for instance, been in my place, it would never have occurred to him to tell Elizabeth to remember that Isaac was a strong man who stood a good chance of pulling through; and in complete contrast to me, Rowdy would not have felt the urge to advise Elizabeth to take slow, deep breaths, sit down, drink tea, go home and get some rest, or seek a second, third, or fourth medical opinion about her husband's condition. Having learned a bit from dogs, I restrained my stupid human impulses and offered the comfort of physical contact, which is to say that I put my arms around Elizabeth and held her gently.

But after rising to canine heights, I made the inevitable descent. 'Elizabeth, have you eaten anything?' I asked. 'Could I get you anything? Tea? Ginger ale? A sandwich?'

'Nothing,' she said. 'Thank you. If you could just take care of Persimmon?' From a Peruvian shoulder bag, she removed a key chain with a single key and a pewter disk depicting a stylized puli. 'This is a spare key. It's for both doors, front and back. You can just let her out in the yard. It's fenced.'

When Elizabeth had finished telling me where to find Persimmon's food and how much to feed her, I renewed my offer to do anything at all, including drive her home. Then I made my departure. Once I got back to Appleton Street, I parked in our driveway and walked to the Mc-Namaras' house, where Persimmon heralded my arrival even before I'd put the key in the front door. Her barking was energetic rather than threatening. The puli – correct plural *pulik* – is a medium-size Hungarian sheepdog, a lively, charming companion and often a fine watchdog. When I opened the door, Persimmon delighted me by bouncing up and down, thus sending the long black cords of her coat flying in what looked like gleeful abandon. I'm tempted to compare her to a black dust mop in flight, but the image would be misleading, mainly because Persimmon devoted herself more to play than to work of any kind.

'Hey, Persimmon,' I said, 'you must be desperate to get out. Let's go!'

As we made our way to the back of the house, I scanned the shining wood floors and the handwoven area rugs for evidence that Persimmon had been unable to wait, but she'd apparently held it; and when I opened the door to the backyard, she dashed out and immediately squatted, thereby confirming my guess. Following Elizabeth's instructions, I found a metal canister of dry food and a stack of stainless dog bowls in a kitchen cabinet. When I'd given

Persimmon her dinner and refilled her water bowl, I made a quick call to Steve and then cleared the breakfast dishes off the table, loaded the dishwasher, wiped the counters, and took Persimmon back outside.

As I was watching her sniff around, I heard Vanessa's voice from the opposite side of the cedar fence that separated the yards. 'Elizabeth? Is that you?

'It's Holly,' I answered. The fence was about five feet high, so by stepping on one of its wooden supports and standing on tiptoe, I was able to stick my head over it. 'Isaac is in the hospital. Elizabeth is with him. I'm here taking care of Persimmon.'

Vanessa was alone in the yard. 'I would have done that!' She sounded almost insulted. 'Or Tom. Or even Avery. What's wrong with Isaac?'

'Something serious,' I said. 'I don't know exactly what. Elizabeth said that the doctors are talking about liver and kidney damage.'

'Well, I can't say that I'm surprised,' Vanessa said. 'Isaac hasn't been well for years, you know. My father knows all about it. Naturally!'

'Whatever's going on with Isaac was sudden, I think. He collapsed this morning. Elizabeth called an ambulance. He's in intensive care.'

'Huh. I didn't hear the ambulance. I must've been out. My father was with me. At Loaves and Fishes. I wish he'd never discovered that place. He spends hours poking through all the vitamins and remedies and whatever, and the salespeople encourage him. He refuses to swallow any kind

121

of pill, but he spends a fortune loading up on all sorts of disgusting liquids, and he won't listen to a word that Hatch says. But what can I do for Elizabeth?'

'For now, nothing, I think.'

'Where is he? Which hospital?'

'Mount Auburn. At least it's nearby, and Elizabeth knows that if she needs a ride, all she has to do is call me.'

'Well, the same goes for me,' Vanessa said. 'And my father. And even Avery. She's capable of making herself useful when she feels like it. Just let us know.'

'Of course,' I said. 'And thank you.'

'We'll be happy to help,' Vanessa said. 'With Persimmon. With anything. We just love Elizabeth. We'll be more than happy to help.'

FIFTEEN

At ten o'clock that Wednesday night, when we'd finished dinner and after Rita had gone upstairs to her own apartment, I'd heard nothing from Elizabeth and decided to check on Persimmon. Since Kevin and Jennifer were leaving, I walked them to their car, which was actually Kevin's, and was parked in his driveway, which was actually his mother's. If I sound awkward, it's because that's what the situation was – in more

122

ways than one.

Until Kevin met Jennifer, he and his mother lived on Appleton Street in the house next to ours. Kevin still lived there, in a sense, but he increasingly spent his nights at Jennifer's. Many conservative parents could have adapted to the reality of changing times. Mrs Dennehy was not such a parent. She had been a committed Roman Catholic before her conversion to Seventh-Day Adventism, and neither her former religion nor her present one made her inclined to approve of what she sincerely felt to be sin. She was a woman of severe appearance, demeanor, and character. She wore her hair knotted on top of her head in a bun so tight that she must have lived in unremitting pain, and she was forever quoting the Bible. Over the years, I'd come to like and respect her. She and I got along mainly because she had a soft spot for animals and knew that I was on their side. She made a fuss over our dogs, and she was the rare person who appreciated what I'd tried to do for my difficult cat, Tracker, after I'd rescued Tracker, rehabilitated her, tried to place her in a good home, and eventually realized that the only home Tracker would ever find was the one she had, namely, with me, because no one else would want her. Tracker was missing part of an ear and had a disfiguring mark on her face. Unfortunately she was not a *belle laide*, a creature so ugly that she was beautiful. Worse, she was outright unfriendly to absolutely everyone except Steve, whom she adored. He could pick her up and carry her around. In spite of my efforts, she barely tolerated me, and because my initial optimism about teaching Rowdy and Kimi to accept her had been unfounded, she spent most of her life in my office, which was filled with cat furniture and cat toys. Many people thought that Tracker was simply a dreadful cat and that I was a fool to have kept her. Others felt that it was mean of me to doom poor Tracker to an existence of confinement. Mrs Dennehy, however, understood that the life I gave Tracker was better than the alternative – none at all. Furthermore, once I'd married Steve, Mrs Dennehy had decided that I'd become respectable, and she'd abandoned her belief in what she'd groundlessly suspected were my designs on Kevin, who'd never done anything worse at my house than eat meat and drink beer, activities banned at home.

As to the dark-haired, voluptuous Jennifer Pasquarelli, Mrs Dennehy knew perfectly well what Kevin was doing with her and found in Jennifer no redeeming qualities. It counted for nothing with Mrs Dennehy that Jennifer, like Kevin, was a police officer and a runner. In fact, whereas Kevin's career was successful, Jennifer had such trouble getting along with people that she was lucky to have a desk job with the Newton police. In some ways, Jennifer had been a good influence on Kevin. She forced him to eat vegetables and various soy-based products, and although he complained about being fed weeds and slime, he looked great and was clearly crazy about her in spite of her obvious failings, which included a hot temper, a sharp tongue, and a thinly disguised dislike of animals. Mrs Dennehy couldn't stand her. Steve, Rita, and I weren't wild about Jennifer, either, but excluding her would've meant excluding Kevin, whose friendship we valued.

Kevin? Oh, Kevin is a gigantic Irish cop, a powerhouse, a red-haired dynamo with a Boston accent who once took a bullet in the chest in the line of duty and is afraid of nothing except possibly his mother, who was emerging from her back door when Kevin, Jennifer, and I reached the bottom of my stairs.

'Hey, Ma,' Kevin called out.

Mrs Dennehy stood silently by her back door, her arms folded.

'Hi, Mrs Dennehy,' I said.

'Hello, Holly,' she replied.

'Thank you for dinner,' Jennifer said to me. It was probably a line she'd memorized in one of the social-skills courses she'd flunked.

'You're welcome,' I said.

Kevin gave me a hug, and he and Jennifer walked to his car, got in, and drove off.

Mrs Dennehy snorted and uttered one word, 'Jezebel!'

With that, she retreated into her house, and I made my way to Elizabeth and Isaac's. Seeing no sign that Elizabeth was there, I let myself in and gave Persimmon a few minutes in the yard and a bedtime cookie.

Early the next morning, I made another visit and saw no indication that Elizabeth had been to the house during the night. Although I was reluctant to abuse the privilege of having the house key, I didn't want the exhausted and worried Elizabeth to arrive home only to discover that there was nothing to eat. Consequently, I checked the refrigerator. Having noted that the McNamaras were low on milk and eggs, I shopped for Elizabeth and Isaac when I went out to stock up for us. When I returned to their house at ten o'clock, everything was still as it had been. I put away the groceries and spent a little time with Persimmon, who wasn't used to being alone.

Back in my own kitchen, I thought about calling Elizabeth on her cell phone but decided not to intrude. Sadly, at eleven thirty, she called to say that Isaac had died only an hour earlier. She'd been with him all night and at the end. She was now at home. Incredibly, she'd noticed the food I'd bought – I refused the offer of reimbursement – and she thanked me for leaving it as well as for taking care of Persimmon. We talked for only a minute. Her daughters would be flying in, one from Tucson, the other from Dallas. Would I let people in the club know about Isaac? I promised that I would.

The news of Isaac's death took the edge off my happiness about Gabrielle's visit. She was due in the late afternoon. After I'd dusted the guest room and supplied it with towels, I went ahead and worked on an article about research on social cognition in dogs. Example of social cognition: the ability of domestic dogs to understand human communicative signals, including the ability to read the human gaze. The topic was difficult. For one thing, my training in journalism had schooled me to be unbiased, whereas I felt anything but objective on the subject of the research, which I was utterly wild about. Finally, serious researchers understood that dogs *think*! These people went so far as to write dense academic papers not only about the tendency of dogs to follow the human gaze but about the apparent ability of dogs to read the human mind! The principal difficulty I encountered was my own ignorance. My background in ethology consisted of having read Lorenz and Tinbergen long ago, and I had a lot of catching up to do in the field of cognition as well. What a fool I'd been to study journalism! In my next existence, I'd enroll in the Department of Ethology at Eotvos University in Budapest and study with Ádám Miklósi, the guru of canine cognition, assuming that my next existence included the opportunity to become fluent in Hungarian or at least to learn to pronounce *Eotvos*. But in spite of my deficiencies, I was fired up and labored on.

At four thirty, Gabrielle still hadn't called to alert me to her arrival. Because she and I were due at dog training at seven, I stopped deciphering articles that were as fascinating as they were challenging, and turned to the familiar, easy job of feeding my family. Steve, who had India and Lady with him, was having dinner with his fishing buddies to plan the trip to Grant's Camps, but I wanted to offer Gabrielle something other than pizza or subs. Also, in spite of Avery's having spurned the lasagne I'd made after Fiona's death, I intended to cook for Elizabeth, who was older and much more civilized than Vanessa's daughter was. I put two chickens in the oven to roast, washed lots of romaine for two Caesar salads, and reminded myself to omit the croutons from Elizabeth's because of her celiac disease. As I got ready to give the dogs an early dinner – they usually eat around five – it occurred to me that feeding malamutes seemed easy only because I was good at it. An inept or naive person would've let Rowdy, Kimi, and Sammy loose in the kitchen, put three bowls of kibble on the floor, and ended up with a three-dog brawl, bloodshed, and gigantic vet bills. Steve wouldn't have charged me to patch up the dogs – *not* why I married him, by the way – but I still didn't want a fight. Before I'd taken the usual measures to prevent one and before I'd done anything at all about preparing the bowls of food, while I was merely *thinking* about feeding the dogs, Kimi leaped up and began to dance, whirl, zoom around, and emit piercing shrieks of joy. Taking their cue from her, Rowdy and Sammy joined in.

'You've been reading the same articles I have,' I told Kimi. 'What a coincidence! I hope that you understand them better than I do. Actually, if you felt like it, you could probably teach me to pronounce *Eotvos.*'

Malamutes being the food-driven creatures

that they are, they're capable of squabbling not just about dinner itself but about the prospect of eating. To avert catastrophe, I crated Sammy and Rowdy and left Kimi loose, mainly because her reaction to the imminent arrival of food was so violent that she was capable of damaging one of the crates. As I doled out three portions of food into three steel bowls, she switched from flying around to hurling herself three feet up into the air, and her yelps became screams. It's been suggested to me that as a dog trainer, I could and should diminish the intensity of my dogs' lunatic reaction to the arrival of dinner time, as I certainly could but definitely don't want to. I have seen sick and dying dogs become indifferent to food and refuse it altogether. These raucous displays of appetite are confirmations of health and celebrations of life, and I revel in every leap and every shriek. Quick as could be, I put Kimi's bowl down at a safe distance from the crates and rapidly opened the door of each crate, shoved in the bowl, and latched the door. About thirty seconds later, all three bowls were empty. I removed Kimi's from the floor and Rowdy's and Sammy's from their crates before I freed the dogs. After all three dogs had had time in the yard, I left Rowdy and Kimi there, and just as Sammy and I got back indoors, Gabrielle called from her car to say that she was five minutes away.

One of my stepmother's gifts was an emotional radiance that cast an improving glow over everyone she encountered. From the moment she and Molly arrived, I began to feel an increased acceptance of Isaac's sudden death, and despite my lingering sadness, I felt simply delighted to have Gabrielle in our house and, as ever, grateful to her for having married Buck. As we carried her bags to the guest room, I was also aware of another feeling of gratitude concerning my father, namely, a profound sense of relief that he hadn't finagled a way to accompany his wife to Cambridge. It's a tribute to Gabrielle's favorable influence on me that I managed to ask her nothing about the worrisome medical appointment that was one reason for her visit. Gabrielle was skilled at choosing occasions; I trusted her to tell me about her medical trouble when she was ready.

Still, I couldn't help scrutinizing her. As we chatted about her trip from Maine and about what to expect at dog training, and later as we sat in the kitchen eating roast chicken and salad, I was alert for signs of illness. She'd had no apparent difficulty in lugging a heavy suitcase from her Volvo wagon up to her room on the second floor: no shortness of breath, no muscular weakness. After a Maine winter, she was pale, but not abnormally so. As she used a knife and fork to cut a piece of chicken and then raised the piece to her mouth, there was no sign of a tremor. Her eyes were their usual sparkling blue, her expression as animated as ever. After the long drive, she didn't look even slightly tired. On the contrary, she looked altogether terrific. She was as pretty as ever, with spectacu-

130

lar bone structure and lovely features framed by ash blonde hair. A dash of pink blush on her cheeks would've compensated for the effects of winter, and a coating of foundation make-up would've covered the sun damage visible on her face, but she disliked make-up and almost never wore it.

As we were clearing the table, the phone rang. Seeing the familiar 'Unknown Name, Unknown Number' on caller ID, I answered eagerly and was ready to record the call, but whoever it was immediately hung up. 'Sorry about this,' I said to Gabrielle, 'but I've had ... I had a nuisance call, and I'm trying to find out—'

'Just don't tell your father,' she said. 'You know how he fusses.'

'Do I ever! Yes, we mustn't tell him. Leave the dishes!' As I'd done before, I dialed the code to find the caller's number and once again got nothing except the area code, which was again 781. 'Damn it!'

'It's probably one of those telemarketers,' Gabrielle said. 'Or one of those robot things, whatever you call them.'

'The first call wasn't,' I said. 'And a couple other rescue people ... I'll tell you about it later. I want to run this chicken and salad over to my neighbor Elizabeth McNamara. Her husband just died. I'll be back in no time.'

A few minutes later, I was standing at Elizabeth's front door. As I expected, Persimmon began to bark even before I rang the bell, but to my surprise, it was Tom Oakley who answered.

131

Instead of inviting me in, he held the door ajar and stuck his head out.

'Tom,' I said. 'I've brought food for Elizabeth. And I want to return her key.'

'Kind of you,' he said. 'And she'll want her key, of course. But Vanessa has already sent dinner over, and you've probably brought food that Elizabeth can't eat. She has celiac disease.'

Did ungraciousness run in that family? And I didn't like the implication about the key. I wasn't scheming to keep it, for heaven's sake, and even if I'd kept it, I wouldn't have misused it. 'I've brought a gluten-free meal,' I said, probably with a hint of self-righteousness. 'Roast chicken and a Caesar salad. Without croutons.'

'No soy sauce,' he cautioned.

Feeling exasperated, I said, 'It's a plain roast chicken. And the salad is romaine with a dressing I made myself. With no gluten!'

As I was on the verge of demanding to know when he'd been appointed to the position of Elizabeth McNamara's dietitian, Elizabeth herself appeared behind him in the hallway. 'Holly! Tom, let Holly in, please. Persimmon, look who's here! Your buddy has come to see you. Holly, I just can't thank you enough. Come in!'

'I won't stay,' I said as I entered and then reached down to stroke Persimmon. 'You must be exhausted. I just wanted to return your key and leave you some food. And to say how sorry I am about Isaac.'

'Thank you,' she said.

'I'm going to dog training. I'll tell everyone.

132

And when you've made plans...'

'Isaac did that years ago. A little graveside service at Mount Auburn. That's all he wanted. Just the immediate family. It'll be on Saturday. The girls will be here tomorrow.'

'As always,' I said uselessly, 'if there's anything you need...'

'I know that,' she said. 'You and Steve are angels. Thank you.'

I made my departure and hurried home. Because we were running a little late, Gabrielle, Molly, Sammy, and I drove to the armory, which more than makes up for its lack of architectural splendor by offering a rarity in Cambridge, namely, ample free parking, some on nearby streets and, for people attending dog training, plenty in the lot behind the armory. As is inevitable at dog events, most of the cars in the lot had dog crates inside and dog-themed bumper stickers; and as is inevitable in Greater Boston, a fair number of vehicles sported Red Sox stickers, too. With its three crates, a Woo Woo window decal, and a Sox bumper sticker, my Blazer fit right in. Come to think of it, with my Alaskan Malamute National Specialty sweatshirt, my little cooler of perishable dog treats, and, most of all, my carefully bred and lovingly groomed Sammy, I fit in pretty well myself. As for Gabrielle and Molly, I knew from experience that within ten minutes of our arrival, my stepmother and her charming bichon would have made friends with a dozen other pairs of handlers and dogs, as, indeed, proved to be the case.

133

Because we'd entered through the rear of the armory, we had to make our way down the length of the gymnasium-like hall to reach the entryway to check in. Our progress was slow, mainly because we kept stopping so that I could introduce Gabrielle to everyone, including my friend and plumber Ron, who was teaching the Canine Good Citizenship class that Gabrielle and Molly would be joining. Although it was a drop-in class open to anyone, I explained to Ron that Gabrielle and Molly had been taking private lessons and intended to take the CGC test on Saturday. Then Gabrielle took over, and within a minute, Ron was beaming at her and making her feel so welcome that I practically had to drag her to the front desk, where Vanessa and Ulla were checking in.

'Such a shame about Isaac,' Vanessa said, and several members of the club echoed her sentiment.

'So sudden,' someone murmured.

'How is Elizabeth doing?' someone else asked.

Before I could answer, Vanessa said, 'She's exhausted. She was up all night. I sent some dinner over for her, and my father's there with her. She's right next door to us. I'll pop in when I get home. Her daughters are flying in. They'll be here tomorrow.' Spotting Gabrielle, she said, 'Well, hello! For a second, I didn't recognize you ... out of context, so to speak. Is Buck here, too?'

'No,' I said rather too forcefully. 'Gabrielle

134

and Molly are having a visit with us. Among other things, they're taking the CGC test on Saturday. Are you going to the match?'

Exhibiting the real dog person's compulsion to tell other people what to do with their dogs, someone said, 'You should enter Ulla in Prenovice.' Several people echoed the encouragement.

By then, it was time for classes to start, so Gabrielle and I hurriedly checked in and returned to the big hall, where she and Molly joined Ron's class, and Sammy and I went to the class called Novice for Show – or in Sammy's case, maybe Novice for Show-offs. Because he'd been shown in breed – conformation – his best exercise was the stand for examination. From puppyhood, he'd been taught to stack himself in a show pose, and no one had had to teach him to display animation and to accept the touch of strangers. His attitude, however, carried over to what are called the 'group exercises', the long sit and the long down, which he interpreted as additional opportunities to elicit admiration by flicking his plumy white tail and casting come-hither looks at the other dogs and see-how-cute-I-am glances at the other handlers, all of which would have been fine if his excess of high spirits hadn't spilled over into squirming and even crawling forward when he was supposed to be holding still. Like a lot of other obedience dogs, Sammy was great in the backyard, but the presence of an audience put a gleam in his eye and a wiggle-waggle in his hind end. Worse, alone with him the yard, I had the self-control to

135

refrain from reinforcing his antics, but everyone at the club thought that he was hilarious and let him know it. Tonight, in an effort to reinforce calm behavior while shielding him from the grins and smirks he loved, I remained next to him during the long down – three minutes, thus not all that long – and kept tossing tidbits of cheese just under his chest, and all went well until Vanessa called from the next ring, 'Hey, not fair! He's so cute when he's being bad!'

Damn it! But if dog training teaches you nothing else, even if it fails to help you learn to train dogs, it ought to teach you to be a good sport. Consequently, I accepted the teasing with apparent good grace, and in any case, our instructor called, 'Exercise finished.' When I'd kept Sammy in a down for an extra few seconds, I released him, and then we hooked up with Gabrielle, who, as predicted, had somehow managed to train her dog while making friends with what seemed like the entire class. Several people remarked on what a delight my step-mother was, and I, of course, agreed. Ron was filled with praise for Molly, and Gabrielle felt altogether happy about this secret-from-my-father life that she and her dog were leading.

Before we left, Ron called me aside to say that he was sorry about Isaac and also to say that he'd volunteered to take over Isaac's duties at the club's National Pet Week event. 'It was really Isaac who was hot for that AKC award,' Ron admitted. 'If you ask me, the Responsible Ownership Day is enough. But we can't cancel this thing now.'

'Of course not,' I said. 'But I have to wonder how many people we're going to get for an indoor event on a Saturday afternoon in May.'

'Pray for rain,' Ron said. 'And Vanessa's done a lot of publicity. That should help.'

As Gabrielle and the dogs and I made our way past the advanced classes, which were just beginning, Vanessa caught up with us. 'If you're free tomorrow afternoon, let's set up a play date,' she said. 'I don't know how your little one is with other dogs, Gabrielle, but we could give it a try.'

I'm not a big fan of having malamutes participate in playgroups. Sammy and Molly did well together, as did Sammy and Ulla, but I felt uneasy about the combination of Ulla and Molly. And not because of Molly!

Fortunately, Gabrielle said, 'Thank you! But I'm afraid that I'll have to bow out. I have an appointment tomorrow afternoon. Another time?'

'Any time at all,' Vanessa said warmly. Leaning toward me, she asked in an undertone, 'Have you had any more of those calls? Or Katrina? Any of you?'

'I had an anonymous ... well, not exactly a letter. A one-word message. Someone thinks I'm a bitch.'

'It's not the worst thing,' Vanessa said. 'Still, it's the sort of thing that one can say about oneself but not what one wants to be called by others.'

'Exactly.'

'No good deed goes unpunished. So, are you and Sammy free tomorrow?'

I made my excuses, but a little awkwardly, mainly because I was worried about Gabrielle's appointment. With whom? For what? When Vanessa had moved away, while we were crossing the dark parking lot, I decided that I'd had enough of waiting until Gabrielle was ready to confide in me. If our positions had been reversed, she'd have had the whole story out of me long ago. Lacking her subtlety, I said, once we were in the Blazer, 'What's this appointment? The medical stuff?'

'I'm so embarrassed,' she said hoarsely.

Living as I do surrounded by Cambridge shrinks, including Rita, I naturally assumed that she was referring to psychotherapy. Finally, my damned father was driving her crazy!

'Gabrielle, whatever it is, it's OK.'

I heard her take a deep breath. 'Dermatology,' she almost whispered.

'What?'

'I have an appointment with a dermatologist.'

Skin cancer! The sun damage? Melanoma! So serious that she was seeing a Boston dermatologist.

Before I could speak, she said, 'I'm so ... Holly, I have never been vain.'

'Of course not. Is it that serious? Something that will—'

'No! Not at all. That's what embarrassing. It's purely cosmetic. Lasers! I have brown spots and

138

broken blood vessels, and I just hate them! Did you think...?'

'Yes. Yes, I did.' I sighed audibly. 'Gabrielle, it's fine. If you want lasers, fine! That's wonderful! I was so worried! I thought you had some potentially fatal illness or something. I am so relieved.' With that, I shifted into drive, released the brake, and eased the car forward. Because the lot was dark and people were still leading dogs to cars, I crept carefully toward the exit to Concord Avenue, where I had to wait for the two cars in front of me to make the turn into the street. Behind us was a big van that I didn't recognize. In fact, that's why I noticed it. It was black or maybe deep blue or possibly green, and I'd never noticed it in the lot before. I did not, however, wonder whose it was. I assumed that I'd never see it again.

SIXTEEN

"Changed in appearance by artificial means".' Gabrielle bit into a bagel loaded with cream cheese and lox. 'I'll be ineligible for shows!'

My late mother, too, had a habit of assuming that the American Kennel Club's rules applying to dog shows were applicable to all facets of human life. Indeed, my mother often quoted the AKC scripture as Gabrielle had just done.

Gabrielle was, however, speaking entirely in jest.

I laughed. 'There's even something about skin, isn't there?' My mother's daughter, I quoted: '"The removal of skin patches to alter markings." I think that's right. It's one of the examples of change by artificial means.'

'"Anything to improve a dog's natural appearance",' Gabrielle said. 'The poor things! No braces on their teeth, no hair coloring! Well, thank heaven that we're not show dogs. But "to alter markings" is exactly what I want, except that I want them eradicated and not just changed.'

It was ten o'clock on Friday morning. Gabrielle had slept late and was in excellent spirits, presumably because of the change by artificial means that she was going to experience that afternoon. Her appointment was with a dermatologist at Brigham and Women's Hospital, someone she had seen a few months earlier about the laser treatment she'd receive today.

When I'd refilled our coffee cups, she said, 'And you *do* understand why I'm not telling your father.'

'Do I ever! He'd insist that you're fine the way you are, which is true from his viewpoint, but not from yours. Then he'd tell everyone on earth about it. And he'd have a fit because you aren't seeing a dermatologist in God's country, the beautiful state of Maine.'

'I do prefer a Boston doctor,' Gabrielle said. 'But the worst thing would be what I'm going to look like afterward, all splotchy and sunburned. We can't have Buck charging into the dermatologist's office and ... well, being himself.'

'I hadn't though of that. But you're right. Gabrielle, is this going to be painful?'

'Not very. But as everyone's mother used to say, you have to suffer to be beautiful. Not that I'm going to be—'

'Please! You're beautiful now!'

'I have brown spots and broken blood vessels, and among other things, people *will* think that this redness means that I drink! It doesn't. But I simply—'

'I understand. Really, I do. And I don't want to sound like Buck.' I paused. 'Won't he notice?' Then I answered my own question. 'No, of course he won't. And if he ever finds out, he'll say that there was nothing wrong to begin with and that you look the same as ever.'

'Exactly,' said Gabrielle. 'And that the dermatologist was a quack and a thief.'

'But he'll never notice,' I said.

Not that Buck is unobservant. Far from it! But the moment he met Gabrielle – at a dog show, *Ça va sans dire*, as is said in the most romantic of languages – my father fell madly in love with her. I'm tempted to say that given what Buck was like to begin with, his new form of madness should have been imperceptible. It was not. He did out-of-character things, albeit in characteristic ways. For instance, so eager was he to create a favorable impression that he bought himself new clothes. Instead of acquiring them in some

141

normal, ordinary manner such as going to a store and trying on shirts, pants, sweaters, and jackets, however, he called L.L. Bean, described his lovesick situation in great detail, and inveigled a sympathetic customer service representative into choosing the items required to serve his purpose. He was like a male bird in springtime who knew that courting demanded fresh plumage but who trusted L.L. Bean more than he trusted himself to decide exactly which feathers he should sport. Lunatic infatuation is, of course, perilous, blinding its victims all too often to hideous flaws of character in the idealized object of the sufferer's affection; and when *l'amour fou* goes unrequited, misery ensues. But Buck lucked out, and simultaneously, so did I, all thanks to God and L.L. Bean.

'He'd notice right afterward,' Gabrielle said. 'I'm going to be a fright. Speaking of the dermatologist, I need to call a cab now. It's Friday, and if I wait until the last minute to call, I won't get one.'

'Why do you need a cab?'

'I hate Boston traffic to begin with, and you know what it's like on Fridays, and public transportation will take forever.'

So, I ended up volunteering to drive. As Gabrielle predicted – I knew she was right – the traffic was indeed fierce all the way through Cambridge, on the Riverway, and on the block of Brookline Avenue that led to Francis Street, where the hospital was located. The morning's fair weather had given way to torrential rain that made the trip an ordeal. Although we'd left early, by the time I turned onto Francis Street, Gabrielle had only ten minutes to find her way through the hospital to the dermatologist's office, so instead of making her late by hunting for a spot in the big multilevel garage on the right, I dropped her off at the main entrance to the hospital. We agreed that once I'd parked the car, I'd go to the Au Bon Pain in the lobby, where I'd get some coffee and wait for her. The decision proved to be correct. The first free space I found in the garage was all the way up on the top level, and it took ages to find that one. Meeting at the café was also a good idea. Living as I do near Harvard Square, I'm aware of the risk of ordering cappuccino in the afternoon or evening within the Cambridge city limits. I mean, there you'll be, peacefully sitting in a coffee shop in the afternoon or at a restaurant table after dinner, minding your own business, inoffensively enjoying your foamy milk with a shot of espresso, when some self-styled sophisticate just has to pass along the information that in Italy, no one ever drinks cappuccino with any meal except breakfast. Where, I ask you, is Cambridge? Is it in Italy? No, it is in Massachusetts, USA, a country in which it damned well ought to be all right to drink cappuccino whenever you feel like it without interference from supercilious kibitzers.

So, there I was at a table at the Au Bon Pain in Brigham and Women's Hospital in Boston, safely out of Cambridge, stirring sugar into my cappuccino, harming no one, when a male voice said, 'Holly!'

'Hatch!' There was no reason for my surprise. I knew that Vanessa's son was a resident physician here, as Fiona, too, had been. 'Sit down! If you have a minute.'

'That's about what I have.' Hatch was wearing a white coat with hospital ID. Again, I was struck by his resemblance to Vanessa, who seemed to have passed all of her genes to her son and none to Avery. As Hatch took the seat opposite mine at the little table and rested his cup of take-out coffee on it, he moved with the athleticism and grace that his sister lacked, and even though he looked tired and worried, he lacked the air of melancholia so notable in Avery. 'Thank you for your note,' he said. 'Your stepmother and Leah wrote, too. I really appreciate it.'

'Hatch, I am so sorry about Fiona. We all are. She was lovely. So bright, interesting, beautiful. She had everything.'

'She did. It still doesn't seem real. I don't know what I'm going to do. All our plans ... I'm trying to rearrange everything. California. I don't want to go without her. It's all up in the air. But maybe something will open up here. I just don't know.'

'Why should you?'

He smiled wanly. 'Because my mother expects it? Is that a reason?'

'Not necessarily.'

'I shouldn't complain. She's been great. Hey,

144

I've got to run. I'll see you tomorrow. My mother's turning this dog thing into a family picnic. She said you and Steve would be there.'

'And Gabrielle.'

'And your father? And Leah?'

I explained that Buck was in Maine and that Leah had to study. When Hatch had rushed off, I felt acutely aware of Fiona's absence, as if the crowded, noisy café were filled with people in white coats or scrubs whose principal characteristic was that they were not Fiona. Even in this setting, which had been hers, her striking looks and her vivacity would have made her stand out.

'Do you mind if I sit here?' asked a man in a tweed jacket.

'Not at all,' I said.

He put his tray on the table and took a seat. 'You're having cappuccino,' he informed me. 'You know, in Italy, no one drinks it after ten o'clock in the morning.'

'This isn't Italy,' I said. 'Do you live in Cambridge?'

He did. I defiantly finished my cappuccino and left to wait for Gabrielle in the lobby, just outside the café. When she came striding toward me, I almost gasped.

'Is it that bad?' she asked.

'You look sunburned,' I said tactfully. Her cheeks were scarlet, with livid patches and purple spots here and there.

'I have to be very careful tomorrow. Lots of sunscreen. And a hat. Maybe it'll keep raining.'

'No. It's supposed to clear up. Uh, are you

145

allowed to use make-up?'

'Not for three or four days. I never use it anyway. That bad, huh?'

When we reached the lobby of the garage, Gabrielle insisted on paying for the parking. She inserted my ticket and money into the machine, reclaimed the ticket, and tucked it in her purse. After we'd taken the elevator up to the top floor and seated ourselves in my car, Gabrielle pulled down the visor on her side and tried to examine her face in its little mirror. Fortunately, the light was too dim to give her a clear view. To distract her, I told her about running into Hatch Jones; and we talked about him and about Fiona while I drove slowly down, floor after floor, and while we waited for the drivers in front of us. Once we finally reached the contraption that would open the gate, Gabrielle held us up as she ferreted around in her purse for the validated ticket. I clearly remember that as I stretched my left hand out the window to insert the ticket, I caught a glimpse of a dark van two vehicles behind us. Cars all look more or less the same to me, as do vans. When it comes to vehicles, I'm the equivalent of someone who can tell a Dalmatian from a poodle but who compliments me on my malamutes by saying, 'Beautiful huskies.' I practically have to read the writing on a car to know what it is. As to vans, when Rowdy had delivered the coup de grâce to Steve's old rattletrap van by bursting out through one of its windows – in good cause, I might note – my ever-cooperative, endlessly patient husband had tried to solicit my opinion about a new one but had eventually given up. I did express color preferences: white vans reminded me of ambulances, black ones of hearses. So, Steve's new van is pewter. I'm pretty sure that it's a Chevy. All this is to say that the vehicle two behind my Blazer at the exit from the garage was definitely a van. The garage had dim light, so I couldn't be sure of the color: black, dark blue, or green. Was it the same one I'd seen at the armory? I had no idea.

SEVENTEEN

When Betty Burley called at five o'clock that same Friday afternoon, Gabrielle answered. She and Betty had met twice, I thought: once at our wedding and once at a Malamute Rescue event. Even so, Gabrielle greeted Betty as if they'd been friends for decades and had a long chat with her. To the best of my knowledge, Betty never even asked to speak to me. Gabrielle handled everything, which is to say that she listened to Betty's description of the nasty phone calls and conspired with Betty to concoct a cockamamie plan about how to investigate their origin.

I paid little attention during the first part of their conversation, of which I, of course, heard

147

only Gabrielle's side.

'Horrible!' Gabrielle exclaimed. 'Two more? And to think that this is the reward that you people get for trying to help homeless animals ... well, yes, men do turn protective ... I wouldn't say that she's dismissive ... yes, maybe un-characteristically passive...'

Me? Passive? But far be it from me to inter-rupt a call that was supposed to have been mine. My ears perked up only when I started to hear Gabrielle's side of the ludicrous scheme.

'Betty, there's no reason to blame yourself or your organization. How many rescue groups have the resources to follow up with every applicant? And even if you did, what could you do? Fire your volunteers? There are never enough to begin with, are there? But this situa-tion is not routine. I'd be more than happy to ... just a few little questions ... a survey, we'll call it. I'll make it clear that I'm not a telemarketer ... the likely ones ... yes, especially if the alterna-tive is calling the police.'

Fate saw to it that I heard none of the details of this pseudo survey that evening. Steve arrived home with Lady, India, and Sammy. Because Steve's last patient had saturated him in bodily fluids best left unspecified, he went upstairs to shower and change his clothes. I fed all five of our dogs, Gabrielle fed and walked Molly, and then we let the five resident dogs out, brought them in, wiped mud off their feet and bellies, watched the evening news, and ate dinner, after which Steve and I ran Gabrielle and Molly

148

through the test items that make up the Canine Good Citizen test. Because tomorrow's test would take place outdoors, we should have practiced outside, but Gabrielle was proud of Molly's lovely, clean show coat and vetoed the idea, so we ran through the CGC test indoors.

Playing the part of the evaluator, Steve did his best to wear a solemn expression, but I could see that he found Gabrielle's bizarrely crimson and heavily spotted complexion a challenge. In any case, Molly, looking adorable, breezed through the business of accepting a friendly (supposed) stranger and allowing Steve to pet and groom her. She walked politely on leash and continued to behave herself when I played the part of a supposed crowd; and when Lady joined me in the role of a strange dog, Molly was fine. Indeed, everything went well except the seventh item, Coming When Called: the handler puts the dog in a sit, walks ten feet away, turns to face the dog, and calls the dog. Unfortunately, the sight of Gabrielle walking away impelled Molly to follow her. We tried three times. Molly succeeded once.

'Go ahead and take the test,' I told Gabrielle. 'Molly did beautifully on everything else. Besides, that exercise is about coming when called. It isn't supposed to require a perfect stay. For a dog who used to be carried a lot, she's doing just great.'

The next morning, I continued the pep talk as we drove to the match, which was at a park, playground, and picnic area on the banks of the

Charles River in Newton. Although Steve was driving my car and I was in the front passenger seat, I didn't turn around to address Gabrielle, whose face now looked as if she had just spent a day in the sun at the equator while suffering from a ghastly disease. The previous day's rain had given way to brilliant sun. Besides slathering herself in sunscreen, she'd borrowed a Red Sox cap from Steve to shield her face. Her skin and the cap were the identical shade of bright red. Out of her hearing, Steve had said, 'It's like her head is on fire,' but she truly wasn't vain and hadn't even considered staying home.

I then launched into a lecture on setting your own goal when you enter any event, but when I'd barely begun, Steve and Gabrielle interrupted me by laughing. 'I guess you've heard it before,' I said meekly.

'Once or twice,' Steve said.

'But you're perfectly right,' said Gabrielle. 'So, my goal is ... not to trip over my own feet.'

'Mine,' I said, 'is to make sure that everyone entered in Prenovice A gets hooked on showing in obedience and leaves my ring wanting more.'

The Prenovice A class is for rank-beginner handlers. All exercises are performed on leash, so there's no chance that an exuberant dog will go flying around or zoom out of the ring. The class is supposed to be fun, and I intended to see that it was. So, I was looking forward to judging, all the more so when we drove into the parking lot, which was so incredibly crowded that for a second, I imagined that the challeng-

150

ing sport of dog obedience was experiencing a sudden and inexplicable surge in popularity. As it turned out, a local software outfit was holding a company barbecue in the picnic area, and the sunshine and warm weather had drawn families with children to the playground, as well as runners, walkers, and birders to the trails that ran through the park. Still, dog people were there in decent numbers, and more would be arriving. Some were at a table registering for the match and the CGC test, some were setting up the rings, and some were hanging around with one another and with their dogs. Because Steve and I needed to check the conditions of our rings and to speak with our stewards before the judging began, we introduced Gabrielle to a couple of people at the registration table and left her there. The crimson splotchiness of her countenance was more startling than ever in the bright morning light, but she seemed unselfconscious. Several people said how cute Molly was, and even before I left, Gabrielle had hooked up with two other handlers whose dogs were also going to take the CGC, so I felt not at all guilty about leaving her on her own in an unfamiliar environment.

The baby-gated rings had been set up in the middle of a big field that was obviously used for baseball and soccer. Dutiful person that I am, I paced off my ring and took a close look for bumps or holes that might trip a handler and for objects that might distract dogs. Then I spent a few minutes with my stewards, two young women I'd never met before. 'Smile!' I said. 'We want everyone to have fun.'

Finally, clipboard in hand, my score sheets fastened to it, I was ready for my first team, a thin, pale young man with a young black Lab. The dog was a little wiggly and hyper, but they left my ring happy. Next were a girl of sixteen or so and an apricot toy poodle; then a short, wide woman with a pug; a woman with another black Lab; a thin young woman with a golden retriever who had more potential than his handler did; and a man in khaki with a German shorthaired pointer. Even my simple L-shaped heeling pattern was a challenge; and the handlers and the dogs lacked the focus and polish that come, if at all, with experience; but the performances were surprisingly good, and I was having a great time.

When Vanessa and Ulla entered the ring, I smiled as I'd done at everyone else and asked the mandatory judge's question: 'Are you ready?' An amazing number of beginners answer that question without even glancing at their dogs; instead of sitting attentively in heel position at the handler's left side, the dog can be twisted around staring into space, and the handler will say, 'Yes!'

But Vanessa had been taught well. When she looked at Ulla and said, 'Ready,' the glint in Ulla's eyes told me that she heard the word as cue to fix her attention on Vanessa.

'Forward!' I said.

Great heeling, the ultimate test of teamwork,

is incredibly difficult for handlers and dogs. Vanessa made a lot of beginner's mistakes. She should've kept the leash loose, and her changes of pace were awkward and strange. When I said, 'Slow pace,' she barely slowed down, but her fast pace was a sudden gallop that caught Ulla off guard and got her overexcited; and Ulla kept sniffing at Vanessa's left hand for food that wasn't there. But Ulla's stand for examination was quite good; and on the recall, she not only responded but sat straight directly in front of Vanessa, and she did a smooth finish that put her in correct heel position at Vanessa's side. Vanessa left the ring beaming.

When I'd judged my total entry of ten dogs, I called everyone back for the group exercises, the long sit and the long down. In beautiful, lovely, relaxing Prenovice, the leashes stay on, and the handlers remain close to the dogs. On the long sit, the wiggly young Lab broke after about two seconds, thus inspiring three other dogs to do the same. The steadiest dog was the little apricot poodle, who also made it all the way through the three minutes of the long down, during which time the shorthair held perfectly still, too, as did – wouldn't you know – a Border collie. Ulla rolled onto her back and waved her paws in the air, but she refrained from crawling around or rising to her feet.

'Exercise finished,' I said.

The handlers and dogs left the ring to await the results. I took a seat at the little card table by the gate to add up the scores. When I'd finished, one of my stewards checked my addition, and then we called the dogs and handlers back into the ring. Turning to face the small group of spectators, I noticed Tom, Hatch, and Avery, who'd probably been there all the time. Projecting my voice, I gave the standard little speech that obedience judges deliver on such occasions. I said that this was the Prenovice A obedience class, that the maximum number of points required for a perfect score was two hundred, that every dog and every handler who'd participated today represented the future of our wonderful sport, and so on. Then I announced the placements and scores, and presented the ribbons, which fluttered happily in the light breeze. The little apricot poodle was in first place. Second was the Border collie. Ulla was third, and the German shorthair was fourth. The club sponsoring the match had provided little trophies, attractive glass paperweights, that I gave out, too, as I shook hands with each handler and received thanks ... from everyone except Vanessa, who merely nodded at me and didn't return my smile. Maybe I was naive, but it never crossed my mind that she was angry or disappointed. This was Vanessa and Ulla's first time in any obedience ring, and for a first-time handler with what is euphemistically called a 'nontraditional' obedience breed, a third place was more than decent. So, I assumed that some unhappy incident had occurred while I'd been focused exclusively on judging. Had Ulla had an altercation with another dog? Had Tom, Hatch, or Avery said or done something to upset Vanessa?

I had no chance to find out. The young woman – a girl, really – with the apricot poodle wanted to tell me that showing in obedience hadn't been half so scary as she'd expected. In return, I told her that she and her dog were really going to go places. Then, as the handlers were picking up their score sheets and moving away, I thanked my stewards and headed off to find Gabrielle. Predictably, she and Molly were in the center of a congenial group near the refreshment table.

Gabrielle looked so happy that I didn't hesitate to ask, 'How'd you do?'

'We flunked the Sit and Down on Command and Staying in Place. She just would not stay. All she wanted to do was come to me. It was all my fault. I knew we had ten minutes before our turn, so I ran back to the car to get the special liver treats for when we were done–' Steve had given her the key to my car – 'and I took just two little minutes to brush Molly, and then I was afraid we'd be late, so we went flying back, and I'm sure I threw her off. But she did everything else right, didn't you, Molly?'

'She is just adorable,' said one of Gabrielle's new friends.

'And she knows it, too!' someone else added.

'Vanessa!' Gabrielle called out. 'Congratulations! And you, too, Ulla. Ulla, CGC.'

Vanessa hung back, but Tom, Avery, and Hatch approached, and Gabrielle greeted everyone. 'I'm not contagious,' she said. 'It's just

155

dermatology.' She was more fiery red than ever. 'I should put my hat back on.'

'We'd better get you out of the sun,' I said. 'Steve should be finishing up. Let me go check.'

'You're welcome to stay and have lunch with us,' Hatch offered. 'All of you. There's plenty.'

'Fried chicken,' said Avery, who sounded and even looked more animated than usual. For once, her hair wasn't lank, and she was wearing a cheerful yellow sweater. 'Enough for everyone.'

'A few slices of poached chicken for me,' said her grandfather. 'I cannot tolerate anything fried.'

'Avery is an excellent cook,' Vanessa said.

I'd have been glad to accept the invitation, but Gabrielle said, 'Oh, we just can't! I'm sorry. We have plans.' Directing a knowing look at me, she continued, 'In fact, Holly, you'd better go run and see whether Steve's done. We don't want to be late, do we?'

Late for scraping paint? In case my face gave me away, I took off for the ring where Steve was handing out the ribbons in Open B. Because he's often serious, it's always a special pleasure to see him having fun. As is a fact of his life wherever he is, the eyes of all the women in the ring were on Steve, whose blue-green eyes were on the dogs. There's an old saying that it's as easy to love a beautiful dog as it is to love a homely one. Well, it's as easy to love a handsome man as it is to love a homely one, too.

As I waited, Ron from my club came up to me

and said, 'We need to talk about doing something in Isaac's memory.'

'A trophy, maybe,' I said. 'Let me ask Elizabeth.'

'For the highest scoring puli in our fall trial,' Ron said.

'Or maybe a trophy for Beginner Novice A. Isaac would've liked something to encourage beginners. Let's see what Elizabeth says. But we do need to do something.'

When Steve was free, we headed back to find Gabrielle. On the way, I told him about the picnic invitation and warned him about Gabrielle's refusal. 'She said that we had plans, so don't contradict her.'

'Huh. That's not like her. What's up?'

'I have no idea. But she's beet red, so it's probably a good idea to get her indoors. Oh, and Molly didn't get her CGC. But that's not why Gabrielle wants to leave. She's being a model of good sportsmanship about it.'

When we reached Gabrielle, Vanessa and her family had left. Steve, Gabrielle, and I, with Molly trotting happily along, made our way to my car. As Gabrielle was crating Molly in the back, I glanced across the parking lot, which was less crowded than it had been when we'd arrived. Parked in a far corner was a midnight-blue van.

'Steve,' I said. 'You see that van over there? The big blue one. What kind is it?'

'A Dodge. It's a Dodge Ram panel van.'

'I'll be right back,' I said.

'Panel van' apparently meant a vehicle that looked like a delivery truck, as it did. The side I could see had a passenger window but no other side windows and none in the back. I took brisk steps toward the van, but before I got close, it suddenly began to move and then headed to the exit from the lot and disappeared. I hadn't been close enough to read the license plate or see the driver. Even so, I had the feeling that I'd seen that same van before.

EIGHTEEN

Gabrielle's white lie about our plans for the afternoon made it impossible for me to carry out my actual plan: if I climbed high on the extension ladder, I'd be plainly visible from the front of Vanessa's house. Furthermore, we couldn't walk dogs without running the risk of encountering Vanessa, Tom, Hatch, or Avery.

Over tuna sandwiches at our kitchen table, I asked, 'Why didn't you want to share their picnic?'

Gabrielle hesitated, took a bite, chewed, swallowed, and finally said, 'Vanessa is just a little too interested in Buck.'

'What?'

'Go ahead and laugh! But she is.'

'She's met him exactly once.'

158

'She asks about him.'

'She asked about you before you got here.'

'It's the way she does it. There's a little gleam in that woman's eye. And something about her tone of voice.'

Steve said, 'Buck isn't interested in her. You've got nothing to worry about.'

In unison, Gabrielle and I said, 'That's not the point!'

'But,' I added, 'I think that you're imagining things.'

'I'm not. And I'll tell you something else. That young woman, Avery, takes an unhealthy interest in her brother.'

'You must kidding,' I said.

'While you were off judging, I spent some time with them. She sidles up to him. She flirts with him.'

In defense of Avery, I told Gabrielle about seeing her with Quinn Youngman. 'So,' I finished, 'she's attracted to older men. Even if Hatch weren't her brother, he'd probably be too young for her.'

The mention of Quinn triggered a conversation about Rita, whose response to the news about Quinn and Avery had been to take off for a week on the Cape with Willie. The vanishing act was totally unlike her. She was devoted to her patients and never took time off without giving them notice weeks or months in advance. I had no idea what explanation she'd offered, but she'd probably stayed close to the truth. Willie was a member of her family, and she'd hoped that Quinn would become one, so maybe she'd pleaded a family crisis. By now, Steve had excused himself. I couldn't usually read his mind the way I could read Rowdy's or Kimi's, but on this occasion, I plainly saw what he was thinking: *Girl talk.* (And Sammy's mind? I envisioned it as a complex series of interlocking roulette wheels. Although I could see them turning, I had no better than chance luck in guessing where the ball would land.)

Anyway, Gabrielle decided that since we had a few free hours, we should put them to productive use by working on the ridiculous mock survey that she and Betty had concocted. At her insistence, I got out one of the folders in which I kept applications that I'd printed from our Malamute Rescue website, the folder that included rejected applications.

'I don't like this,' I said. 'These are ... well, they're somewhat confidential.'

'Of course they are,' Gabrielle agreed. 'We aren't sharing them with anyone outside the organization. Besides, there's nothing really personal in them, is there? Of course not. All we need are names and phone numbers, and anyone can get those online. Now, once we have a list of likely candidates, I'll get on one phone, and you'll get on another, and you'll—'

'Not on our phones,' I said. 'They're cordless. One person only. And no speakerphone, either. The, uh, system was one of my bargains,' I confessed. 'And not one of my better ones.'

Gabrielle rejected my suggestion that we use a

cell phone or a computer. 'We need maximum fidelity,' she declared. 'We need a *real* phone. If you can't hear his voice clearly, that defeats our purpose.'

Our?

So, that's what happened to the rest of the afternoon: we shopped for new phones. When Steve heard about the project, he said that it was nuts and that he wanted nothing to do with it. I agreed with him, but I couldn't bring myself to take on both Betty and Gabrielle.

NINETEEN

It wasn't until Monday morning that my would-be-crime-solving stepmother got into action. By the time we'd returned from the Saturday shopping trip with Gabrielle's idea of a real phone, that is, a corded phone, the dogs needed to be fed, and we had to get ready to go to Newton to have dinner with Ceci and Althea, elderly sisters who were dear friends of ours. On Sunday morning, Gabrielle was itching to make her first call, but the plan required her to use the speakerphone while I listened in, and she was convinced that Steve would voice his opinion of our endeavor and give us away. Her suspicion was probably unwarranted. In the same circumstances, my father would've bellowed and

161

butted in. There was, however, nothing loud or interfering about Steve. Still, to my discredit, instead of standing up for Steve and challenging her insistence on viewing him in Buck's image, I took advantage of her irrational distrust to postpone the ludicrous survey. The weather was again clear and dry, and I was aching to rid the house of the peeling paint.

My determination to do the work myself had irked Steve from the moment I'd told him of my intention, and on Sunday morning, we had probably our tenth argument on the subject.

'I don't like you using the high ladder,' he said.

'You use it. You used it when you installed all the outside lights, which you did, if you remember, even though I don't like you to do electrical work.'

'We can hire a painter.'

'We could've hired an electrician, only you refused.'

'We can afford a painter.'

'No, Steve, *you* can afford a painter. I've been doing repairs and maintenance on this house since the day I moved in.'

'It's always going to be *your* house, isn't it, Holly?'

'No, it is not! It is *our* house. All I'm trying to do is my share, and the way I can contribute my fair share is to do the work myself. And I am very careful with the ladder.' That was true. When I first owned the house, I was timid about extension ladders, but the cost of hiring painters eventually got to me. Old wood-framed houses like this just don't hold paint, especially on the north side and especially when they are battered by New England winters. I'd hired professional painters, and I was still willing to hire them, but not all the time, not when I was perfectly capable of doing touch-ups and maintenance myself. 'You're the one who walks the ladders, Steve.' Walking a ladder means moving it by rocking it from side to side ... while you're standing on it. 'I never do that. I always make sure that the ladder is level, I check the ropes, I'm careful to lock the rungs, and I never use the ladder when the dogs are in the yard. I am a model of ladder safety.'

'You sound just like your father,' Gabrielle said.

When I was growing up, it was actually my mother who did almost all the repairs. She could install plumbing, and she was a whiz at laying tiles. But I didn't want to say so in front of Gabrielle. 'I'm much more careful than Buck is,' I said.

Steve said, 'But just as stubborn.'

The argument pretty much ended there, except that I made one concession: I allowed Steve to convince me to hire someone to fix the gutters and downspouts instead of tinkering with them myself. I also agreed to quit in the early afternoon so that we could spend time together grooming our dogs, but that agreement didn't count as a concession. We'd have fun.

So, in the mid morning, there I was high on the

163

ladder scraping paint off the trim around one of Rita's windows when what did I find lodged next to a sash, way up there on the third floor of the house? A great clump of what was instantly identifiable as malamute undercoat! When you're prepping a house occupied by shedding dogs, you don't just have to remove peeling paint; you also have to scrape off dog hair. Anyway, the discovery led me into deep philosophical speculation about free will: does there exist an agent of any sort capable of taking rational control of actions? Of making decisions? Answer: yes! And the reason that all those philosophers had debated endlessly without reaching a clear, definitive conclusion, I realized, was that none of them had owned Alaskan malamutes. If they had, you see, they'd have nearly choked to death on the humble answer to the classic problem of free will: dog hair! It not only controls its actions but habitually makes malicious decisions about where to go and what to do. 'A *free agent* is he that *can do as he will*, and *forbear* as he will, and that *liberty is the absence of external impediments.*' Thomas Hobbes on the subject of dog hair. I rest my case.

Have I digressed? Sorry. To return to my observations from the top of the ladder, as I was up there working, I heard first Vanessa and then Ulla, both of whom called out to me. Vanessa confined herself to hallooing and using my name, but Ulla broke into her irresistible I'm-crazy-about-you version of *woo-woo-woo*. Looking down, I saw them at the gate to the yard.

'Hasn't anyone told you that Sunday is a day of rest?' asked Vanessa.

'I'm having fun,' I called. 'Fun counts as rest, doesn't it? And this side of the house is in terrible shape. The downspouts are practically falling off. Hey, congratulations on the CGC. It's very well deserved.'

'Thank you! Too bad about Molly. She almost made it.'

'She will next time,' I said.

We said goodbyes. Maybe a half hour later, after I'd climbed down the ladder, carefully moved and repositioned it, and climbed back up, I took a moment's break, glanced down Appleton Street, and spotted two women emerging from the McNamaras' house with Persimmon on leash. Assuming that the women were Elizabeth and Isaac's daughters, I descended the ladder with the intention of introducing myself and saying how sorry I was about their father. When I reached the ground, I realized that in my paint-stained jeans and ragged T-shirt, I was ill-dressed for offering condolences. Still, if the daughters were anything like Isaac and Elizabeth, they'd care about nothing except my sincerity.

But as I reached the gate, a conversation taking place on the sidewalk just on the other side of the wooden fence brought me to a halt.

'With Daddy barely cold!' a woman exclaimed. 'What *can* Mommy be thinking?' And then: 'Do you have a plastic bag? Good girl, Persimmon!'

The other woman spoke. 'I am so sick of hearing about Tom that I could scream! And after what Daddy went through, how can Mommy go on and on about her ailments! When there's nothing wrong with her.'

'She does have celiac disease.'

'Big deal! She's used to it, and she never used to harp on it, and she wouldn't now except that she's being encouraged.'

'Plus, she can hardly wait for us to...' The voice trailed off.

I climbed back up the ladder.

What's the best thing to do when you're guilty of eavesdropping, even unintended eavesdropping? Nothing, I decided. Besides, even if I'd wanted to interfere, what could I have done? Order Elizabeth and Tom to end what was evidently becoming more than a friendship? Have a little talk with Elizabeth, who'd hardly welcome the advice of someone who was no more than a neighbor and a member of the same dog-training club? Explain to Vanessa that she had to make her father quit courting the widow next door until a decent interval had elapsed? Ask Rita for her professional opinion of the situation? Or ask Gabrielle to apply her admirable social skills? No! Furthermore, I knew without asking that Rita and Gabrielle would offer the same good advice, which would be to mind my own business. Ah hah! Therein lay the source of my urge to interfere. Especially because dogs were my business, I was at great risk of succumbing to the real dog person's compulsion to offer unsolicited observations and advice: *Your dog is twenty pounds overweight. Get him on a diet right now! You should get rid of that prong collar and use an Easy-Walk Harness instead. Take that dangerous toy away from your dog this minute!* And on and on! But dogs really were my business. If I had to issue advice, I should confine myself to my field of expertise.

Consequently, I climbed back down the ladder, went into the house, and said to Steve, 'These dogs are getting fat and lazy. What they need is a good long walk.'

They got one. The route we had in mind was a bit much for Lady, so we left her with Gabrielle and Molly. After supplying ourselves with bottles of water, folding fabric bowls, sand-wiches, and dog treats, we headed to the river with Rowdy, Kimi, Sammy, and India. When we reached the Charles, we followed the path on its banks upstream to Watertown Square and beyond before we turned around and retraced our route. The round trip was about twelve miles. During the entire time that it took us to cover that distance, I refrained from quarreling with my husband, from sounding like my father, and from handing out free advice. According to one of the old saws of the dog world, a tired dog is a good dog. Maybe the same is true of human beings.

TWENTY

That evening, Steve, Gabrielle, and I were in the living room watching the Red Sox. Gabrielle was on the couch with Molly in her lap; India, tuckered out, was sleeping on the floor in a corner of the room; and Steve was in a chair with Lady lying down on the rug to his right. Doglike, I was sitting on the rug just to the left of Steve's chair, and Sammy was cuddled up next to me. Kimi then strolled into the room, paused to size up the situation, and did something so unprecedented that all of us stared at her: with obvious deliberation, she marched up to Sammy, planted herself directly in front of him, and executed a classic front-down, rear-up play bow. In the past, it had absolutely always been Sammy, the baby of the family, our permanent puppy, who had initiated play with Kimi; she was often happy to accept his invitations and to tear around with him, but never before had I seen Ms Queen of the Castle stoop to begging her serf for anything. Sammy was as astonished as I was. With no hesitation, he leaped to his feet, ready to fly around the house after her. A second later, Kimi's true intention became clear: having enticed Sammy into vacating the prize spot next to me, she flung herself down and occupied it in his stead. With a smug expression on her face, she rested her head on my legs.

Sammy knew that he'd been outfoxed, as he certainly had been. Kimi had walked into the room, analyzed the situation, and observed that Sammy occupied the position that she wanted and, in her view, deserved. The play bow had been a mere means to an end. Instead of using force to get Sammy to move so that she could take his place, Kimi had applied her considerable intelligence. Interestingly, the means she had chosen, the play bow, was way down at the bottom of her own behavioral repertoire but was an element of canine body language that Sammy was guaranteed not only to understand but to react to in an absolutely predictable way. Kimi had also known that if she had shoved Sammy out of the way or used some other forceful or even aggressive tactic, I'd have stopped her, whereas I'd been as charmed as Sammy had been to see her unexpectedly issue the beguiling invitation to get up and play.

It's possible, of course, to see Kimi's tactic not only as brilliant but as shamelessly manipulative: there was Sammy, innocently and happily curled up next me, when mean Kimi came along and tricked him into ceding his position to her; it's possible to judge Kimi as if she were a human being. But even in our own species, rank has its privilege. The British monarch isn't expected to defer to a commoner unexpectedly discovered on the coronation throne. In our little canine kingdom, Kimi greatly outranked Sammy. In a way, she behaved nobly. And in his own way, so did Sammy, who happily settled down next to Kimi, content to have been gently put in his place.

So, the next morning, when Gabrielle decided that we finally had time to implement the ill-conceived plan to conduct a mock consumer-satisfaction survey, I thought of Sammy and tried to show comparable good grace in accepting the reality of having been outranked. As Sammy was no match for Kimi, so I was no match for the combined forces of Gabrielle and Betty, especially Betty, who was, of course, the human incarnation of Kimi.

'Now,' said Gabrielle, who was seated at the kitchen table with the new corded phone and a great pile of papers in front of her, 'while you and Steve were taking your walk yesterday, I called Betty, and we've come up with a list of survey questions. We also decided that the tactic to take is newest first. Betty pointed out that it's unlikely that this dreadful man is someone who's been harboring a grudge for months or years. It's probably someone who was rejected shortly before the calls started. And we think it's one of your applicants, or that's our working hypothesis. You're the one he called first, and he bothered to find out Vinnie's name.'

'Would you like some coffee?' I asked in the first of my efforts at delay.

'No, I don't think so. Thank you, but we want

170

to sound professional, don't we.' The tag was not a question. 'We don't want kitchen sounds in the background.'

'What about dog noises? Rowdy and India are in the yard. India might bark.' The noisiest of the dogs, Molly, was crated upstairs in Gabrielle's room; and Sammy and Lady were at work with Steve. The only dog loose in the kitchen was my radical feminist, Kimi, whose strong presence was intended to remind me to stand up for myself if the mock survey became more than I could tolerate. 'And if someone comes to the door, Kimi might *woo-woo*.'

'That'll just lend verisimilitude,' Gabrielle said. 'After all, the survey does have to do with dogs.'

'I thought that you were supposed to represent a market-research company.'

'Specializing in dogs. So, first of all, we have to make sure that this number doesn't show up on anyone's caller ID.'

'There's a code for that. We'll have to enter it before every call.' Even though Kimi's dark, intelligent eyes were on me, I dutifully entered the code. 'But, look, Gabrielle, you have to understand that I am far from sure that I'll recognize the voice. When I got that call, the kitchen was full of people, and then when he started asking for Vinnie—'

Gabrielle smiled sweetly. 'Just do your best.' She pressed the speakerphone button. Over the sound of the dial tone, she said, 'Since Betty and I think that the most likely culprit is one of *your* applicants, we're starting with your recent ones.' She picked up the application on top of one of the piles. 'Irving Jensen. What's this you've written here? I have a little trouble reading your writing.'

'So do I.' I took a quick look at the application and at the notes I'd scrawled on it. 'Oh, he was impossible! He doesn't believe in fences, he wants an intact dog, and he said he'd owned lots of dogs, but he didn't give a vet reference, and the reason, according to him, was that all the dogs were healthy. And on top of that, he swore at me.'

'A propensity for obscenity.' She took back the application and dialed Jensen's number.

A man answered.

'Good morning,' said Gabrielle in a voice higher and lighter than her own throaty, seductive alto. 'This is Gail with Canine Consumer Satisfaction. May I speak to Irving Jensen, please?'

'This is him. We don't want none.'

'I'm calling to find out whether you were satisfied with your recent experience with Alaskan Malamute Rescue. Were you treated courteously by the organization's representative?'

'We already got one.'

'A malamute?'

'My daughter come home with some damned little yapper.'

In gracious tones, Gabrielle asked, in an effort to keep Jensen talking, 'And what kind of little dog is it?'

'One of them bitchin' frizzies. Pisses all over the place.'

Gabrielle's expression was as severe as I'd ever seen it. 'Bichon frise. I see.'

By then, I was shaking my head, mouthing 'no', and gesturing to Gabrielle to hang up.

'Well, Mr Jensen, thank you for your time. Goodbye.' She ended the call. 'What a dreadful man! Bitchin' frizzy, indeed!'

'I hate to tell you, but I've heard it before, presumably as a joke. A bad joke. Anyway, he's not the one. I didn't think I'd be able to tell anything, but I'm positive. For one thing, I notice grammatical errors. I'm a writer. "My daughter come home"? And Jensen sounds ... he sounds coarse. The caller was obscene, eventually, but he didn't sound coarse.'

'Scratch Irving Jensen. The poor bichon! I hope his daughter is better than he is.'

'I hope so, too.' My surprising certainty about Jensen boosted my confidence in what I'd previously seen as a loopy enterprise. 'Who's next?'

'A couple. Don and Diane Di Bartolomeo.' She handed me the application.

'He actually might have it in for me. The wife was the one I talked to. The husband, Don, was the one who wanted a malamute. The wife, Diane, said that he could get any medium-sized dog that didn't shed. That's why she agreed to a malamute. I broke the news.'

Again, I blocked our number from displaying on caller ID, and Gabrielle dialed. To her obvi-

173

ous disappointment, a woman answered. Even so, Gabrielle ran through the same introduction she'd used before.

'Were we treated courteously?' asked Mrs Di Bartolomeo. 'Well, frankly, no. I can't say that I find it courteous to be told that a dog would be better off dead than in our home. I find that highly insulting.'

'Let me make sure I understand. The, uh, representative threatened to—'

'Not in so many words. And not that it matters now.'

I was rolling my eyes and mouthing, 'I told her no such thing!'

Gabrielle asked, 'So, you've changed your mind about wanting a malamute?'

'Not at all! We found a wonderful, knowledgeable breeder. She explained that the rescue person didn't know what she was talking about. Malamutes come in all different sizes, you see, and the puppy we're getting is going to be a medium-sized dog. He won't get to be more than forty or at most fifty pounds. And they don't shed anything like what that rescue woman said, either.'

I mouthed, 'Who?'

'Why, that's wonderful,' Gabrielle said. 'I'm very happy for you. This breeder sounds like a gem.'

'Oh, she is!'

'I wonder if she's someone I happen to know.'

'Her name is Pippy Neff. She is *very* well known.'

'Well, the best of luck with your puppy! And thank you for your time.'

When Gabrielle had hung up, I said, 'At most fifty pounds! And for a male! Damn Pippy! Yes, once in a while there's a malamute bitch that small, but hardly ever. And not from Pippy's lines.' I removed a dog hair that had somehow ended up in my mouth. 'And shedding! Well, let the Di Bartolomeos find out for themselves. They had a dog that was killed by a car, and the husband lied about it on his application, but who knows? Maybe they'll turn out to be great owners. Once the puppy grows up, maybe they'll love him and forgive him for being a big hairy dog. And keep him on leash.'

Gabrielle then placed a couple of other calls, reached answering machines, and did not, of course, leave messages. We took a coffee break and resumed.

'Next is Flood. Eldon,' she said.

'With the farm stand. He was interested in one of the dogs on our website, Thunder. Anyway, according to Mr Flood, he has a special gift with dogs, and my problem is that I just don't train 'em right. That's why I have to use a leash and why I need a fence. But I was perfectly polite to him. I probably told him that this was the wrong breed for his situation. I think maybe he did hang up on me. I'm pretty sure he didn't swear at me, though.'

'The perfect gentleman.'

'I've talked to worse. Well, his application said that he had a farm when it's a farm stand, but that's no big deal. I looked at the website for the farm stand. It does exist. He has a wife, Lucinda. Anyway, he didn't really lie about anything, at least that I know about.'

'Bully for him. Ready?'

I nodded. Gabrielle dialed, and a machine answered the call. 'Thank you for calling Flood Farm.' The voice was a man's. 'We are open Wednesday through Sunday from ten to six until May 15. After May 15, we are open seven days a week. For directions, press...'

By then, I was sitting upright and pointing a finger at the phone. Gabrielle hung up.

'I'm not positive,' I cautioned. 'But he could be the one. What I'm sure of is that we can't rule him out.'

'Well, it's just too bad that this is May fifth. We'll have to wait until Wednesday to take a little drive into the country and stop at a farm stand. What on earth do they sell at this time of year? Radishes? What else is ready?'

'Plants, garden supplies. You can visit their website if you want. Pies, Native American crafts, dried flowers, jam, stuff like that, and later on, fresh produce, probably pumpkins and then Christmas trees and wreaths.'

'I find myself overcome with an acute longing for pie,' said Gabrielle. 'And a Native American craft object, dried flowers, and jam.'

'Gabrielle, I'm not positive. All I said was that we can't rule him out. And we don't even know whether Eldon will be there on Wednesday.'

'Of course we don't! But we'll find out.'

176

TWENTY-ONE

In case you wondered, I really did have the sense it could have been Eldon Flood who'd made the nasty call. Still, my statement that we couldn't rule him out had the happy effect of bringing the sham survey to a halt. Thus instead of having to spend the rest of Monday and all day Tuesday listening to Gabrielle ask people whether they'd been treated courteously by Malamute Rescue, I had the time to finish scraping the paint on the north side of the house and to complete the preparations assigned to me for Saturday's National Pet Week event at the armory. I called Max Crocker to confirm that he and Mukluk would help with the Malamute Rescue booth and to tell him that we still didn't have a cat-friendly rescue female for him. I did not, of course, add, 'But I do have the right woman!'

The right woman, Rita, returned from the Cape looking more relaxed than she had since the unfortunate episode with Quinn Youngman. She went back to seeing her patients and agreed to help out on Saturday. Steve, bless him, solved the problem of taking Willie to a public event for which he was temperamentally unsuited by offering to handle Willie himself. Unlike Eldon Flood and lots of other people who bragged about possessing a special gift with dogs, Steve, the most unassuming of men, quietly exerted an almost hypnotic power over animals. It's possible that in some previous existence, he was a snake charmer, not that I've seen him with snakes, but something about his presence had a soothing effect on dogs and cats, including challenging ones like Willie. Even the ultimate challenge, my cat, Tracker, had trusted Steve from the moment I'd rescued her. In spite of all my efforts, she still occasionally hissed at me when I entered her abode, my office, but from the beginning, she'd purred for Steve and for Steve alone. Did Steve in fact cast a spell on animals? Maybe not. It's possible that animals trusted him for the simple reason that he was trustworthy. In any case, with his leash in Steve's capable hands, Willie would be trustworthy, too.

Late on Tuesday afternoon, Sammy and I went to Vanessa's so that he could dash around the yard with Ulla, who greeted me by plopping her rear onto the ground, raising a paw in a charming wave, and issuing melodious peals of *woo-woo-woo* readily translated into English as, 'You are soooooooooo special!'

'Ulla, you say that to all the girls. And boys. But you're pretty special yourself,' I told her.

While Ulla and Sammy chased each other and ran in giant figure eights, Vanessa and I chatted in the usual way that owners do while dogs play.

178

She told me about the new car that her father was buying for her. 'He spoils us rotten,' she commented.

'My father is generous, too,' I said. 'We're both lucky.'

'But your father doesn't dwell on illness! He has other topics of conversation.'

'Dogs,' I said. 'And fishing.'

'Better than everyone's ailments!'

After we'd talked about a couple of other things, Vanessa said that I was brave to use the high ladder and enterprising to do so much work myself.

'*Enterprising* isn't Steve's word for it,' I said. 'He thinks I'm a cheapskate, and he doesn't trust me to do everything to his satisfaction. Besides, he hates watching me up on the ladder. It's been a subject of some debate, but I know what I'm doing.'

When we switched to the topic of the National Pet Week event, I said that I'd seen posters and notices all over and that she was doing a great job of publicity. Vanessa thanked me and confirmed that she'd be managing the food table. 'I've promised Ron I'll run it, but malamutes and food tables don't mix, so I've roped my family in.'

'Thank you,' I said. 'I'm afraid that the event has lost its momentum without Isaac. He was the driving force. He was the one who wanted the club to get whatever this award is from AKC.'

'All the more reason to do it well,' Vanessa

179

said.

As Sammy and I were leaving, we ran into Elizabeth and Persimmon, who were returning from a walk with Tom. Although the temperature was in the low seventies, Elizabeth wore a handwoven shawl, and Tom's neck was swathed in a wool scarf.

'Our daily constitutional,' Tom remarked.

'The cardiovascular benefits of dog walking!' Elizabeth exclaimed. 'Tom is a convert. Oh, Holly? Ron asked about a trophy in Isaac's memory. That would be lovely. Something for Beginner Novice A or Novice A, I think. He had a soft spot for beginners. Tom is making a dona-tion–' she beamed at him – 'and I'll want to, too.'

When I'd mumbled something appreciative, Sammy and I headed home. As we made our way there, I tried to squelch the thought that Elizabeth had buried her husband only three days earlier. 'Tom,' I said to Sammy, 'is a widower himself. He understands what she's going through. It's petty and small of me to judge something I don't understand. Besides, Elizabeth and Tom have a lot in common. For example, hypochondria!'

TWENTY-TWO

'According to the website,' said Gabrielle as she drove us toward Flood Farm on Wednesday afternoon, 'they have chicken pot pies, so at a minimum, we won't have to cook dinner. And it really is a splendid day for a drive in the country.'

To avoid tipping off Eldon Flood to the true reason for our visit, we'd decided to take Gabrielle's Volvo station wagon instead of my Blazer. As dog-person vehicles go, mine was relatively unornamented, but the rear window had three *Woo* stickers that I'd bought from Alaskan Malamute Rescue of North Carolina, and I was unwilling to remove the happy transcription of my dogs' vocalizations. We also left the malamutes themselves at home and took only Lady and Molly, who, Gabrielle reasoned, might be produced if we wanted to stimulate talk about dogs without giving ourselves entirely away.

'I'm more interested in finding that dark van than I am in buying a chicken pot pie,' I said. 'It's one thing to get anonymous calls and letters – not that I like them – but I really hate the sense that a threatening person is lurking around. Or

181

following me. And there's something ... oh, this is ridiculous! But that kind of panel van? It's stupid. It's a cliché. I've seen too many movies. But that kind of dark van—'

'You expect the doors to fly open and thugs to pop out,' Gabrielle said. 'But they're all over the place, aren't they?'

'Thugs?'

'Dark vans.' She glanced in the rear-view mirror. 'Well, I don't see it now, but there was one in back of us. It's gone now. The point is that it's like pregnant women or Cadillac trucks or—'

'What?'

'All you have to do is notice one of them, and then you start noticing all of them, and it feels as if they're all over the place when, really, they've been there all along.'

'Are there Cadillac trucks? They exist?'

'Yes.'

'If you say so. But there's nothing sinister about them, is there? Well, or about vans, either. I get the point. But the one in the parking lot at the match? As soon as I started walking toward that van, it suddenly took off, and, yes, *post hoc, ergo propter hoc*, as Leah would say – it didn't necessarily leave because of me. Even so.' I took a look at the Google map we'd printed out. 'We should be almost there. Yes, there it is – on the right.'

'On this busy road! All I can say is that it's a good thing that you people don't just give rescue dogs to anyone who asks. Now, remember! Not a word about malamutes. We're out for a drive in the country on this beautiful spring afternoon, and we've never heard of Lucinda and Eldon Flood before.'

Gabrielle's exclamations to the contrary, we were not exactly in the country, but we were on a busy route, almost a small highway. The big wooden Flood Farm sign announced that the enterprise was open year round. In case the words didn't register on passers-by, the sign depicted corn stalks, tomatoes, pumpkins, Christmas trees, wreaths, and double-crust pies with what at first glance appeared to be a three-dimensional rendition of flaky pastry but turned out on close inspection to be peeling paint. The farm stand itself was a low, wide, rickety-looking building with glass-paned doors across the front and a faded awning above them. To the left of the structure was a small beige ranch house; to the right were greenhouses covered in clear plastic; and on both sides and in the back were fields. Three vehicles were parked in a dirt and gravel parking area in front of the stand. Two belonged to the farm: a red pickup truck and a white minivan had tiny versions of the roadside sign painted on their doors. The third vehicle, an environmentalist's nightmare, was a gigantic black luxury SUV. Its apparent owner, a deeply tanned blonde woman in tennis whites, was examining the flats of annuals and the pots of perennials arranged in front of the glass doors to the building. She then opened one of the doors and entered.

'So,' said Gabrielle, 'we aren't the only custo-mers.'

Leaving the dogs in the car with the rear win-dows open, we strolled to the display of plants, not one of which would've lasted more than two minutes in my yard before being stomped on or dug up by malamutes.

'There are some unusual varieties here,' said Gabrielle. 'I do like verbascum. You know, you could grow that in front of your house. It would be safe from the dogs there.'

'Shall we go in?' I asked. Hint, hint.

The interior, although somewhat dark, had a rustic appeal. The promised jams and jellies were neatly arrayed on shelves that also contain-ed tins and bottles of maple syrup, boxes of candy, and jars of herbs and spices. The Native American crafts promised on the website turned out to be authentic and local: the baskets, made of ash and sweet grass, were typical of those produced by Maine tribes. Across the back of the shop were refrigerator and freezer units with glass doors, and the walls displayed herbal wreaths and bunches of dried flowers. To the right was a long counter with loaves of bread in plastic bags and a dozen or so pies at one end, and, at the other, a computer and an old-fash-ioned cash register. Behind the cash register was a thin, tired-looking woman of forty, I guessed. Her face was lined, and her short brown hair had been chemically fried by a bad perm. She wore a pink tracksuit at least two sizes too big for her.

The tennis player was talking to her. 'Apple, I

think. And one blueberry.'

'Blueberry pie!' Gabrielle exclaimed. 'Do you have blueberry? My husband just loves it, and I make rotten crust.' Both statements were true.

'Lucinda's pies are the best,' the customer said.

'The berries are frozen,' Lucinda said apologetically. 'But we did grow them here.'

'Well, of course they're frozen,' said Gabrielle. 'At this time of year? We'll take a blueberry pie and ... something for dinner. We'll take a look in the freezer, shall we?'

'Do you happen to have any anemones?' the tennis woman asked. 'The biggish ones? I didn't see any out front.'

Just then, a tall, thin, blue-eyed man with a long braid entered through a rear door, a big flat of snapdragons in his arms. He wore earth-stained blue work pants and a plaid flannel shirt.

'Eldon will know,' Lucinda said. 'Do we have any anemones out back?'

Gabrielle and I were examining the chicken pot pies in the freezer. She didn't quite dig an elbow into my ribs, but I saw her arm twitch. As if I needed a reminder to listen carefully!

'You want the ones they call Japanese?' Eldon asked.

'Yes. Pink. I have a gap in the border, and I want a fall bloomer. And not mums!'

'I've got Queen Charlotte, but they're small.'

'Oh, I just love Queen Charlotte!' Gabrielle explained. 'They do have a tendency to take over, but they're lovely. They do beautifully in

185

partial shade.'

'How small?' the woman asked.

'Small,' Eldon said. 'They take a while to get established.'

'Let me mull it over,' the woman said. 'So, just the apple and the blueberry for today.'

As the customer was paying, Gabrielle carried two large chicken pot pies to the counter, set them down, and said to Eldon, 'And I'll have that flat of snapdragons, too, please.'

I hoped that Gabrielle was footing the bill.

'They're dwarf.' He set the flat on the counter.

By then, I was certain. 'Yes,' I said. 'That's exactly what we were hoping for. Exactly.'

Gabrielle nodded. 'And I have a little question about something out front.' She marched off with Eldon following her. I trailed after the two of them. Gabrielle paused and pretended to examine some potted delphiniums. As she was about to say something, the blonde woman emerged with two boxes of pies in her arms. Leaving the door to the interior ajar, she got into her SUV and started the engine.

With speed and directness that surprised me, Gabrielle said, 'My question, Mr Flood, is not about plants. It's about phone calls. And an anonymous letter.'

In the bright outdoor light, it was easy to see the blood drain from Eldon Flood's face. I thought that he was about to faint. He must have thought so, too. Reaching down, he rested a hand on a big pot of white geraniums and slowly bent from the waist as if he were going to touch his toes.

Before Gabrielle or I had the chance to respond, Lucinda suddenly appeared. Seeing her outdoors, I realized that she was far younger than I'd assumed, probably no older than twenty-five. With a jolt, I realized that both she and her husband were younger than I was.

'Eldon, not again!' she pleaded.

Without asking whether Eldon was given to irritating fits of hysterical syncope, I cleared some flower pots off a wooden crate and said, 'Maybe it would help him to sit down.' Then I addressed Eldon himself. 'Here. Put your head below your knees.'

Ignoring both Eldon and my effort to minister to him, his wife turned to Gabrielle. 'What's he done this time?'

With an expression of infinite understanding on her face, Gabrielle said gently, 'Phone calls. A letter.' A stranger who knew nothing about the situation would've assumed from Gabrielle's manner and especially from her confiding tone that she was sharing a secret with a close and valued friend.

Lucinda responded by pouring out her troubles, albeit somewhat incoherently. 'He was supposed to be cured! After the last time, he was in court-ordered therapy, and they kept saying that he did it because he didn't know how to confront people directly, but now that he knew how, he'd quit!'

'But he didn't quit,' Gabrielle said. 'Did you, Mr Flood?'

Eldon, who had made a subtle shift from lowering his head below his knees to hanging his head in shame, mumbled something inaudible.

His wife was incensed. 'You see, Eldon! That's what they told you not to do! You're supposed to express your frustrations and anger and all that shit loud and clear the second you feel pissed off instead of bottling it all up and moaning and stewing about it and sneaking around making dirty phone calls and the rest of that same old crap, and what are you doing now but bottling it all up and acting like you're going to faint and—'

Leaping to his feet, Eldon knocked over the wooden box he'd been sitting on and accidentally bumped into me. 'Lucinda, shut up!' he roared. 'And you, too, lady!' he hollered at Gabrielle.

He took a step toward her, but I blocked his path. 'You are way out of line,' I told him.

'You stay out of this,' he growled.

'No, I will not stay out of it. I did nothing to deserve that nasty phone call you made to me, and no one deserved the other nasty calls you made. You applied to adopt a malamute, and I did my best to turn you down politely, and what was your response? Your response was to harass and offend and frighten people whose only crime is trying to help homeless dogs! And you did it in a sneaky—'

'Holly,' Gabrielle said softly. 'Holly, this—'

Lucinda cut her off. 'So that's who you are!

Eldon told me all about you, and I don't see that you're in any position to call us sneaky. There we were offering a wonderful home to a dog, and not only did you insult us, but now here you are showing up under false pretenses and—'

'I did not insult your husband. All I did was turn down an application, and what your husband did in response was—'

'You *thwarted* him,' Lucinda said. 'That's what triggered his relapse. It's all your fault. Eldon doesn't do these things unless he's *thwarted*. That's what the doctors say.'

Although I was ripping mad, I tried to stay cool. 'So, he's entitled to get all his own way because that's what prevents him from making obscene phone calls and sending anonymous letters? You may buy that argument, but I don't.'

Gabrielle, the eternal diplomat, said brightly, 'Well, we've all had the chance to voice our frustrations and clear the air, and we've reached a sort of agreement.'

We'd voiced a lot more than mere frustrations, and far from clearing the air, we'd polluted it, or so I thought. And what was this agreement we were supposed to have reached? I gritted my teeth. 'Positive reframing,' as Rita calls this kind of Pollyannaish ploy, always irritates me. According to Rita, psychotherapists do it to introduce helpful new perspectives on seemingly bleak or horrendous situations: problems aren't problems; they're challenges. If your life has crashed down around you, you're having a potentially beneficial learning experience. Your beloved dog has just died, and you're supposed to reinterpret your agony as a significant part of your life experience. Lies, lies, lies! But if positive reframing, aka lies, would give us an easy exit, great!

As if sensing my thoughts, Gabrielle rested a hand on my arm. 'All of us have expressed our feelings clearly and directly, and that's the most we can expect to accomplish. When you think about it, that's quite a lot, isn't it? So, we'll pay for our pies and our snapdragons and—'

I'll never know exactly what part of Gabrielle's little speech sparked Eldon's outburst. Maybe it drove him wild to imagine us eating his wife's pies or planting his dwarf snapdragons. Maybe Gabrielle's positive reframing awakened bitter memories of his court-ordered therapy. For whatever reason, he suddenly started shouting at me about wanting Thunder, the dog he'd seen on our Malamute Rescue website, and he began jabbing his finger at Gabrielle and calling her a nosy loudmouth bitch. Now, besides being angry, I was alarmed, even frightened. Why hadn't I realized that what lay beneath Eldon Flood's cowardly phone calls and anonymous letter was the potential for raw violence? Why had we left the big dogs at home? Since I myself had ended up mentioning Malamute Rescue, we might as well have had the malamutes with us, and not in the car either, but at our sides. In most circumstances, the malamute attitude is: *We're equal partners, OK? I watch out for myself, and I expect you to do the*

190

same. If, however, these dogs decide that we thickheaded, weak-bodied bipeds are imperiling ourselves by engaging in stupid, ineffective dithering, they sometimes take action. Rowdy would've calmly blocked Eldon's access to us by transforming himself into a canine barricade, and Sammy might've done the same. As for Kimi, I had no desire to imagine what she'd have done if Eldon had actually attacked. The only sure bet was that she'd have given no warning.

In taking my eyes off Eldon and Lucinda to glance around, I obviously did not expect to see my dogs. My action was pure reflex: *when scared, seek malamutes.* If I was looking for anything, it was for the malamute strength and courage that might infuse me in the absence of the dogs themselves. What actually caught my eye was neither a bold, bounding, double-coated savior nor was it a mystical, strength-infusing vision thereof; rather, it was a midnight-blue panel van parked just off the pavement, perhaps fifty feet from us. Damn it all! On the ride to Flood Farm, I'd been hoping to discover that not only had Eldon Flood made the nasty phone calls and sent me that horrid message but that he had also been the person tailing me in what Steve had identified as a Dodge Ram panel van. Arriving at the farm stand and seeing the two Flood Farm vehicles in the parking area, I'd given no further thought to the van, as if the presence of the red pickup and the white mini-van made it impossible for the Floods to own a third vehicle, for example, a big panel van sometimes used by Eldon and sometimes – now, for instance – driven by an employee.

In the few seconds that it had taken me to glance quickly around and spot the van, Eldon had launched into the obscenity that I'd heard on the phone. As I moved my gaze away from the van and back to him, maybe the slight motion caught his eye, or maybe it was just my turn to become his target. Shouting filth, he lurched toward me. I took a quick step backward, and he again went after Gabrielle, first with words, then with gestures. Now, instead of jabbing a finger at her, he pounded his fist into his own palm and then into the air in front of her. I cursed myself for having let Gabrielle drive. If I'd had my car and my keys, we'd already be zooming off.

Gabrielle, however, was still trying to talk her way out. 'Mr Flood, let's all calm—'

I put my hand on her purse and shouted to make myself heard. 'Gabrielle, your keys! We—'

The roar of an engine interrupted me. The blue panel van, the Dodge Ram, thundered toward us and abruptly halted. By the time the passenger door flew open, I'd seen the driver and thus expected the bellow that followed.

'You son of a bitch!' my father thundered. 'No one treats my wife like that!'

Eldon Flood was tall, but Buck had a good four inches on him and must have outweighed Flood by forty pounds of angry, protective muscle, the force of which shot down my

192

father's right arm, through his massive fist, and into Eldon Flood's jaw. As Flood toppled backward into the display of potted perennials, Buck lowered his voice and growled, 'Stand up, you yellow-bellied piece of shit!'

'Buck, stop it right now!' Gabrielle screamed. 'Stop it!'

'Yes, stop it!' I echoed.

Instead of joining in, Lucinda took the practical step of bending over her husband, who was clutching his face while floundering among the injured delphiniums. Incredibly, she asked, 'Eldon, are you all right?'

'Ice,' my father recommended.

I wanted to strangle him.

Addressing Lucinda, he said in tones of sweet reason, 'Hey, I can't stand by and watch someone threaten my wife, who happens to be–' he paused dramatically – 'a brave woman battling–' his voice dropped to a hoarse whisper – 'cancer.'

TWENTY-THREE

'Buck, you are an idiot!' Gabrielle told him. 'You are a *blithering* idiot!'

'Cancer is nothing to be ashamed of,' my father told her. 'It's a disease that strikes—'

'I do *not* have cancer. All I have is vanity.

193

Vanity! Not that it's any of your business. Now, go home! I am staying with Steve and Holly until I cool down, and until I do, I do not want to see you. Go home! Get in that van you've been using to *stalk* us and *frighten* us, and go home!'

My father looked astonished. 'I never meant–'

'Buck,' I said, 'at the moment, no one particularly cares what you meant. In case you've forgotten, I'm a dog trainer. I care more about behavior than I do about intentions, and no one is happy about your behavior right now. I think that you should do what Gabrielle is telling you. Return that van to wherever you got it from, and go home.'

With an appropriately hangdog air, my father nodded to everyone, got back into the Dodge Ram, and drove off. By then, Eldon was sitting on the wooden box he'd used earlier. His head hung down, and he was clutching his jaw.

'Do you need an ambulance?' I asked.

'He hates doctors,' Lucinda said. 'And we don't want a fuss.'

I suddenly understood. 'Is he on parole?' I asked.

'Go away,' she said. 'He's been decked before. He's used to it. Just go away.'

It would've been exactly like Gabrielle, despite what had just happened, to try to form some kind of positive connection with Lucinda and, God help us, even with Eldon Flood himself. What motivated her to seize the opportunity to leave was, I soon realized, her need to vent her

194

anger at Buck. The second we were in her Volvo and heading out of the parking lot, she said, 'Have you ever wanted to strangle your father?'

'Yes,' I said. 'More often, I've wanted to muzzle him.'

'What was he *thinking*?'

'He wasn't. But where on earth did he get the idea that you have cancer?'

'Oh, I can tell you that. He followed me. The nerve! Theodora, our dog trainer, is married to a doctor. Her husband has an office at their house. We see Theodora there because I was afraid that if we went to her training facility, Buck would find out. Hah!'

'He had no business following you. Or us.'

'Where did he get that van? I hope he didn't buy it.'

'You know, once he thought that you had cancer, he must have been horribly worried.'

'As if I wouldn't tell him! I am not an independent, stoical type. I didn't tell him about training Molly because he would have taken over.'

'Yes. He would have.'

'And I didn't tell him about the dermatologist because I was embarrassed. And ashamed. Ashamed of being so vain.'

'You are not vain. Is it vain to get haircuts? Or, uh, touch up the color? You just wanted to look your best. And you wanted privacy. Recognizing people's need for privacy is not one of Buck's strong points.'

'Because of dogs!' Gabrielle exclaimed. 'He

195

assumes that since dogs have very little need for privacy, no one else does, either.'

'He does have his good points.'

'At the moment I am having trouble remembering what they are,' Gabrielle said.

My father was outstandingly loyal, faithful, devoted, affectionate, gregarious, and playful, but I paused before answering in case I made him sound like a golden retriever. Eventually, I came up with a virtue that dogs don't possess. 'Buck,' I said truthfully, 'is very generous.' Of course, if dogs had bank accounts, they'd be generous, and in other ways, they are generous, but they don't have bank accounts, and I was desperate. Buck's marriage to Gabrielle was a godsend. If she became disenchanted with him, what would happen? On inspiration, I said, 'He worships you. What's behind all this is his deep fear of losing you.' I borrowed that explanation from Rita, who was always attributing people's nasty moods and rotten behavior to a profound fear of loss. 'He suffers from a profound fear of loss,' I said. In a way, he did. After my mother died, he fell into such a deep state of grief that he became more than a little odd. Or that's my view. Rita has her own opinions. But then Rita never knew my mother. Anyway, I didn't want to dwell aloud on Buck's prolonged mourning, particularly so soon after he'd eulogized my mother at someone else's funeral.

'I really should have told him about the dermatologist,' Gabrielle said. '"What a tangled web we weave!"' She sighed before adding, a second later, 'But I'm still not telling him about training Molly.'

'No, don't tell him. You were right about that to begin with. With the best of intentions, he'd take over. It's your project. And Molly's. And eventually we can present it to him as a lovely surprise.'

'A surprise! Yes. Exactly. And the day isn't a total loss. We've resolved the whole matter of the phone calls and the letter, and at least we don't have to worry about a menacing stranger following us in a dark van!' To my relief, she laughed.

'But we left without our chicken pot pies,' I said. 'And our blueberry pie. Not to mention the dwarf snapdragons.'

'Oh, I hate dwarf snapdragons, and the dogs would have killed them, anyway.'

'That's true,' I said. 'And I'm not that crazy about chicken pot pie, either.'

'So all we're really missing out on is one blueberry pie.'

'We'll make our own,' Gabrielle said.

And we did.

TWENTY-FOUR

After Gabrielle had gone to bed that night, I reached my father on his cell phone. I had mixed feelings about making the call. On the one hand, he'd had no business following us, and I certainly didn't approve of his having punched Eldon Flood in the jaw. On the other hand, I thought that Buck deserved to know some of what was going on.

'What Gabrielle meant by *vanity*,' I told him, 'is that she went to a dermatologist for laser treatment. She's spent a lot of time in the sun, and she wanted to get rid of—'

'She's beautiful!' he boomed. 'What did she want to do that for?'

'She had brown spots and redness that she didn't like. Buck, people do it all the time. There's nothing wrong with it. And the reason she didn't tell you is that you'd tell her not to. I'm not even supposed to be discussing this with you, so please do not mention it to her. And don't you ever follow me again! Where did you get that van, anyway?'

'Chet Smith.'

Chet was a foul-mouthed, hard-drinking old fishing buddy of Buck's who lived in Newburyport. I barely knew him because my mother didn't want him in the house, in part because he was obnoxious and in part because he never bathed. 'Him,' I said. 'Did you stay with him, too?'

Sounding insulted, Buck said, 'Of course not. I got a room at a motel on Route 2. Gateway Inn.'

'Five minutes from here.'

'I got the idea I wouldn't be welcome,' he said.

'Even if the alternative was stalking us? Speaking of which, how did this whole mess get started?'

'I was worried she was ... Gabrielle is a straightforward person. And all of a sudden, she started sneaking off. What was I going to think?'

'Oh, Buck, really!'

'And then when I saw her going to this doctor in Ellsworth, I was half relieved and half worried about her, of course.'

'And you decided that whatever she had was so serious that she needed to see a Boston doctor.'

'Nothing wrong with Maine doctors!'

'And if she actually had been seriously ill and had wanted to come here to one of the big teaching hospitals, that's exactly what you'd have said.'

'It's the truth.'

'I am not having this argument with you. In fact, I'm not arguing with you at all. I just wanted you to know what Gabrielle meant. You must

199

have been worried sick about her, and I wanted to make sure that you knew that she is perfectly healthy.'

'She could've told me,' he said.

I pretended to be Rita. 'Say that to her. Say exactly that. Once she's speaking to you again.'

We then turned to the topic of Eldon Flood. If I'd told Buck about my obscene phone call and the anonymous hate mail, he'd probably have returned to Flood Farm to sock the perpetrator in the gut. Consequently, I passed off the dispute as a minor matter concerning Flood's supposedly know-it-all attitude about growing perennials. Then I diverted Buck in the way that never fails: I switched the subject to dogs.

That night, curled up between Steve and Kimi, I prepared to descend into the oblivious sleep of the deeply relieved. I'd called Betty and Katrina, and I'd posted to our little local Malamute Rescue list, so I had the satisfaction of knowing that others, too, were rid of the worries that had plagued us. My father no longer had to deal with the fear that Gabrielle had cancer. She was still angry at him, and he was hurt and insulted that she'd failed to confide in him, but I felt optimistic that they'd resolve their differences. The presence of the dark van was no longer mysterious; the explanation for its pursuit of us was ludicrous but benign. Rowdy was asleep on the floor under the air conditioner. Steve was out cold. Kimi pressed her spine to mine. I blacked out.

TWENTY-FIVE

My relief lasted throughout Thursday. In the morning, I made some phone calls and sent emails to encourage people to show up at the armory on Saturday. In the afternoon, during Sammy's play date with Ulla, Vanessa promised to bring her whole family and asked whether my family would all be there, too. As I told Vanessa, Leah would attend, and Gabrielle would be there, but my father would not. Vanessa looked disappointed and said what a charming man he was. Feeling slightly disloyal, I told her the whole story of his recent misdeeds, but far from being horrified at what Buck had done, she said, 'He borrowed a van and stalked his own wife? And then he slugged this SOB in the jaw? Good for him! You don't find a lot of men like that anymore.' She paused and added, 'Especially in Cambridge.'

I was tempted to reply that yes, indeed, not a single John Wayne movie had been set in Harvard Square and that the local scarcity of men who went around throwing punches was one reason I'd moved here, but I kept the remarks to myself. By now, I was beginning to feel sorry for my father, who'd suffered terribly after my mother's death, who truly was afraid of loss, and who really did have good qualities. In fact, I felt happy to hear someone say something good about Buck, who, besides having enraged his beloved wife, was not only being excluded from Steve's fishing trip to Grant's Camps but was the object of a conspiracy to keep the trip secret.

I settled for saying that Buck could be charming, as was true. Dogs, for instance, reliably responded to his fascination with them by falling under his thrall. With his fellow human beings, he was, of course, sometimes delightful and sometimes maddening, but when he felt like it, he *could* be charming. Besides, he was my father. In other words, I didn't exactly tell Vanessa a lie. Or a bad lie, anyway.

At dog training that night, everyone was optimistic about the upcoming event. In particular, all of us were happy about the forecast for dismal, rainy weather on Saturday. With luck, we'd attract people who might otherwise have gone to the beach or done yard work. Because the project had been Isaac's idea, I wanted it to be a success, as did everyone else in the club. So far as I knew, no one else had a matchmaking agenda for Saturday, but I sure did and could hardly wait to introduce Rita and Max, who were bound to have the same happy realization I did that they were made for each other.

Then, on Friday afternoon, trouble started again.

My father called.

The dogs and I were alone in the house when the phone rang. Gabrielle was in Harvard Square with Leah, whom she was treating to a shopping spree for clothes to wear at commencement activities. I didn't know and hadn't asked Gabrielle whether she and Buck had spoken since their encounter at Flood Farm, and I hadn't asked her when she planned to go home, either. She was due to leave on Sunday, but for all I knew, she intended to prolong her visit. Anyway, my first thought when I heard Buck's voice was that he was calling to announce his impending arrival.

I was wrong, as I realized within seconds. Ordinarily, instead of asking how I am or how Steve is, he booms, 'And how's the beautiful boy?' That's Rowdy. He then asks about Kimi, Sammy, Lady, and India, and before he's even heard how the dogs are, he begins handing out advice. Typically, he advises me that I should be showing Rowdy, Sammy, or both to Judge So-and-So, who'd appreciate them. And if I'd have to drive to Ohio or Michigan or some other distant show site for the privilege of getting Judge So-and-So's opinion, so what? 'These dogs are serious quality!' he admonishes. When he's fervently nagging me to get my dogs out on the show circuit, he quotes the Bible: 'Neither do men light a candle, and put it under a bushel, but on a candlestick; and it giveth light unto all that are in the house.' He uses the same passage to urge me to enter the dogs in performance events, including those in which I already show –

obedience, agility, and rally; and to try to convince me to put Bermudan championships on Rowdy and Sammy and to take out ads in our national breed club's newsletter and membership directory. No matter what I'm doing with the dogs, I should be doing more of it or doing it differently. All this to me, when in my absence, he bores and irritates people with his incessant bragging about the accomplishments of my dogs!

So, the second he began the conversation, I knew that something was wrong. 'How are you?' he asked. For once, he sounded nothing whatsoever like a moose.

'I'm fine.'

'How is Steve?'

'Steve is fine, too. All of us are fine. Gabrielle, Leah, the dogs, the cat. We are just fine. And how are you?'

'I got something in the mail.'

I waited.

'It's got to be ... what do you call those programs that let you change photos? It's got to be from one of those damn things. Gabrielle's been acting ... well, she isn't quite herself, but...'

Well, what would anyone assume? Yes, that someone had inexplicably sent Buck a doctored image of his wife that showed her in the nude, perhaps, or in a compromising situation. That's precisely what I thought, but as so often happens in connection with my father, I was wrong. What he'd actually received was a four-by-six photo on glossy paper that appeared to show

Gabrielle hitting Molly. In the same envelope was a sheet of paper that asked, 'Is this how you want your wife to treat a dog?'

'Buck,' I said sternly, 'listen to me! It's impossible. Gabrielle would never hit Molly. Or any other dog. Never! I don't know who sent this thing to you – or why – but what we're dealing with is a vile, malicious piece of mischief, and if you have even the slightest notion that what this picture seems to show actually happened, you can forget it right now. I want to see this thing. I want you to scan it and send it to me right now. And the sheet of paper that came with it. What's the postmark?'

'Boston.'

'Regular mail? Not ... if there's no return address, I guess it must be. You can't use Express Mail without a return address, can you?'

'Plain white envelope with a flag stamp. Probably just dropped in a mailbox.'

'When did you get it?'

'Today.'

'Look, scan this stuff and send it to me, and we'll talk then.'

My father is an egregious and unapologetic violator of online etiquette – email in ALL CAPITAL LETTERS – but he is computer literate and has had plenty of practice in sending and receiving pictures of dogs, so he scanned and sent the photo and the message in almost no time. I opened both files and printed the images, the photo on the same kind of four-by-six glossy paper he'd described, the message on plain paper; I wanted to see exactly what he'd been sent. One glance at the photo told me that it had been taken the previous Saturday at the match where Steve and I had judged and where Molly hadn't quite passed her CGC test. That was the only occasion when Gabrielle had worn Steve's Red Sox cap. The quality of the photo was poor, maybe because the picture had been taken through a car window, maybe because this image had been cut from a larger one, or maybe both. Still, the subject and setting were unmistakable: Gabrielle, wearing the Sox cap, was standing at the back of my car, and Molly was perched on the open tailgate. Gabrielle's right arm was raised high, and her head was turned to reveal her crimson face, which bore an expression of unbridled fury. The accompanying message showed exactly what my father had reported: 'Is this how you want your wife to treat a dog?' The font was ordinary Times New Roman, 12 cpi.

I called my father. 'I know how it looks,' I said, 'but things aren't always what they seem.'

Sounding like himself again, he boomed, 'I hate Gilbert and Sullivan!'

'It was an accidental quotation. I didn't mean skim milk masquerading as cream. What I mean is that there is a benign interpretation, and as soon as Gabrielle gets back, I'll find out what it is.'

'There is nothing benign about sending me—'

'Of course not! Sending this picture was vicious. But whatever Gabrielle was doing, she was not hitting Molly. I don't know what she was doing or why she had that expression on her face, but she had some innocent reason, and I'll find out what it was.'

So eager was I to hear Gabrielle's explanation that when she walked in, I had to restrain the impulse to thrust the picture in her face and blurt out the story before she'd even had a chance to say hello and put her purse down. The impulse was the result of having been raised not only *with* golden retrievers but *as* a golden: I have a tendency to go bounding up to people with my emotions written all over my face. My tongue practically hangs out, and if I had a tail, it would be wagging. Gabrielle was probably surprised that I didn't rise up and jump on her. I'd never do such a dreadful thing, of course. My mother trained me not to.

So, it was a good ten minutes after Gabrielle's arrival before I told her what had happened and showed her the photo and the vile message. I'd supplied both of us with coffee, and we were sitting in the kitchen surrounded by dogs. Molly was in Gabrielle's lap, Lady was playing up to Gabrielle in the hope of pats on the head, and Rowdy and Kimi were engaging in what it's fashionable these days to call their 'default behavior', namely, watching me. *Default behavior* refers to what a dog does without a cue or command whenever he has the slightest question about what he's supposed to do; it's a fallback, a favorite contingency, a behavior that's been reinforced fifty gazillion times so that it

207

has become automatic. It is, by the way, no coincidence that my dogs and I share the same default behavior: they watch me, and I watch them. Furthermore, the act of giving and receiving synchronous positive reinforcement strengthens the identical default behavior in the dogs and in me. And there you have a dog trainer's view of love. We're a bunch of hopeless romantics. Truly, we are.

'What a dreadful expression!' Gabrielle exclaimed. 'That grooming spray blew right into my face, and did it sting!' As if I'd never noticed the short-term results of her laser treatment, she lowered her voice and said, 'I was still quite raw and red from the dermatologist, you know.'

'Why were you using grooming spray?'

'Because when I went back to your car for Molly's liver treats, I decided to do a little work on her coat so she'd look her best. I know that grooming doesn't matter the way it does when you're showing in breed, but it matters to me, and Molly knows whether she's clean or dirty, don't you, Molly? Besides, if you remember, I was a little nervous, and I was making Molly nervous, and grooming is such a soothing activity for both of us. So, that's when this picture was taken. What you can't see is that the bottle of grooming spray flew right out of my hand when that horrible stuff hit my face, and I have to tell you, I will never buy that product again. It is supposed to be all wholesome and natural, and all it really is, is rubbing alcohol. But whatever possessed someone to take this picture?'

'I have no idea. But one thing we can be sure of is that Eldon Flood isn't responsible for it. He'd never even heard of you until we showed up at Flood Farm on Wednesday. This picture was taken four days before that. Well, it's remotely possible that Flood could've read something I've written on the web or seen photos there, figured out who you were, and found Buck's address. And he could've seen online that I was judging on Saturday, I guess. But it's totally unlikely. It simply doesn't add up.'

'If Flood thought that I was you? On Saturday, I mean. No. that won't work. Then why would he have sent this picture to Buck? And if he was looking online, he'd have seen pictures of you. No. We're dealing with someone else, maybe a copycat who knew about that other business or who was inspired by it, but someone different. In any case, this is someone else's mean, nasty, cruel meddling. Now if you'll excuse me, I absolutely have to talk to Buck.'

I expected Gabrielle to retreat to her bedroom to call my father. Instead, she refilled her coffee cup and settled herself on the couch in the living room, her cell phone in one hand, the other on Molly, who was curled up next to her. Far from trying to eavesdrop, I went out to the yard with Lady to work on basic obedience. Twenty minutes later, when we got back inside, Gabrielle was still on the phone and was speaking at normal volume. 'I'll never be the trainer that she was,' said Gabrielle, obviously referring to my mother, 'but I don't need to pay people to do *everything* with my dog. I can't trim Molly. It's just too complicated. And I can't handle her in breed. I'd never be good enough. But I wanted...' She listened for a minute and then said in her most husky, seductive tone, 'Thank you. Apology accepted.'

My father had apologized? I kneeled down and silently called to Rowdy, who came to me and buried his great head in my stomach almost as if he intended to return to the womb, not that he had actually sprung from mine, except in the spiritual sense, but I guess that if the primitive longing is ardent enough, any beloved womb will do. Not be left out, Kimi trotted up and nudged me, and Lady followed her. Breathing in dog hair, I whispered, 'Hallelujah!'

TWENTY-SIX

Remember what Groucho Marx said about not wanting to belong to any club that would have him as a member? Gabrielle, in contrast, always assumed that she already belonged to any club in which she found herself; it almost never crossed her mind that she might want to exclude herself from a group, and anything even remotely like blackballing was foreign to her. If she were ever abducted by extraterrestrials, instead of being subjected to the gruesome medical tests commonly described by abductees, she'd soon be pitching in to tidy up the spaceship and chit-chatting with her new friends about which planet *we* should visit next. Thus at noon on Saturday, Gabrielle arrived at the armory wearing a pink Cambridge Dog Training Club sweatshirt and was enthusiastically welcomed by actual club members, all of whom acted as if she'd belonged for decades.

Steve, Leah, and I, together with all five of our dogs, also got to the armory at noon, an hour and a half before the activities were scheduled to begin. Over breakfast, Gabrielle had announced her intention of surprising my father by returning home that evening instead of the next day. She'd gone so far as to pack her car for the trip and drive it to the armory so that she could head directly for Maine when the event ended, at four thirty. After she'd talked with Buck the previous afternoon, he'd called her back, then she'd called him back, and for all I knew, the progressively lovey-dovey murmuring (hers) and infatuated bellowing (his) had continued late into the night. In any case, she was eager to see him and had rejected our efforts to persuade her to spend one more night in Cambridge and leave for Maine on Sunday morning. In response to Steve's ever-so-rational argument that the trip would take five and a half or six hours and that Buck might be asleep when she arrived home, Gabrielle had replied, with coy defiance, 'If he is, I'll just have to wake him up, won't I?'

The rainy weather was less than ideal for the

long drive but perfect for the National Pet Week event. Opportunistic proselytizers that we dog people are, we were shamelessly pleased that the cancellation of plans for yard work, picnics, and outings to lakes, beaches, and theme parks would boost attendance at what was, in effect, our revival tent. All too often, efforts intended to educate the general public about responsible dog ownership are wonderfully effective in reaching responsible dog owners and no one else. A sunny day could've meant preaching to the choir.

Setting up for any sort of dog event is, I suspect, a lot like readying a church hall or a school gym for a festivity or fund-raiser, which is to say that it involves lugging around heavy, bulky objects that inevitably require arrangement and rearrangement. Because Rita, for all her virtues, was not the kind of person who happily hauls metal folding chairs, unfolds melamine banquet tables and baby gates, or drags around rolls of grubby rubber mats, she did not arrive at the armory until quarter past one, but when she did get there, she made herself useful by fastening my Malamute Rescue banner across the front of our assigned table, stacking my flyers in neat piles, and performing other such civilized tasks. Firebrand that he was, Willie remained crated in Rita's car, where he would stay until Steve got him. Consequently, when Max Crocker and Mukluk showed up, I was able to present them to Rita without whatever distraction Willie might have caused; and in the absence of the only potential hitch in my matchmaking, the introductions went well.

As is understood by everyone who shows dogs, first impressions count, so I was delighted to observe that Rita, Max, and Mukluk were well groomed and altogether fit for the breed ring, so to speak. Rita's red linen blazer and pressed jeans were, by her standards, the height of informality, and she was even wearing flats instead of her usual heels; but as always, her cap of hair looked freshly trimmed and highlighted, and her make-up was as perfect as it was subtle. Max, who had on chinos and a white sweater that I'd have bet was real cashmere, had the rugged, outdoorsy good looks I'd noticed when I'd visited him, and to my relief, he was wearing ordinary tan athletic shoes rather than Quinn Youngman-style hiking boots. As I knew from my considerable experience in matching up rescue dogs and adopters, it's one thing to contemplate the match and quite another actually to see the potential partners together in the flesh. In some cases, the person and the dog click as fast the shutter of a camera. In others, they need time to figure out whether they are made for each other. Now and then, it's obvious that they are not. When the pairing is wrong, it's usually the dog who lets me know pretty quickly. If a friendly, talkative malamute responds to a potential adopter by keeping his head down and silently sniffing the ground, he might as well come out and say, 'Not this one! Sorry, but you've got to send this one home alone!'

To my relief, Mukluk greeted Rita with the melodious caroling that translates as: *Oh, I like you! I really like you a lot!* Constrained as they were by the repressive conventions of our inferior species, Rita and Max did not follow Mukluk's joyous example by blurting out the same happy sentiment about each other. Still, they said that they were pleased to meet each other, and Rita told Mukluk that she was glad to meet him, too, and took the paw he proffered, and before long Max and Rita were removing the banner from the front of the table and fastening it to the wall and unpacking the cartons of books that Steve and I were donating in the hope of attracting potential adopters to the booth. As I've mentioned, one of the books, *101 Ways to Cook Liver,* was a dog-treat cookbook and treatise on training with food that I'd written myself, and the other, *No More Fat Dogs*, was a doggy diet book that we'd co-authored. Thus neither was specifically about Alaskan malamutes except in the sense that malamutes are always convinced that they are on the verge of starvation and consequently are easy to train with goodies and highly skilled at persuading owners to overfeed them. Our own books were, however, what Steve and I had available to offer as freebies, so they were what Rita and Max arranged on the table in the hope of luring people in with the promise of something for nothing.

Leaving Rita, Max, and Mukluk together, I floated around helping here and there and seeing what was what. In addition to our Malamute Rescue booth, there were booths promoting the adoption of other breeds, including the Great Pyrenees and the keeshond, heaven help me, two breeds I am utterly crazy about, but we had five dogs now! When Molly visited we had six! Another dog was out of the question. So, no Pyr for me! No gorgeous giant white dog! As to a kees, damn! Keeshonden look so much like little fluffy malamutes, and the breed is so bright and cheerful, and ... I dragged myself away to a particularly appealing booth that offered free canine-themed face painting, mainly but not exclusively for children. Ron, who'd taken over Isaac's job of running the whole event, sported a shiny black nose and curly black whiskers on his cheeks. Local pet-supply shops were ready to give away sample-size bags of dog and cat food; a local groomer with a white standard poodle in need of a trim was ready to demonstrate the art of clipping; and white baby gates marked off rings to be used for demos of obedience, freestyle, rally, and agility and for CGC testing.

In a far corner, Vanessa and Avery had spread out a greater quantity and variety of food than I'd ever before seen at an event like this one. Indeed, Vanessa, who'd just started training with the club, had entirely misconstrued the meaning of 'refreshments'. Arrayed on two long tables were elaborate cheese and fruit platters, pans of lasagne on heating trays, big baskets of fried chicken, a large baked ham, bowls of green

215

salad, and cakes, cupcakes, and cookies of all sorts, many decorated with stylized figures of dogs. Coffee perked in a big urn, and two metal tubs of ice held bottled water, little cartons of fruit juice, and cans of soft drinks. Ashamed though I was of my ingratitude, I couldn't help thinking that this incredible spread was so wildly overdone that when people told Vanessa, 'Oh, you really shouldn't have,' they'd mean precisely what they said.

'Vanessa,' I said. 'Avery. This is incredible. You really shouldn't have!'

'It's my treat,' Vanessa hastened to assure me. 'I'm donating everything. And we all pitched in. We even put my father and Hatch to work washing lettuce and helping us transport it all. And Avery does love to cook. Really, we've had fun.'

'Everything looks delicious. Thank you.'

'In case you're wondering, I haven't forgotten Ulla. Her crate is back here. Hatch is out taking her for a little walk. They'll be back in a second. Doesn't Leah look spectacular today! Lovelier than ever.'

Following Vanessa's gaze, I turned to see Leah and Kimi in a nearby ring, where they were warming up for the agility demonstration by checking out the A-frame and the tunnel. As perhaps I need to explain, agility is a timed obstacle course, and of the many performance events, it's inevitably the great crowd-pleaser, in part because people love to watch dogs negoti-ate the A-frame, zip through tunnels, sail over jumps, and conquer the other obstacles, and in part because a race against time is always fun. Like Gabrielle, Leah had on a Cambridge Dog Training Club shirt, but whereas my stepmother's sweatshirt was pink and oversized, Leah's T-shirt was bright yellow and at least one size too small. The vivid color picked up the red-gold of Leah's long curls, and the shirt clung to her voluptuous bosom. I felt sure that the effect was unintended. Leah had a cavalier attitude toward laundry, which she did at our house. Having thrown her clothes into the dryer, she'd forget to remove the all-cotton items until they were, in my view, ruined. She dressed appropriately for shows and trials, but she was always more concerned about Kimi's appearance than about her own and tended to assume that others, too, would focus on the dog and ignore the handler. When she'd arrived at our house this morning, I'd been tempted to deliver one of my little lectures about sartorial respect for the sport, but Steve, having read my mind, had murmured, 'Holly, let her alone. Between working and studying for exams, she's got other things to think about besides what she's got on, and at least she's recovered from that phase of wearing nothing but black.'

Vanessa continued. 'Beauty and brains. She's the girl who's got everything.'

Was Avery by implication the girl who's got nothing? I strained not to look at her. On this rainy day, she wore a drab grey sweatshirt. Her face was expressionless, her life directionless.

The contrast with Leah's colorful animation nearly made me want to point out Leah's petty faults: *Well, yes, she's beautiful and brilliant, and she's going to veterinary school, but she's a lousy laundress.*

'We think so,' I said, 'but we're biased.' I ached to lift Avery's spirits but was afraid to open my mouth, probably because I was frightened of speaking the raw truth, which was that in almost every possible way, poor Avery suffered by comparison with Leah. At a guess, Avery felt herself to suffer by comparison with almost everyone. My rescue impulses are not limited to dogs.

For good or ill, the squeal of feedback from a microphone cut off the conversation. Clapping my hands over my ears, I turned to see that it was time to get ready for Meet the Breed.

'We'll need Ulla now,' I told Vanessa. 'Up there where all the chairs are. I'll see you there in a few minutes.'

Excusing myself, I hurried off. The point of Meet the Breed was to introduce the public to a variety of different breeds and thus to help people to make wise, educated choices when getting dogs. In the area I'd mentioned to Vanessa, a couple of dozen folding chairs were arranged in a big circle. Taped to the back of each chair was a sign with the name of a breed. The plan was this: when the handlers and dogs had taken their places, the announcer, Ron, would introduce a breed and go on to say a few words about its origins and characteristics as the representative or representatives were gaited around the ring. After each breed had had a turn, spectators would be free to meet the dogs and handlers close up. Our little obedience club did not, of course, provide a representative of every one of the hundreds of breeds in existence, but we did have dogs ranging in size from giant to toy, namely a Great Dane and a chihuahua, and we also had four or five mixed-breed dogs, including a darling terrier mix, Misty, who excelled in the sport of agility, and two pit bull mixes, Lewis and Clark, who were far less adventurous than their names suggested. In fact, they were certified therapy dogs whose explorations consisted of weekly visits to a children's hospital. Yes, those notorious pit bulls, sicked on sick kids! So much for stereotypes.

Because Steve, the dog hypnotist, was in charge of Rita's spunky representative of the Scottish terrier, Willie, Leah had agreed to handle India, the German shepherd dog, and I was handling Lady, whose timid temperament made her a less than ideal example of her breed but who was the only pointer the club could provide. The representatives of the Alaskan malamute were Ulla and Mukluk, but control-minded dog trainer that I am, I'd made sure that Lady and I would be seated next to the malamutes and their owners. As far as I knew, both malamutes had stable, sweet temperaments and would behave themselves when meeting the public, but if a problem arose, I wanted to be right on the spot. I'd also arranged to have Leah and India next to Lady and me, not because India, Miss Perfection, was likely to misbehave, but because I wanted to soothe Lady by surrounding her with trusted members of our family. Happily, the arrangement worked. When I led Lady to the Meet the Breed area, Leah and India were already there, and to my surprise, Lady seemed to interpret the situation as more or less a big family party. When I took the seat between Leah, on my right, and Vanessa, on my left, I kept a calming hand on Lady and felt none of the trembling that signals her tendency to turn to canine Jell-O.

'Good girl, Lady,' I whispered. 'You see? India and Leah are here, and Steve and Willie are over there with the other little dogs. You have so many friends here, don't you?'

'Speaking of which,' said Vanessa, 'where's Sammy?'

'In his crate in the van.'

Turning to Max, on her left, Vanessa gushed, 'Holly has the most beautiful malamute you've ever seen! Sammy, his name is. He takes my breath away. And he's just as good and gentle as he is gorgeous. He's Ulla's boyfriend. Isn't he Ulla? Who loves Sammy, huh?'

Ulla, far from showing any regret about Sammy's absence, flung herself to the floor at Mukluk's feet and then leaped to all fours, the better to give the bewildered Mukluk come-hither glances.

With commendable restraint, I said, 'From the looks of things, I'd say that Ulla is a love-the-one-you're-with girl.' In fact, I was seething. So what if Mukluk had Dumbo ears, a collie head, mile-long legs, and all the rest! His doting owner, Max, was right there listening. Furthermore, in response to Ulla's provocation, the wonderfully calm Mukluk remained the perfect gentleman, as my admittedly gorgeous Sammy might not have done. Directing myself to Max, I said, 'Mukluk is so mellow. You're really lucky.'

'He's thunderstruck,' Max said. 'He isn't used to this kind of female attention.'

'I still don't have a dog for you,' I said. 'I'm sorry. The ones good with cats are hard to find. But yours is out there somewhere. We'll find her for you.'

'Max is waiting for a rescue malamute,' I told Vanessa, 'but because of Mukluk, he needs a female, and also he has a cat, so it's taking a while to find the right match.'

'Well, you can't have Ulla,' Vanessa said with a laugh. 'She likes cats, but I can't stand them. Besides, my father is allergic to them. Anyway, Ulla is my pride and joy. She's not going anywhere.'

Why will people make a show of disliking cats, as if the prejudice were commendable? And why will people insist on giving particularly loud voice to the senseless dislike in the presence of cat-loving cat owners? Did Vanessa honestly expect Max and me to pipe up and agree with her?

I said, 'Of course she's not going anywhere,

221

are you, Ulla? And we will find Max's malamute. We just haven't yet.'

Before Vanessa had the opportunity to indulge
herself in yet greater excesses of tactlessness,
Ron, still in dog-face make-up, got Meet the
Breed under way. The sound system was now
working properly, and Ron did an excellent job
of limiting himself to thumbnail sketches of
each breed instead of boring the spectators by
going on and on. He started with the small
breeds and went around the circle. Consequently, Steve and Willie had their turn early, and I
have to brag about both of them and indirectly
about Rita, too, for keeping Willie groomed like
a show dog. As I watched Steve gait Willie
around, it occurred to me for the millionth time
that if Steve would only take an interest in
conformation handling, he'd save us the money
we spent hiring professional handlers for
Rowdy and Sammy. He moved with just the
right smoothness and grace, and he had that
magic knack of bringing out the best in the dog.
Steve's good looks didn't hurt, either, and Willie
had the incomparable style of his dashing breed.

Leaning toward Max, I said, 'That's Rita's
dog, Willie.' Belatedly, I added, 'And my husband, Steve.'

'First things first,' Vanessa commented dryly.

'Steve would be the last person to mind,' I
said. 'In fact, he'd agree. Dogs first.'

'Beautiful dog,' Max said.

'Willie is very spirited,' I remarked. 'He has
real terrier character.'

222

'Mine did, too,' Max said. 'A little too much so.'

'What does that mean?' Vanessa asked. 'That he bit ten people?'

'No, he never actually got anyone. But he did think about it. Or so we always assumed.'

Gabrielle and Molly were in the ring after Steve and Willie. Molly, an experienced show dog, could practically have handled herself, and Gabrielle pretty much let the little bichon do exactly that.

'Your stepmother looks tired,' Vanessa whispered to me.

'Do you think so? She looks fine to me. I hope she isn't tired. She's driving home to Maine as soon as she's done here.'

'How does she keep up with your father? He positively radiates energy.'

'He does,' I agreed. 'But Gabrielle is pretty energetic herself.'

Soon thereafter, as Ron announced that the puli was a medium-size sheepdog originating in Hungary, Elizabeth McNamara rose from her seat and gaited Persimmon around. Elizabeth wore black, perhaps as a sign of mourning, perhaps as an indication of oneness with her dog. The latter explanation seemed the more likely, mainly because Elizabeth's flowing shawl had cords of fringe identical to the cords of Persimmon's coat.

Whispering in my ear, Leah asked, 'Isn't this a little soon after...?'

'That's why she's here, I guess,' I murmured.

'This was Isaac's party.'

If Isaac had been alive, he'd have been the one at the other end of Persimmon's leash, but it seemed to me that if he were looking down from heaven, he'd be glad to see how pretty Elizabeth looked and what a beautiful picture she and Persimmon made. Elizabeth's white curls, the fringe of her shawl, and Persimmon's cords all bounced in harmony. If Isaac was in posthumous attendance, I hoped, however, that he had a bad seat, his view partly blocked by some cosmic object that hovered between him and Tom Oakley, who stood behind Elizabeth's chair and regarded her with unabashed adoration.

When it came time for the malamutes to have their turn, Vanessa and Max did a capable job of leading Mukluk and Ulla around the ring while Ron said the Alaskan malamute was the largest and strongest of the Northern breeds. As he was adding that the malamute was a challenge to train and thus suitable for experienced dog owners, Ulla, with the breed's uncanny ability to identify the head honcho in any group, suddenly plunked herself down in a sit in front of him, raised a paw, waved, and issued peals of *woo-woo-woo*s that rang throughout the hall and had everyone smiling.

'The call of the wild,' Ron said. 'Next, we have the pointer, a member of the AKC's Sporting Group and...'

I'm proud to report that Lady mustered her entire supply of self-confidence to present a lovely image of her breed. Her eyes showed apprehension, but only a little, and when we'd made our way around, pride won out, and she looked delightfully pleased with herself. Leah and India were predictably wonderful, and when the breed-by-breed part of the event ended, we were surrounded by a gratifyingly large number of strangers, which is to say, miracle of miracles, people who were not members of the Cambridge Dog Training Club. Out of the corner of my ear, I monitored Vanessa's and Max's replies to questions about malamutes and was relieved to hear the general public being informed that malamutes don't just steal food but often extend the definition of *food* to include firewood, wild rabbits, and songbirds caught on the wing. Meanwhile, I was happy to sing the praises of the pointer, a breed sadly displaced in popularity by the German short-haired pointer for reasons I have never understood. I love German short-hairs, but not to the exclusion of the pointer, an intelligent, handsome, and affectionate breed adaptable to life as a lively family pet as well as to fine performance as a gun dog.

For the hour after I'd returned Lady to her crate in Steve's van, I was busy non-stop signing copies of our books, running Sammy through a mini version of a rally obedience course, and handling Rowdy in a demonstration of advanced obedience. Formal obedience never draws the crowds that flock to demos of flashier sports. Only an educated eye is equipped to appreciate perfect heeling, and as to the scent discrimination exercise, few spectators realize that they're witnessing a miracle. Suppose that I ask you to examine a set of identical articles and to pick the one that I, behind your back, have just handled. Could you do it? Of course not! Neither could any other mere human being. But the dog's nose knows, as does his brain: once trained to understand the point of the exercise, the dog selects the recently handled article by using a power that his species has in abundance and that our own species almost entirely lacks. The astonishing feat does not, however, wow crowds. When Jesus turned water into wine, there were probably a lot of spectators who shrugged their shoulders and said, 'Big deal! So what!' When miracles look easy, they're pearls before swine.

TWENTY-SEVEN

On the other hand, Rowdy knew what he'd done, as did I, his disciple, and when I crated him in the van, I told him how proud I felt and gave him a big handful of treats from my never-empty pockets. By then, I was so hungry that the lint-dusted liver brownies looked almost appetizing. Consequently, my first stop when I went back inside was at the refreshments table. In front of each of the platters, bowls, and trays was a card with information about the ingredients in the dish and thus about its suitability for people with particular dietary needs. The fried chicken, which contained cornstarch and cornmeal, was gluten-free and lactose-free, and had not been cooked in peanut oil. The lasagne, suitable for ovo-lacto-vegetarians, contained cheese but no meat. The flourless chocolate cake had been flavored with gluten-free vanilla, but it did contain eggs. And so forth, all very Cambridge.

As I helped myself to chicken, lasagne, and salad, I said to Avery, 'Your food has been a big hit.'

Ever morose, she said, 'There's still a lot left. I know what we're having for dinner for the next week.'

'But a lot has been eaten, too. Your mother did a great job with publicity. That's why we had so many people. I'll be back for seconds. And dessert.'

Carrying my plate to the Malamute Rescue table, I found Max, Rita, and Gabrielle. Max had a plate heavily laden with desserts, Rita was nibbling on a strawberry, and Gabrielle, with Molly in her lap, was diving into a plateful of lasagne, ham, chicken, and salad.

'Fortifying myself for the drive home,' Gabrielle explained. 'Molly passed! She got her CGC.'

'I knew she'd do it! Good for you, Molly! Gabrielle, congratulations.'

Gabrielle slipped a piece of chicken meat to her dog. 'Now she gets to eat from the table,' said Gabrielle with a naughty smile.

'You'll arrive home with good news,' I said.

'Buck really will be pleased. Speaking of going home, I think we can start to pack up whenever we're ready. A lot of people have left. We had such a crowd!'

'All of your books are gone,' Max said. 'We talked to a couple of possible adopters.'

'And discouraged a couple of others,' Rita added.

'Was that your job, Rita?' I asked.

We both laughed. Rita loves my dogs, and they return her affection, but she refuses ever again to help me out by feeding them. She just can't seem to understand that for malamutes, it's perfectly normal to herald the prospect of dinner by jumping three feet in the air and issuing shrieks that shake your brain loose from your skull. I've tried to convince her that the dogs are doing their best to clink wine glasses and say, *'A votre santé,'* but she maintains that she'd rather carry a side of beef into a cage of hungry lions than ever again to dole out kibble to Alaskan malamutes.

'I told the truth,' Rita said. 'Didn't I, Max?'

'You did.' Was that admiration in his voice? 'We both did.'

'Where's Steve?' I asked between bites. I don't hurl myself into the air and scream, but the impulse was there. 'This food is wonderful,' I added. 'Has he eaten yet?'

'He's over there talking to Vanessa.' Gabrielle pointed to one of the doors to the parking lot. 'He doesn't look awfully happy. Maybe she's hitting him up for free veterinary advice.'

'He's used to that,' I said. 'People do it all the time. And he isn't even Ulla's vet. I'll rescue him.' I waved and beckoned to him.

Catching sight of me, he looked relieved, and when he got to the Malamute Rescue table, he said, 'Successful event. Let's wrap it up. I'm going to help clean up, and then we'll go.'

I finished eating while simultaneously packing up Malamute Rescue materials, thanking Max and Rita for their help, and saying my goodbyes to Gabrielle, who had returned with a plate of desserts and was continuing, as she'd said, to fortify herself.

'Are you sure that you don't want to stay here tonight?' I asked.

'Positive, but thank you. I'm just going to zip home. I won't have to stop for food, and I have a Thermos of coffee that I just filled. We'll be there in no time.'

Leah showed up, and she, Steve, and I follow-ed Gabrielle to her car, hugged her, bade fare-well to Molly, again congratulated them on passing the CGC test, and saw them on their way. As Gabrielle drove off, Max, Mukluk, and Rita appeared in the parking lot. Max and Rita did not leave together. Willie was crated in Rita's car, and Max would need to take Mukluk home. But with luck, Max and Rita had made plans to meet later. The rain had become nothing more than mist. It would be a lovely evening for Rita and Max to stroll through Harvard Square together. They'd poke in bookstores, enjoy a romantic dinner, linger over dessert, and return to her place or his to watch one of those depressing foreign films that Rita likes and that Max probably did, too. As Steve, Leah, and I helped to break down baby gates, roll up mats, and put away folding tables and chairs, I imagined Max and Rita happily discovering, at either his house or her apartment, that they had identical taste in literature, music, liqueurs, and who knew what else.

As we were about to leave, I noticed Avery, Vanessa, Hatch, Tom, and Elizabeth at the dismantled refreshments table. My arms were full, but I said to Leah, 'Why don't you go help Vanessa and Avery get all that stuff to their car. There's a lot left to carry out. There are heating trays and big coolers and all those bulky things, and Tom and Elizabeth aren't going to do a thing. They're just standing around.'

'If you don't mind, I'd rather not,' she replied in an undertone.

'Why not? Leah, that's not like you!'

'I'll tell you later.' She made a face.

'Steve,' I said, 'why don't you—'

Cutting me off, Leah replied for him, 'Because, Holly. Because he doesn't want to.'

'Aren't we mysterious!' I said.

'Yes, aren't we,' Leah agreed.

TWENTY-EIGHT

Instead of taking advantage of the privacy of Steve's van to spill everything, Steve and Leah tacitly agreed to utter not one damned word to satisfy my curiosity. Ever the dog trainer, I resolved not to reinforce their annoying collusion by begging for explanations. Far be it from me to tumble into the most common pitfall in dog training, which is, of course, unintentionally reinforcing undesired behavior. Instead, I spent the brief drive home exclaiming about what a great success the day had been, as it truly had. The combination of Vanessa's excellent publicity and the bad weather had meant much better attendance than we'd dared to hope for. Ulla and Mukluk had been model malamutes during Meet the Breed. Lady had shown remarkable self-possession and had even had fun. Kimi, Rowdy, and Sammy had performed well during the demos. Molly was now an official Canine Good Citizen. I was, I proclaimed, happy for all of us and proud of the club's accomplishment. Furthermore, Max and Rita had really hit it off, hadn't they! And Willie had made an excellent impression on Max, as had Mukluk on Rita. Then I made the mistake of adding that Isaac McNamara would have been very pleased to have his plans carried out so well.

'He'd have been thrilled at the sight of his all-too-merry widow,' Leah commented.

'People deal with grief in different ways, Leah,' I said pompously.

'Well, if Steve dies, I hope that you—'

I took the bait. 'Leah, stop! That is not funny.' As I've said, the most common pitfall in dog training is ... failing to ignore behavior you don't like.

Steve said, 'She'll run personal ads in the *AKC Gazette* and the *Journal of the American Veterinary Medical Association*.'

'That'll be after she's replaced you with a dog,' Leah said. Mimicking me, she added, '"People deal with grief in different ways."'

I had to wait for more than an hour after we got home to get the truth out of Leah and Steve, in part because they persisted in their irritating game and in part because we had to unload the van and feed the dogs. Finally, at six o'clock or so, we decided to take advantage of the clear skies to sit in the yard and give the dogs a chance to play. Because all three of us had eaten heartily only a few hours earlier, we weren't hungry, and neither was Rita, who, to my disappointment, was alone rather than with Max Crocker when she joined us. She did, however, arrive with a more expensive bottle of Australian Shiraz than I'd have sprung for, and I felt certain that the wine and the presence of a good psychotherapist would combine to loosen Steve's and Leah's tongues.

I'd finished wiping off the picnic table and padding its damp benches with old towels when Rita made her way down the back steps, the bottle of wine in one hand, a wine glass in the other. Leah followed with three more glasses. Sammy was delivering the coup de grâce to a doomed peony plant by rolling on its crushed remains. As he wiggled blissfully on his back, Kimi kept a close and astonished eye on him, as if to say, 'Yet one more instance of this puppy's brainlessness! Isn't he ever going to grow up?' Rowdy was taking care to lift his leg on a wet forsythia branch without actually touching it. When Steve took a seat at the table, India stationed herself next to him, and Lady settled for me.

Pouring wine, Rita said, 'Your friend Max is such a lovely man.'

'Isn't he!' I said.

Handing a filled glass to me, she said with a sigh, 'Damn shame.'

'What is?'

'That all the best men are married or gay or both.'

'Max isn't married. I've been to his house. He lives alone. Beautiful house, by the way. Anyway, his application says that there's no one else in the household. We ask. And he doesn't wear a wedding ring.'

'Who said that he was married?'

I rolled my eyes. 'Rita, you're wrong.' I

sipped my wine. 'This is really good. Thank you.'

'You're welcome, and I'm right, more's the pity.'

'Rita, when we screen adopters, we look for this stuff. I do! Rita, most rescue people are very biased in favor of gay adopters because there's a fair chance that they'll have dogs instead of children. A nice, stable gay or lesbian couple? Preferably older. Settled. Lesbian couples do have babies sometimes, and gay men adopt children, but especially with an older adopter, the odds are heavily in favor of the dog, so it can be the perfect home.'

'Without the bothersome complication of human relationships.'

'No! Well, in a way, but that's no more true for gay people than it is for anyone else, except that for gay people, the gigantic advantage of a dog is the absolute certainty that the dog isn't harboring any lurking prejudices or stereotypes or negative feelings. The dog cares whether the owner is gay or lesbian about the way Rowdy cares whether I'm a Capricorn or whether I read Jane Austen or like the color blue, OK? He just doesn't care.'

'Holly, Max is gay.'

'I take it that he didn't ask you out,' I said.

'Holly, I meant what I said. I like him a lot. We have a great deal in common. I hope that I'll see him again.'

'And when you do,' I said, 'you'll realize that I'm right and you're wrong.'

234

'Truce?' Rita asked.

'Truce,' I said. We both laughed.

Then everyone had a little more wine, and Rita said to Leah, as casually as if she were asking about the weather, 'I saw you with the good-looking young doctor.'

Leah made the same face she'd made at the armory. 'Don't remind me! He is so disgusting!'

'Are we talking about the same person?' I asked. 'Hatch Jones. Vanessa's son?'

'Hatch,' said Leah. 'Hatch. As in cracking open and producing fowl, f-o-w-l. Cluck, cluck, cluck. And foul, f-o-u-l. Foul.'

'You must be kidding,' I said.

'Holly, for God's sake, she is not kidding,' Steve said. 'Leah, what—'

Practically tripping over Steve's words, Rita said, 'Of course Leah's not kidding. Leah, let's drop the light tone, if you don't mind.'

Butting in, I said, 'Leah, I'm sorry. From the way you and Steve were acting, I assumed that he knew about whatever was going on.'

'No,' Steve said grimly.

Rowdy and Kimi came bounding up to me but fixed their intelligent dark eyes on Leah. India was watching Steve, and Lady was training a worried gaze at India. Even Sammy noticed that something was up. He planted himself a few yards from our group and surveyed the scene, his expression baffled.

'Leah,' Steve said, 'we need to hear exactly what happened.'

'It wasn't that big a deal,' she said.

235

I started to demand the account that Steve had requested, but he caught my eye in time, and I kept quiet.

'This was at the armory,' Steve said. 'This afternoon.'

'Yes.'

'Inside? Or out in the parking lot?'

'Inside. In the armory with people all over the place. Besides, Kimi was with me.' Addressing Kimi, she said, 'You don't like Dr Chicken any better than I do, do you, Kimi? We both think that he's revolting.'

'I take it,' I said, 'that whatever he did was verbal rather than physical.'

'He tried to put his hand on my arm, but Kimi got in his way, so he had to settle for whispering in my ear, and in case you wondered, I am not giving you the details. Let's just say that he made a disgusting suggestion – actually, two disgusting suggestions – and he had the chance to do that because for a second I could hardly believe what I was hearing. At first, it practically didn't register.'

'Leah,' said Rita, 'no one is blaming you.'

'I should've ... but I didn't want to ... but that was my choice! I could've punched him in the gut or screamed at him, OK? Kimi's leash was in my hand. I could've wrapped it around his neck and strangled him. I had all kinds of options.'

'Did you say anything to him?' I asked.

'Me? Of course not. Remember? I went to Montessori schools. I'm the product of progressive education. All I did was walk away. And that's pretty much what I'd like to do now. As far as I'm concerned, we've exhausted this topic.'

Although we respected her wish, I have to admit that I was a little disappointed, mainly because I was almost positive about what Steve and Rita were on the verge of saying, and I wanted to know whether I was right. Steve, I predicted, would tell Leah that she had behaved in a sensible, mature way, whereas Rita would praise her for being in touch with her anger.

'If you want to let it go, Leah,' I said, 'that's what we'll do. But I must say that I find it hard to reconcile this incident with ... with Fiona. With their engagement.'

Leah said, 'I thought about that, too, but we spent all of one evening with Fiona. We didn't really know her. Maybe she liked ... or maybe he was different with her. But could we please just drop the whole thing?'

'Of course. So, Steve, who whispered what in *your* ear?'

'Vanessa cornered you,' Leah said to him. 'If she wants free advice, she ought to ask her own vet. She isn't even a client of ours.'

'She should've cornered Rita instead of me,' Steve said. 'She wasn't asking about Ulla. She was asking me about Avery. She says that Tom is spoiling Avery and that if he'd quit, Avery'd be forced to do something with her life.'

'Why did she ask you?' I blurted out. Steve is intelligent, rational, practical, compassionate,

237

and a million other good things, but psychological he is not. 'Not that you're ... so, what did you tell her?'

'I told her that Avery should get a job.'

'That's perfectly good advice,' I said.

'It's probably what I'd have ended up telling her myself,' Rita said.

'What Vanessa really wanted,' Steve said, 'was for me to hire Avery.'

'As what?' I asked.

'She thought Avery ought to take over Leah's job.'

I shook my head. 'What on earth is Vanessa thinking? Avery? Avery has no interest in animals. She doesn't have all that much connection to Ulla. She doesn't have a dog or a cat of her own. Or birds, fish, anything, as far as I know. And she's never shown any particular interest in our dogs. Vanessa is crazy about Sammy, but Avery probably can't even tell our malamutes apart. What a stupid idea.'

'Leah's job,' said Rita in that low, ponderous tone beloved by psychotherapists.

'It may be a meaningful idea, Rita,' I said, 'but it's still a stupid one.'

Rita said exactly what I knew she was going to say: 'Holly, it's a good thing that you didn't become a therapist.'

On cue, I gave my standard reply: 'And it's a good thing that you didn't become—'

All five dogs interrupted me. Led by India, the only one who'd even dream of guarding our property, they flew to the wooden gate, and once

India started barking, Lady joined in, and Sammy, looking pleased with himself, produced a copycat woof that would've fooled no one. He himself looked surprised, as if he could hardly believe that the unexpected sound had erupted from his chest. Rowdy and Kimi just stood there wagging their lovely white tails, presumably in the happy expectation that the new arrival was bearing food. Over the din, I heard a car door slam.

By then, Steve was at the gate. One look from him silenced India, and when she quit barking, Lady did, too. Peering through the narrow space between the gate and the fence, Steve called, 'Gabrielle? We're out here.'

'What's she doing back here?' I asked. 'Steve, don't open the gate until I get the dogs. Leah, could you crate Kimi and Sammy? India, down. Stay. Rowdy, this way, please, Mr Handsome. Good boy! Rita, just keep an eye on Lady, would you? Not that she'll try to bolt.'

When Leah and I had finished incarcerating the malamutes, we both ran out the back door and down the steps to the driveway, where Rita's little BMW, my Blazer, and Steve's van were parked. Instead of pulling her Volvo wagon into the driveway, Gabrielle had barely maneuvered it off the street and left it blocking the sidewalk. The rear windows were down. Looking inside, I saw that the keys were in the ignition. In the rear were Gabrielle's suitcase and Molly's crate, with Molly still in it.

'Something's wrong,' I said to Leah. 'Gabrielle knows better than to ... Steve? Open the gate, would you? We're out here. Leah, could you move Gabrielle's car? And get Molly.'

I entered the yard to find Gabrielle seated at the picnic table. Her eyes were heavy, and her face was so pink that the spots left by the laser had re-emerged.

'I'm so sorry to make a fuss,' she said. 'Do you think I could have some water?'

'Of course,' I said. 'Leah is getting Molly. She'll pull your car in all the way. What's going on?'

'I should've found a motel,' she said. 'That's what ... but I couldn't stay awake. I got off the highway ... that's what they tell you to do, you know. You're supposed to pull over, but there were all these trucks roaring by, and there was an exit right there, and so I got off. And *then* I pulled over.'

'Where was this?' I asked.

She yawned. 'Woburn, I think. Somewhere near there.'

Rita, who'd gone into the house, returned with a tall glass of ice water. Gabrielle emptied it, and Rita went back for more. As she was entering the house, Leah came out with Molly at her heels. Uncharacteristically, Gabrielle didn't thank Leah. It was as if Gabrielle had forgotten that she'd left her car half on the sidewalk and almost as if she'd forgotten all about Molly.

'Woburn is no distance,' I said. 'What is it? Half an hour?'

'That's why I decided just to drive back here.'

240

Molly ran to her, and Gabrielle lifted her up and settled the little white dog in her lap. 'I woke up, and there I was near a park of some sort, and I just couldn't face looking for a motel that would take dogs. And I thought about a taxi, but—'

I started to say that we'd have gone to get her, but Steve took over. 'You look warm. Do you feel hot?'

'Yes. And thirsty. Odd. I feel odd. But the main thing is that I'm so tired. I've gone and overdone it.'

'Have you ever had an episode like this before?' Steve asked.

Rita returned, and once again Gabrielle drained the entire glass.

'Steve, I'm just tired,' Gabrielle said. 'That's all it is. I shouldn't have eaten so much with the long drive ahead. Maybe I'm a little feverish.'

'Have you taken anything?' Steve asked. 'Medication of any kind?'

'Not a thing. Well, my thyroid medication, but that was this morning.'

'Any nausea? Pain anywhere?'

'Gabrielle,' I said, 'the truth is that you don't look well. I think maybe we should get you to the ER at Mount Auburn. It's five minutes from here. Less.' My own heart was pounding. What particularly frightened me were Gabrielle's lapses in judgment. When she'd first felt unwell and pulled off the highway, she should immediately have called us; and when she'd awakened from what must have been a fairly long nap, she certainly should not have driven back to

241

Cambridge.

'No,' she said flatly. 'If you don't mind, I'd like to go to bed.'

I threw Steve a questioning look. He said nothing, but his expression told me that we'd discuss his thoughts out of Gabrielle's hearing. Everyone pitched in to get her resettled. While Rita waited with her, Leah brought in her suitcase, and Steve and I made the guest room bed, which Gabrielle had stripped that morning. As we worked, he said, 'Holly, remember that what you said is true. Mount Auburn is five minutes away. We'll keep a close eye on her. If anything changes, we'll get her there.'

'But what's wrong with her?' I demanded.

He shrugged. 'She says she's just exhausted.'

'I know that's what she says! But she looks terrible, and she seems a little ... dopey. Confused.'

He nodded. When we went back downstairs, he tried his best to persuade Gabrielle to go to the ER. She absolutely refused. The only thing wrong with her, she insisted, was exhaustion, and the only thing she needed was sleep. I found our fever thermometer and took her temperature, which was 98.8, and I made Steve check her pulse, which was a little high, 103, but nothing to panic about. We gave in. As I followed Gabrielle upstairs, she leaned on the railing, and instead of having Molly stay in her room, she asked me to take care of her little dog.

'She'll need to go out,' Gabrielle mumbled.

'Of course,' I said. 'We'll take care of Molly.

Don't worry. She'll be fine.'

I wished that I could feel equally confident about Gabrielle. After Leah left, Steve, Rita, and I watched the Red Sox, but we checked on Gabrielle every twenty minutes or so. During the night, Steve kept getting up to look in on her, and I kept asking, 'Is she OK?'

'So far,' he'd say. 'So far.'

TWENTY-NINE

On Sunday morning, Gabrielle admitted to having slept deeply. Still thirsty, she drank four glasses of orange juice. Otherwise, she was fine, or so she insisted, especially to Steve. Her face was no longer flushed, her eyes were bright, and she looked like herself again. Even so, she decided to postpone her departure until the following day.

'We aren't going to say a word to your father about any of this,' she informed me as she loaded our breakfast dishes into the dishwasher.

Succumbing to Gabrielle's inevitable 'we', I asked, 'What are we going to say to him?'

'That you're giving a little dinner party,' she said, 'and you want me to stay for just one more day so I can help you with it. Well, it's not really a dinner party. It's just a little Sunday-night supper.'

'Why think small? Since it's imaginary, let's invite forty guests for a fourteen-course meal with service à la russe.'

After checking to make sure that Steve wasn't in the kitchen, she murmured, 'It's not quite that imaginary.' At normal volume, she said, 'Now, I know I've kept you from that painting you want do on the side of the house—'

'You haven't. The weather has. Today is beautiful, but the wood is still damp.'

'You're just saying that, but I *would* like it if we could take a little walk.'

'Of course! I'd love to.'

As it turned out, Gabrielle's true objective was to have a tête-à-tête when Steve couldn't possibly overhear us. She, of course, walked Molly, and I took Kimi. At the time, my choice of Kimi seemed almost random, but I realize in retrospect that I picked the dog most likely to inspire me to stand up for myself if this not-quite-imaginary dinner proved to be a hare-brained scheme that I'd want to veto. As I should have remembered, it would've taken the brute strength of all three malamutes combined to deflect my stepmother from her goal.

My suspicions began to arise soon after we stepped out of the house. As I started to turn left at the driveway and head down Appleton Street, Gabrielle said, 'Let's take Concord Avenue. We can go down Sparks Street to Brattle. If we go down Appleton, we might run into Vanessa, and we don't want her tagging along.'

'Any route is fine with me.' To the best of my

knowledge, Kimi approved of the statement of polite agreement and didn't construe my pleasant neutrality as a sign that I was spinelessly buckling under.

'Well,' said Gabrielle, 'I've been doing some serious thinking.' She paused, possibly in the hope that I'd speak up, as I did not. 'And,' she continued, 'I've realized, among other things, that my little episode last night was ... foreign. Foreign to me.'

For half a second, I entertained the horrible idea that Gabrielle had decided that far from having fallen asleep in her car, she'd been the victim of alien abduction. Were the guests at this mysterious dinner going to be her new extraterrestrial friends?

To my relief, she quickly said, 'No, not foreign. Provoked. Deliberate. That's what I mean. Holly, I am not someone who falls asleep at the wheel. That's not who I am. No, someone tried to make me doze off on the highway. Just the way poor Fiona did.'

'We don't know that Fiona fell asleep. We don't know what happened. Except that she had an accident. And that she died.'

'Exactly. She died in an *accident*. A one-car accident. Or an *apparent* accident.' At a curb, where we paused before crossing Huron Avenue, Gabrielle said, 'Molly, sit. Good girl! We don't want any car accidents, do we?'

'Kimi, good girl,' I echoed, even though it was second nature to Kimi to sit before we crossed a street. When we reached the opposite side, I said, 'Steve and I have talked about it. We're both ... we're mindful, I guess you'd say, that Fiona left from our house. It's not as if we'd let her start out when she'd been drinking. She hadn't. She did take an antihistamine, but she was a doctor, and she must've known what she was taking. She had allergies. It must've been an antihistamine she was used to, something she took all the time.'

Instead of saying that she'd already thought of everything I'd just pointed out, Gabrielle said, 'Well, yes. So when there were antihistamines in her system ... they'd have checked, I assume. They would, you know, after that kind of accident.'

'There must have been an autopsy. There had to have been.'

As if changing the subject, Gabrielle said, 'I ate a bit of everything yesterday. Well, more than a bit. And then there's that picture of me with grooming spray in my face.'

'You've lost me.'

'Three incidents. The dinner before Fiona left. That picture, which was taken in the parking lot at the match in Newton. And yesterday at the armory.'

'Yes?' I waited as Kimi lifted her leg on a tree. I'd been afraid that spaying her might decrease her political activism or possibly even moderate her extremism, but my fears were unwarranted and, in any case, senseless. I mean, would a hysterectomy make Germaine Greer start acting like Phyllis Schlafly?

With a smile, Gabrielle said, 'You think I'm paranoid, but I'm not.'

'I'm just having trouble following you.'

'Those three incidents. Now, what do they have in common? Well, I'll tell you what they have in common: Vanessa.'

'What?'

'I know she's a friend of yours. But stop and think who was there all three times.'

'For a start, you and I were. So was Steve. And there's no solid reason to believe that Fiona's accident was anything other than an accident. Well, there's reason to wonder, but there's no proof.'

'Of course there isn't. Holly, the point was to have it *be* an accident, which it was. It *was* a car accident. Except that it was no accident.'

'Gabrielle, I didn't know about your change of plans until yesterday morning. How could Vanessa have known that you were planning to drive to Maine last night? Unless you think that she always carries a supply of ... whatever caused Fiona's accident.'

'But she did know! She walked Ulla down Appleton Street while I was loading my car, and I told her.'

'OK. But Vanessa wasn't the only person present all three times. Besides us, I mean. What about the rest of her family? Tom. Hatch. And Avery, especially Avery, at least according to you. If Avery really does have some sort of ... unnatural affection for her brother, then she was the one with a motive to get rid of Fiona. And at dinner at our house and then again yesterday, she was hovering over the food.'

'So was Vanessa. But I'll concede that at the match, Avery was the one I saw with a camera.'

'I didn't see any of them with a camera.'

'You were judging. After Ulla passed her CGC test, Avery took her picture with Vanessa and the evaluator. But the camera could've belonged to someone else in the family. I don't know. Something I do know, though, is that that's a woman who doesn't want her children far from home.'

'What devoted parent does? Look at how happy all of us are that Leah's going to Tufts. We're elated! In a lot of ways, Steve and I are better parents to her than her parents are. All they're doing right now is blaming us because she's going to veterinary school instead of going to Oxford or Cambridge, the other one, so she'd end up as a professor of classics. They're more interested in what she could become than in who she is. And it's their loss. So, if Vanessa wants her children nearby?' In spite of my heated defense, I thought back to the morning when Vanessa had told me of Fiona's death. I clearly remembered that Vanessa had no sooner broken the news than she'd gone on to speak of re-arrangements in Hatch's plan to go to California. 'Tom,' I said. 'If you're looking for motives, he's the one who'd just love having a doctor in the house. And you'd better believe that Tom's endless griping about his ailments doesn't get him far with his own doctors, so it would be convenient for him to have his

248

grandson right there. Hatch couldn't just tell him that the only thing wrong with him was hypochondria.' We were on Sparks Street, almost at Brattle. My mind's eye had been on the people and the events we'd been discussing, but Gabrielle was in the here-and-now. 'Don't they look like a couple!' she exclaimed. 'Out walking the family dog.'

Catching sight of Tom, Elizabeth, and Persimmon, I hastily said to Gabrielle, 'Look, don't mention any of your ideas to Steve, OK? You know how straightforward he is.' He'd probably decide that Gabrielle was delusional.

'Oh, I don't think he'd say anything to her.' Waving merrily, she called out, 'Good morning!'

Tom and Elizabeth waved back as they approached us. Elizabeth was wearing a navy woolen top embroidered with folk-art designs, and Tom had on a heavy tweed sport coat. No wonder they both worried about their health! I was comfortable in my short-sleeved T-shirt. In wool, I'd have felt feverish. The warm clothes or the exercise had made their cheeks pink and their eyes bright. As Gabrielle had remarked, they did look like a couple, and an especially healthy one.

I greeted both of them, and Persimmon, too, and then Tom said to Gabrielle, 'I must have misunderstood. I thought you were on your way home.'

'Oh,' said my stepmother in that confiding tone of hers, 'I had a little change of plans.'

Patting her throat, she added, 'My thyroid acts up now and then.'

Tom and Elizabeth were, of course, as fascinated as if she'd just announced that she'd won a Nobel Prize. They all but congratulated her, and in response to their inquiries, she made little remarks about the trials of finding the ideal dose of medication. Happily, Tom, Elizabeth, and Persimmon then turned onto Sparks Street, while we continued down Brattle.

When they were out of earshot, I asked, 'What's this with your thyroid?'

'I was creating an opportunity,' she said proudly.

'For what?'

'For our opportunistic murderer to strike again.' After a second, she added, 'That sounds a little melodramatic, doesn't it.'

'Yes,' I said flatly. 'And I do have to admit that I'm skeptical.'

'Have you ever wondered what happened to Elizabeth's husband? What was his name?'

'Isaac. Isaac McNamara. And what happened to Isaac was that ... I think that all systems failed. He'd had some ordinary GI illness, some kind of stomach virus, but he recovered. Then all of a sudden, a few days later, he developed ... kidney failure, I think. His liver was involved, too. I'm not sure. I was concentrating on trying to help. Getting the house key, taking care of Persimmon, making sure that there was food in the house. And when Elizabeth called to say that Isaac was dead, I couldn't ask for details. I'm

250

not a ghoul, and it wasn't as if—'

'Of course not. And then there's Tom's wife.'

'Vanessa's mother? Gabrielle, you aren't accusing Vanessa of murdering her mother!'

'I'm not accusing anyone, Holly. All I'm doing is, uh, enumerating unexplained deaths.'

'They aren't unexplained. Well, Fiona's is, I suppose. But the others? We don't happen to know the explanations, but someone presumably does, and since most people die of natural causes, it's a fair bet that these people did, too.'

'Well, guesswork will get us nowhere. We'll have to find out.'

I almost never sense the age difference between my stepmother and me, but our thoughts about how to find out how these people had died revealed the generation gap: I'd have trusted the web to reveal everything, whereas Gabrielle's plan called for asking subtle questions during what I persisted in thinking of as the imaginary Sunday supper. When we reached the Longfellow House and turned around, she began outlining the menu, and by the time we got home, she was ready to issue invitations and shop for food. Gabrielle's scheme called for leaving her thyroid medication in plain sight in the kitchen, thus giving Vanessa, Tom, Avery, and Hatch the chance to tamper with it. Furthermore, Gabrielle and I were supposed to collect information on how Tom's late wife and Vanessa's late husband had died. While we were at it, we were also to make unobtrusive inquiries about the exact cause of Isaac McNamara's death. I remained so

251

doubtful about the enterprise that Gabrielle was forced to point out that her last plan, the consumer-satisfaction survey that she and Betty had cooked up, had succeeded, hadn't it? As Gabrielle phrased it, we'd tracked Eldon Flood to his lair. Although Flood Farm didn't seem to me to qualify as a lair, I had to admit that she was right. In the end, her faith in this Sunday-supper nonsense triumphed: I capitulated.

THIRTY

Because the plan hinged on the presence of Vanessa and her family, I naturally hoped that when I called to issue the invitation, she'd say that she, together with her father and her children, had a previous commitment. What she actually said was that they'd be delighted to come, but would I mind including Elizabeth? Not at all, I said. I'd intended to ask her, anyway. Coached by Gabrielle, I absolutely refused Vanessa's offer to contribute food. Because Gabrielle had some loopy notion that we'd be re-enacting the events that had preceded Fiona's death, she insisted on inviting Leah, who begged off once she heard that Hatch would be present. I didn't press her. Seven o'clock found eight of us gathered in the dining room. That business about a little Sunday supper had made me worry that Gabrielle would insist on hot dogs and beans with canned brown bread, but she'd decided that the perfect food to set a tone of relaxed informality was spaghetti, a big platter of which I was now dishing out. Because of Elizabeth's celiac disease, there were already rice noodles on her plate, and we'd bought gluten-free bread for her to have instead of the French bread that sat on a wooden cutting board. We'd made the sauce ourselves, so I knew that it was safe for her, and I'd checked its ingredients and those in the salad dressing with her to make sure that they were OK. At Steve's insistence, we were also serving sausages, hot for him, and a choice of hot or sweet for the rest of us, and since he considered supposedly hot sausages to be bland, he'd put a bottle of hot sauce on the table and offered to share it with anyone who was interested. No one but Hatch had taken him up on the offer.

Steve was at one end of the table, with Elizabeth on his right and Hatch on his left. At the opposite end, I had Avery on my left and Tom on my right. Vanessa sat between Avery and Elizabeth, Gabrielle between Hatch and Tom. Gabrielle, with a little input from Steve, had worried over the seating arrangement. Reasonably enough, Steve had asked us to avoid the topic of his hiring Avery, so Gabrielle had buffered him from both Avery and Vanessa. Since Gabrielle wisely trusted herself to draw Tom out on the details of fatal illnesses and death, she'd placed herself next to him. Steve, I

253

should mention, was not in on Gabrielle's true intentions; she'd respected my request to say nothing to him about her suspicions. Consequently, he'd expressed puzzlement about why we were having these people to dinner, but he'd accepted my statement, which was true enough, that the whole thing was Gabrielle's idea.

'Spaghetti?' I asked Tom.

'With a minimum of sauce,' he said, 'if you can manage it.'

'Of course. There's butter for the bread. You could have that if you want. Is cheese OK? Vanessa, could you pass the cheese to your father?'

'Sausage?' Steve offered. 'Hot or sweet.'

'None for me, thank you,' said Tom. 'I'm forced to follow a restrictive diet, I'm afraid. Not as limiting as Elizabeth's, of course. Wasn't it thoughtful of you to get rice noodles for her!'

'Very,' said Elizabeth. 'Holly, thank you.'

By then, I was beginning to feel more than a little irritated at Gabrielle and irked at myself for having given in to her. Marooned as I was between the depressed, dull Avery and her tedious grandfather, I was in no position to learn anything about fatalities, unless, of course, I found myself dying of boredom. What did Gabrielle expect me to do? Suddenly blurt out the questions she wanted answered? *So, Tom, what did your wife die of?* Even the ordinary obligation to make conversation with those on either side of me at the table felt challenging. I

254

could hardly ask Avery whether she'd seen Quinn Youngman after their dinner at Legal, could I? Tom would've been all too happy to blather on about infirmities, but I couldn't even think of an excuse to ask him about one. Desperate, I thanked Avery for helping with the refreshments at the armory.

'Everyone pitched in,' she said.

'But your mother always says that you're the real cook in the family.'

'Kind of.'

Reluctantly, because of the association with the dinner preceding Fiona's death, I said, 'My father just loved your cherry crisp. That was yours, wasn't it, Avery?'

'Yeah.'

'Do you share your recipe?'

'Yeah.'

In spite of my supposed expertise in using positive reinforcement to shape behavior, I wanted to grab her and give her a hard shake. If she didn't want to make conversation, why had she come to dinner at all? Briefly turning my attention to the rest of the table, I noticed that Steve, Elizabeth, Vanessa, and Hatch were engaged in a lively discussion of the Red Sox while Gabrielle and Tom were speaking to each other in low tones. It seemed to me that I could make myself useful only by leaving Gabrielle free to continue her effort to pump Tom. Consequently, I plodded on.

'Well, we'd love the recipe,' I said.

'Sure.' Then, to my surprise, she added, 'Men

like it.'

'It's a favorite of Hatch's, isn't it?'

'Yeah. And Isaac. He just loved it. I don't know what it is about it, but men really like it.' The wistful note in her voice suggested that the whole matter of pleasing men was a mystery to her.

'I didn't know that you cooked for Isaac.'

'Well, yeah, we used to take him stuff. Sometimes I make too much, more than we can eat, and he must've gotten hungry for stuff that Elizabeth can't have. There's flour in it.'

'In the cherry crisp.'

'Yeah.'

'It's a good thing that Elizabeth didn't eat it by mistake.'

'She knew. I always put labels on their stuff, like we did yesterday. And she's careful. She doesn't take chances. But if she did, if she made a mistake, she'd just get sick. Nothing really bad would happen.'

After that, the conversation became general. Steve repeated my thanks for everyone's efforts on the previous day. Elizabeth said how happy Isaac would have been. We served seconds, and Gabrielle reminded all of us to save room for dessert, which would be ice cream with a variety of toppings.

When dessert time came, I finally got to liberate myself from Avery. Although the idea was that each of us would carry our plates and silverware to the kitchen, where we'd then make our own sundaes, Avery insisted on doing more

256

than her share by carrying the serving dishes, too. Prepped by Gabrielle, I tried to see whether anyone was even looking at the little prescription bottle of thyroid medication that she'd left on the counter next to the sink, but with eight of us in and out of the kitchen, I simply couldn't tell, and I lost track of who was and wasn't alone there. The one little incident that caught my attention occurred when Avery offered to make Hatch's sundae for him. She said, 'I always know what Hatch likes, don't I?' On this occasion at least, what she served her brother was an innocent hot fudge on vanilla with whipped cream and walnuts, but when we returned to the table, she got there before Gabrielle, took a seat next to Hatch, and all but snuggled up to him.

Having been an investigative failure, or so I thought, the evening ended early. As I learned after our guests had left, Gabrielle had, however, managed to extract quite a lot of information from Tom. Because we'd agreed not to discuss her speculations in front of Steve, she waited until he was in the yard with the dogs before she passed along what she'd learned. As we cleaned up the kitchen, she said, 'Well, Tom and I had a little talk about widowhood. I told him that I was a widow when I met Buck, as I was, of course, and I asked him whether he'd been widowed for long. And he has. His wife died fifteen years ago.'

'Of what?'

'Cancer.'

'Well, you can't suspect anyone of causing that.'

'But Vanessa's husband is another matter. Jim, his name was. He died of a heart attack while she was alone in the house with him. It was a Sunday night. Hatch and Avery had been there for the weekend, and Hatch had left for Boston, and Avery had gone back to Bennington, and Tom was in his own little apartment in the house. By the time the ambulance got there, the husband was dead.'

'Gabrielle, I admit that there's a pattern of people dying or, in your case, feeling ill after they've eaten food that Vanessa or someone else in her family could've tampered with. But most of us eat three times a day, and we fairly often eat when there are other people around...' I paused. 'Not that I'm exactly eager to accept if Vanessa invites me to dinner.'

'We did leave some of the food unwatched tonight. The toppings for the ice cream. The strawberries, the chocolate sauce. Do you feel all right?'

'Yes, of course.'

'So do I.' A few seconds later, she said, 'Tom won't take pills, you know. Or capsules.'

'What does he do if needs a prescription?'

'He gets children's versions, or he uses a special pharmacy. He has things compounded. That's what it's called.'

'Anyone can buy over-the-counter liquid medication. And Steve dispenses liquid medication all the time. I don't like to use it, even for cats, because if an animal spits out some of it, I can't tell how much, so I don't know how much more to give. Besides, I have a knack for getting animals to like swallowing pills. And if I had trouble, I could always ask Steve to do it. But the point is that anyone can buy children's liquid medicine. Anyone! Gabrielle, look. There's no proof. There's no proof of anything at all.'

THIRTY-ONE

As I'd never have admitted to Gabrielle, her departure on Monday morning came as something of a relief. Because she and Molly were house guests as well as family members, we'd been making accommodations. I'd felt obliged to serve lunch instead of wolfing down my writer's substitute – a sandwich eaten while standing at the sink – and I'd had almost no time to write. Although our dogs did well with Molly, adding a sixth dog had inevitably meant short-changing the other five. Also, Steve and I had both felt guilty about concealing his forthcoming trip to Rangeley from Gabrielle, and we'd become increasingly apprehensive about accidentally letting his plans slip out. He was leaving on Friday, and with Gabrielle around, he'd been unable to assemble his fishing gear. Furthermore, he and I had both been worried that one of his buddies might carelessly leave a message on our machine that Gabrielle would overhear. To confess the full truth, I was looking forward to having the house to myself while Steve, India, and Lady were at Grant's Camps, by which I mean, of course, having the house all to my true self: the unity that consists of the malamutes and me, since it's impossible to determine where I end and they begin. It seemed to me that once Rowdy, Kimi, Sammy, and I were alone, I'd be able to ignore Gabrielle's ideas about the deaths that she'd insisted were unexplained. Unless my father received another nasty photo or message, I'd forget that episode, too.

Not that I intended to cultivate amnesia! I'd once taken a bad fall that had resulted in a brief experience of the real thing, and when it comes to amnesia, once is a lifetime's worth. But in the absence of evidence, there was nothing to be done except to take basic precautions. I'd made sure that Gabrielle's cell phone was charged, and she'd promised to call me every hour until she got home. I'd avoid consuming food prepared by any member of Vanessa's family, especially if I intended to drive. But I'd never been targeted, except by Eldon Flood, and Gabrielle was now far away. Maybe she hadn't actually been targeted, anyway, I told myself. For all I knew, she'd been suffering from the effects of overeating or exhaustion. It was almost impossible to believe that anyone would wish her harm. On the contrary, everyone loved her.

My mood of self-confident denial lasted

throughout Monday. As promised, Gabrielle called every hour, and she arrived home safely. I made ambitious to-do lists of tasks to accomplish in the next few weeks: I'd write articles, update my blog, screen applications for rescue dogs, finish painting the north side of the house, and hire someone to repair or replace the gutters and downspouts. Leah's exams would begin on Thursday, and I wanted to give her some kind of special treat to compensate her for all the effort she was putting in. Although Rita was beginning to recover from Quinn Youngman, she deserved more sympathy and distraction than I'd been offering her. We'd spend time together, I vowed. We'd go out to dinner. I'd rake, brush, and blow every last bit of loose coat off the malamutes, and when I was done, I'd vacuum the entire house and every inch of the interior of my car.

Then, on Tuesday morning, I got a call from some people named Snell who wanted to surrender their eight-month-old dog, Buster, to rescue because he was destroying their house. As usual, I asked where Buster had come from. Pet-shop puppies come from mass-breeding operations in the Midwest. The commercial producers in Missouri, Oklahoma, the Dakotas, and elsewhere take no responsibility for their dogs, and neither do the brokers who act as middlemen in transferring puppies from puppy mills to pet shops. Of equally little help are the scumbags who mass-produce puppies and sell them on the Internet. Also useless are what are known as 'backyard breeders', local ignoramuses who do

261

no genetic screening of the dogs they breed, who are unequipped to educate buyers about the breed, and who sell puppies to anyone willing to pay the asking price. But every once in a while, a call is about a dog from a breeder who will immediately take full responsibility. So, the question is always worth asking.

In this case, Buster turned out to have been bred by Pippy Neff, who, according to the Snells, had refused to take him back. Experienced rescue person that I was, I knew better than to take the Snells' word. The owner who says that the breeder won't take the dog back sometimes means: 'I called the breeder, got voice mail, and didn't leave a message', or 'The breeder won't take the dog back until tomorrow'. Consequently, my first step after hanging up was to call Pippy.

'I've had a call from some puppy buyers of yours,' I told her. 'The Snells. With Buster.'

'Oh, them! What'd they tell you?'

'That you won't take the dog back.' The thought crossed my mind that if Pippy had, in fact, refused responsibility, my call might be persuasive, especially if she was still harboring the hope of using Rowdy.

'Is that what they said? Well, what we agreed on when I talked to them was that they'd give it another week. That puppy is ten months old, and they're giving him free run of the house, and then they have the nerve to complain that he's chewing on shoes and ripping up pillows. What do they expect?'

'A stuffed animal?'

She laughed. 'Well, that's not what they've got. They're supposed to use a crate like I told them in the first place. But if they give it a week and it doesn't work out, back here he comes.'

'Fair enough.'

'You know, you can never tell for sure when you sell a puppy. People can seem fine, but who knows? And you never know what damned thing's going to happen out of the blue. Take that girl Olympia. How was I supposed to know she'd drop dead?'

'Who?'

'The girl I sold that puppy to. Ulla. The bitch that's with that friend of yours who was at the show with you. What's her name?'

'Vanessa. Vanessa Jones. What happened to Olympia?'

'Like I said, out of the blue, she's dead as a doornail! Healthy young girl. Single. Good job, stable life. And then, wham!'

'That's terrible. I knew she was dead, but I had no idea ... how did she die?'

'Car accident. She fell asleep at the wheel, or maybe she got blinded by the lights of the on-coming cars. This was at night. She was alone, so nobody knew for sure. She crashed into an overpass or something. Out of the blue! It wasn't like she had a heart condition. She wasn't sick. Matter of fact, she'd had dinner with that friend of yours, Vanessa, and she was fine. She didn't complain about feeling sick. And then, wham! She was gone.'

263

Pippy's revelation left me, for once, almost speechless, but I somehow managed to end the call before she had a chance even to mention Rowdy's name, never mind to pester me about using him. For a minute or two after hanging up, I sat motionless at the kitchen table. Kimi roused me, as she sometimes awakened me from sleep, by fixing her gaze on my face. Without getting to my feet, I reached out, put my hands on either side of her head, and lowered my own head so that we were at first face to face, and then eye to eye. At one with Kimi, I felt strengthened. Releasing her, I was suddenly aware of being chilled to the core, horribly cold, as if the temperature in my kitchen had dropped below zero. Thanks to Kimi, my common sense returned. I switched on the electric kettle, dropped a tea bag in a mug, and put on a heavy sweater. As I waited for the water to boil, I wrapped my arms first around Kimi and then around Rowdy, as if I needed their body heat to keep me from freezing to death.

When the tea was ready, I almost gulped it down, and as I began to warm up, my power of speech returned. 'Questions I should've asked Pippy,' I said to the dogs. 'When Olympia had dinner with Vanessa, was it at Vanessa's house? Olympia's? Or at a restaurant? Was anyone else there? Tom, Hatch, Avery? Not that Pippy necessarily knows. And not that I'm about to call her back. Or ask Vanessa. But I wonder. OK, so, Pippy says that Olympia was a *girl*, meaning that she was young, maybe close to the age of Vanessa's children. Vanessa told me that Ulla's first owner was a friend and neighbor, so presumably the rest of the family knew Olympia, too. Was she a friend of Avery's? Or maybe Hatch's? A girlfriend of his? Yes, I know that you don't know, either. But what we know for sure is that her death bears an uncanny resemblance to Fiona's.'

THIRTY-TWO

If dogs could talk, they'd be blabbermouths. For example, the second Steve got home from work Rowdy and Kimi would've gone running up to him to blurt out, 'Guess what? Gabrielle thinks that Vanessa's family is murdering people, and now Holly thinks so, too! Isn't that exciting!' Sammy would've happily shared Gabrielle's theories not only with Steve but with all the prime suspects. Not to be left out in the matter to total disclosure, India and Lady would've innocently informed Rita that Steve and I had never been able to abide Quinn Youngman. I could just hear them: 'They think you're well rid of him, you know. Isn't that interesting!' I cringe to imagine what any or all of the five, possibly in unison, would've revealed to Elizabeth McNamara. 'The bipeds keep saying that your husband was barely cold before you took up with Tom Oakley. Did you know that? Isn't that fascinating? Feed us! Rub our tummies!' And you can bet that if dogs could talk, they'd make phone calls. 'Hey, Buck, Steve is leaving on Friday for a fishing trip at Grant's Camps. How about if you show up there? Wouldn't that be fun!'

As it was, when Steve got home, Rowdy and Kimi did go running up to him, but they limited their speech to *woo-woo-woo*, and I didn't say a word about Gabrielle's theories or Pippy's revelation. At the time, I told myself that Steve, rationality personified, would cite statistics on fatalities attributable to car crashes, heart attacks, and liver and kidney failure. And if survivors benefitted? When people died, the living often did gain in one way or another. Heirs inherited money and property. Matters rearranged themselves in ways that were pleasant or convenient for survivors. Hadn't I ever heard of silver linings? In retrospect, I see, however, that my underlying reason for saying nothing to Steve was the fear that speaking my suspicions aloud to my intelligent, logical husband would give them a credibility that they now lacked. In other words, if the suspicions remained crazy ideas, they were easy to dismiss, but if they became reasonable hypotheses, I'd have to take them seriously. Worse, I'd feel the need to do something about them. And what could I do?

As I failed to realize at the time, the problem should have felt familiar to me and to any other dog trainer who has ever worried that a relatively unknown dog is likely to bite someone. You don't know the dog's history. You have no proof that he's ever bitten anyone. He isn't growling, snarling, lifting his lip, or baring his teeth. You can approach his food bowl. If you hold his collar, he makes no objection. But there's a look in his eye, there's a knot of fear in your stomach when you're in his presence, and you just don't trust him. Why? Because you love and trust dogs, and if this one scares you, your reaction is information about the dog. So, what do you do? Remain vigilant. Watch the dog. Trust your gut more than you trust him. And that's what I did, perhaps to the point of hyper-vigilance: during the small encounters I had with Vanessa's family throughout the week, I was nervy and jumpy.

The first occurred on Wednesday morning in Loaves and Fishes, where I ran into Tom, who was kneeling in an aisle of shelves packed with natural remedies. When he rose to his feet, I was puzzled by the extreme embarrassment of his expression until I saw that he'd been examining the bottles and packets in a section labeled Men's Health. Taking care to avoid staring at the contents of his shopping cart, I greeted him and rather reluctantly asked how he was.

For once, he merely said that he was doing well, but just when I thought that I'd escaped his usual harping on ailments, he said, 'Gabrielle told me that you'd once had a traumatic head injury!' He made it sound as if I'd neglected to mention that I'd once climbed Everest.

267

'Yes,' I said, 'but I'm fine now.'

'No after-effects? No special precautions?'

'Not really.' I laughed. 'I've been warned to avoid another head injury, but it isn't exactly the kind of thing I'd seek out, anyway.'

For a few seconds, his face was flat. 'Well, of course ... oh, yes! Very funny! No, it isn't something anyone would go looking for, is it? Still, it's sound advice for all of us.'

The second encounter took place that same afternoon when Avery unexpectedly appeared at my back door with a big wicker basket in her hands. She was dressed entirely in white – white jeans, white T-shirt, white sandals – as if she were costuming herself as chef, perhaps, or as a bride about to be married on a beach.

'Come in,' I said.

'I can't stay. I'm just dropping off food. As usual, I made too much, and I thought that you and Steve could use it.'

The combination of the basket and the phrase 'could use it' made me feel like an object of charity. Even so, I was gracious. 'Thank you.'

'It's home-made bread and a lamb stew.'

'Thank you,' I said again.

When she'd left, I threw everything out, of course, but felt foolish and wasteful.

The third little incident occurred on Thursday morning. The day was bright and dry, perfect for painting. Careful to keep the dogs indoors, I'd raised the high ladder on the north side of the house and had then gone out by way of the gate and into the cellar through the door near the driveway. When I returned to the yard, I was carrying a caulking gun, a can of paint, and brushes. Since my arms were full and the dogs were inside, I left the gate open. Ladder-safety fiend that I am, I rechecked the ladder to make sure that it was level and that the pitch was correct, not straight up and likely to make me fall over backward, and I needlessly re-examined the ropes to make sure that the ladder wouldn't slide down and take me with it. Caulking gun in hand, I climbed up and was beginning to caulk an area by one of Rita's windows when Hatch Jones hailed me from below. With him, on leash, was Ulla.

'Hi, Hatch,' I called.

To my dismay, he pulled the gate shut.

'Do me a favor,' I said. 'Keep Ulla on the leash! Steve keeps warning me not to have a dog loose when I'm up here on the ladder.'

Although I tried to keep the warning friendly, I must've sounded sharp, because Hatch said, 'Sorry. I was just passing by, and I saw you and thought we'd say hello.'

'I'm sorry if I snapped at you.' Again passing the responsibility to my husband, I added, 'Steve worries that a dog could zoom around and collide with the ladder and knock me off. And some dogs will climb ladders. That's a situation I'd rather not face.'

My effort to smooth things over apparently succeeded, and Hatch and Ulla left. Although there'd been no danger, I felt a sense of unease, as if I'd somehow left myself vulnerable. At the same time, I was a little ashamed of having overreacted. It wasn't as if Hatch had marched in and turned Ulla loose; she'd been on leash every second.

That same afternoon, Vanessa called to invite Sammy to play with Ulla. I couldn't think of a good excuse to refuse, and it seemed a pity to deny Sammy the chance to burn off energy and have fun with his buddy. When I got there, still in my ragged painting clothes, Vanessa let me in through the gate, and at the sight of Sammy, Ulla did a flirtatious little dance and led him on exactly the kind of wild chase he loved and needed.

'A match made in heaven,' Vanessa said. 'Tea?'

'No!' I blurted out. Recovering, I said, 'Thanks, but I'm already pumped full of caffeine.'

'Herbal tea? Juice?'

'No, thanks.'

'Well, I think I'll have something. You're sure...?'

'Yes, but go ahead.' I sat on one of the patio chairs.

Vanessa went inside and soon returned with a cup of tea. 'Would you like something to eat? Cookies? Or cake. Avery has been on a cooking binge. My father bought her some sort of bread machine and a couple of cookbooks. He spoils her rotten.'

'Oh, please thank Avery! I should've called. She brought us bread and a lamb stew.'

Taking a seat, Vanessa said, 'I'm glad some-one other than Ulla got to enjoy it. Avery left ours uncovered on the counter, and Ulla ate all of it. You can't trust her for a second. She is an incurable counter surfer. Avery should've known better. It was her fault. She knows what Ulla's like. Ulla will watch and watch for an opportunity. She'll wait endlessly for her chance, and then she'll strike!'

The statement made me uncomfortable, sum-marizing, as it did, the strategy that Vanessa or a member of her family had perhaps been using to get rid of unwanted people. 'My dogs are the same way,' I said. 'Sammy less than Rowdy and Kimi. Kimi is the worst. She's so smart, and she's lightning fast. The second you realize that you've left food unattended, it's already in her stomach.'

'Sammy is such a good boy,' Vanessa said. 'He's the perfect dog. He's wonderful with people, he's good with other dogs, and he's gorgeous.'

Inevitably, I was tempted to expand. *Gorge-ous? Vanessa, you don't know enough about this breed to begin to understand how beautiful Sammy is. His temperament? He's sweetness itself. And funny! He makes me laugh aloud ...* Then I came to my senses. According to the old Sippie Wallace song, 'Women Be Wise', as belt-ed out by the incomparable Bonnie Raitt, it's a mistake to advertise your man; and in the pre-sent, somewhat comparable, situation, my wise course of action was not to advertise my dog.

271

The song would've had me keep my mouth shut, but silence seemed an inadequate defense. 'Thank you,' I said. 'We think so. We co-own him. Steve and I do. And his breeder is crazy about him, too. If anything happens to us, Sammy goes back to her.'

Having thus eliminated a possible motive to kill off Sammy's present owners, I felt awkward and foolish about defending myself and Steve against a ridiculously improbable threat. When survivors benefit, it's almost always because they're just that, survivors, and not because they're murderers. Looking around, I was struck by the ordinariness and innocence of the scene. The spring day was bright. Vanessa's house and yard were attractive and safe. I was not wandering down some urban alley at midnight! Vanessa herself was a familiar Cambridge type and a person I knew. Dressed in ever-so-Canta-brigian beige jersey, she had her gray-streaked hair fastened at the nape of her neck. On her feet, for God's sake, were Birkenstock sandals! She loved Jane Austen. Her son was a doctor. She was wholesomeness itself. And if her father was an annoying hypochondriac who'd taken up with a neighborhood widow, and if her daughter was having an identity crisis, so what! As Buck's daughter, I of all people should know that some of us have difficult relatives. As to Vanessa's late husband and Ulla's first owner and poor Fiona, not to mention Isaac McNamara, people die! My own mother had. After her death, Buck and I had inherited everything she

272

owned, including her dogs, but we certainly hadn't killed her.

As if to reinforce my sense of the innocuousness of the situation, Sammy and Ulla came bounding up to me. Ulla was panting lightly.

'Tuckered out already?' I asked. 'Ulla, do your trick for me! Wave!'

Ulla promptly sat and raised her paw.

'Good girl!' I exclaimed. 'You really are a cutie.'

After the dogs had played a bit longer, I said that Sammy and I had to leave.

'See you at dog training?'

'Not tonight. For once, I'm playing hooky.'

'You? A truant? I'm shocked!'

'Steve's leaving on a fishing trip tomorrow. We're going out to dinner tonight. I need to get ready.'

'How long is he going for?'

'A week.'

'Well,' said Vanessa, 'you'll have to come and have dinner with us while he's gone.'

'Sure,' I said. 'Thank you. I'd like that.'

I almost meant it.

THIRTY-THREE

'I wish you were coming with me,' Steve said. Lady and India were already crated in his van, which was loaded with his fly rods, fishing tackle, rain gear, warm clothes, and enough bug dope to repel every black fly in the state of Maine, or so I hoped. Spring is black fly season.

'Fishing trips are a male-bonding ritual,' I said. 'My favorite one. What if you were going to one of those men's workshops to beat on drums and chant?'

'What?'

'Quinn Youngman went to one. Rita told me about it.'

'He should've gone fishing instead.'

'Exactly. You'll have fun. And you know that I hate being stuck in a canoe in the rain, and I hate black flies. It's a wonder that I survived my childhood without being bitten to death. I have scars.'

'I know you do. I've seen them.' He pulled me toward him and whispered in my ear, 'I saw them last night.'

'You'll have to wait a whole week to see them again. Hey, bring me home some trout! Better yet, catch a salmon. Have fun. I love you.'

'I love you, too, Holly.'

When he drove off, it was noon. As if to remind me of why I wasn't going with him, light rain was falling. My father, a dedicated fisherman, used to try to indoctrinate me by taking me out in a canoe at dawn and keeping me captive there all day with nothing to eat except a couple of squished chocolate bars and a flattened tuna sandwich. He always refused to pack anything to drink. His rationale was that since we were in God's Country, the beautiful state of Maine, all I had to do was dip a metal cup over the side of the canoe and partake of water that practically sprang from heaven itself. I could equally well have tilted my head up and held my mouth open. It always rained. If it wasn't raining when we left, rain soon started, and as if to prove that he lacked the sense to come in out of the rain, Buck always responded with enthusiastic booming about how lucky we were to have weather that made the fish bite, as it did not. Rather, it made the flies bite. My father devoted himself to issuing advice about how I could improve my casting. To boot, we never caught anything.

I love Cambridge. It has no black flies. My father lives far away.

After Steve drove off, I went into the warm, dry indoors and made a delicious ham sandwich and good coffee. Remembering those miserable fishing trips, I told the dogs, 'I am free! Never again! Never ever!' Then I worked on my column until quarter of five, when I fed the

275

dogs, gave them a few minutes in the yard to relieve themselves, took a shower, and got dressed to go out for dinner with Rita. Luxury! Restaurant meals two nights in a row! Steve and I had just had divine Arabic-influenced Mediterranean food at Oleana. I'd have been more than happy to go back there, but Rita had persuaded me to give another chance to a lesser Cambridge establishment for which she had an inexplicable fondness, a bistro with condescending waiters, mediocre cooking, and high prices. Cambridge being the unorthodox place that it is, you can wear anything anywhere, but since I work at home, I spend most my time in kennel clothes and enjoy the occasional opportunity to dress up. So, a few minutes before six, outfitted in a pale-rose linen suit that Rita had picked out, I was in front of the computer in my office, where I was checking my email and spending time with Tracker, when I thought I heard a car pull into the driveway. Rita's office was in easy walking distance, so she never drove there, even when she had on stiletto heels. Besides, I'd seen her car earlier, and I didn't expect her for another half hour. My best guess was that someone desperate for a parking place had ignored my threatening sign about not blocking the driveway.

After grabbing a raincoat, I ran to the back door, peered out, and saw Quinn Youngman, of all people, getting out of his car, pardon me, his Lexus, which he'd parked in back of Rita's BMW, pardon me, her car. He looked ghastly, as if he'd just learned of the death of someone he loved. His face was pale, and his eyes were red and swollen.

'Holly,' he said hoarsely. 'I have to talk to Rita. Is she home?'

I was less than cordial. 'No.' Then I took pity on him. Maybe someone actually *had* died. 'She'll be here in half an hour or so.'

As Rita had pointed out during their fight, Quinn typically affected serious-looking hiking boots for a stroll to Harvard Square. He wore them now. In other respects, he did not, however, look like himself. He had on a light-blue sweater and khakis, but the sweater was rumpled, and his hair was messy and tufted, as if he'd been running his hands through it. Standing there in the rain, he looked stricken and pitiful. Could he have been diagnosed with a terminal illness?

'Come in,' I said.

When we reached the kitchen, he surprised me by asking whether he could sit down.

'Of course,' I said. 'Has something terrible happened?'

'Yes,' he said. 'Well, no. Not terrible. Not terrible at all.'

In preparation for going out, I'd crated Sammy in another room, but Rowdy and Kimi were loose. Having met Quinn many times before, they offered him none of the greetings that they typically bestowed on promising strangers, which is to say, all newcomers whom they assessed as likely to offer treats, tummy rubs,

277

sweet talk, or admiring glances; nor did they perform the routines they'd perfected for welcoming beloved personages. Their favorite visitor was Kevin Dennehy, who not only fell all over them but slipped them sips of beer when he thought that I wasn't looking. Now, neither dog trained gorgeous brown eyes on Quinn, and neither dog issued peals of *woo-woo-woo*. Kimi didn't fall to the floor at Quinn's feet. Rowdy didn't bother to fetch his fleece dinosaur and drop it in Quinn's lap. In brief, instead of turning on the charm and radiating that irresistible you're-so-special message, Rowdy and Kimi evidently agreed that Quinn was no fun at all and acted accordingly. Rowdy went so far as to yawn ('This guy is boring, boring, boring!') before lying down. Kimi, however, monitored Quinn or perhaps studied him almost as if she were a curious social scientist engaged in observing the behavior of a subject in a psychological experiment.

I sat at the kitchen table across from Quinn and waited.

'I've been a total jerk,' he said. 'Could I bother you for a tissue?'

I supplied a whole box.

He blew his nose. 'I have a new therapist, and for the first time in my life, I'm doing deep work.' He repeated the phrase, 'Deep work. I've just come from a therapy hour, and I have to see Rita. I have been such a jerk.'

That's therapy? Realizing what a jerk you've been? Maybe sometimes it is.

'Rita should be home soon,' I said.

'I owe you an apology.' He paused. 'For making a scene.'

'Scenes don't bother me,' I said. 'And Willie's not my dog. But if you want to apologize to Rita, that's—'

'He didn't even break the skin,' Quinn confessed. 'What am I saying? He didn't—'

'He didn't bite you. He didn't actually bite you at all.'

'He didn't even nip me. Christ! I am such an asshole.'

'For what it's worth, Willie probably does think about using his teeth,' I said.

'I stepped on his foot,' Quinn admitted.

'On purpose?'

'By accident.'

I took a deep breath and said, 'But you didn't take Avery Jones to dinner by accident.'

'I should've been seeing her in my office.' He started to cry.

'She's a patient of yours?'

'No! No. She should be. But she isn't.'

'She was referred to you?'

'No! We took a cooking class together. It was a one-shot deal, Saturday afternoon, at the Cambridge Center for Adult Education. Yeast breads.'

And you rose to the occasion? I didn't say it. When I feel tense, I have a deplorable tendency to think in puns.

'We got paired up,' Quinn continued. 'Partners. The instructor put us together. And then after the class, we ended up going to Legal. It's right down the street.'

The Cambridge Center for Adult Education is in the Blacksmith House, as in Longfellow's poem. The spreading chestnut tree is no more, but the Blacksmith House is on Brattle Street, near the corner of Story Street, maybe a ten-minute walk from Legal Sea Foods, not far away, but not exactly right down the street, either.

'I know where the Blacksmith House is,' I said.

'She was looking for a therapist.'

'Avery asked you to recommend someone?'

He shook his head. 'That's what she was looking for in me. She's a troubled young woman. Father died recently, and she's dealing with a certain amount of guilt about that.'

'Guilt?'

'The parents fought all the time, and there's bound to be a sense of relief that the fights are over, so Avery's feeling guilty.'

'She looks depressed.'

'She is depressed. That's what I meant when I said that I should've been seeing her in my office.'

I heard the outer back door open.

'That's Rita,' I said. It occurred to me to offer Quinn a few quick bits of advice about valuing Rita's high tolerance for difficult creatures and remembering her many virtues as a therapist and a friend, but it's probably just as well that Rita rapped on my kitchen door before I'd uttered a word. As I let her in, I said, 'Quinn is here. He needs to talk to you.'

'I saw his car. You and I are having dinner.'

'Rita, come in. Quinn really needs to talk to you.'

Out of the corner of my eye, I saw that Quinn was standing up. 'Rita,' he said.

'Holly and I have plans,' she told him. 'We're having dinner.'

'Rita,' I said, 'for the moment, let's say that we are post-feminist or third-wave feminist or—'

'We're not.'

'We're human beings! The two of you need to talk more than you and I need to have dinner. If you want me to take Willie out, I'll be glad to.'

'Thanks. He should be OK. I was here between patients a couple of hours ago. But thanks.'

Rita and Quinn exchanged what I'm tempted to call a meaningful glance, but I had no idea what it meant. As he followed her, his face looked simultaneously old and young, lined and unguarded. Rita's whole body was rigid, her face expressionless. Hearing their footsteps sounding on the stairs to Rita's apartment, Kimi shook herself all over, and I, too, felt the impulse to shake myself off, as if the tension between Quinn and Rita were a sort of invisible powder that had deposited itself on me, where it didn't belong and where I didn't want it.

'All dressed up with nowhere to go,' I told Kimi. 'Except that for all I know, Rita will—'

The phone interrupted me. The caller was

Gabrielle, who had a habit of beginning conversations as if she were continuing them. 'Well, here I am all on my own. Your father took off with the boys.'

'He did? Gabrielle, it's always good to hear your voice. Buck is...?'

'He had an unexpected chance to go fishing, and off he's gone. Someone cancelled at the last minute, and Buck got a call this morning, and—'

The worst thing about my premonitions is that I don't believe in foreknowledge. Actually, in this case, the worst thing about my premonition was its accuracy. With a feeling of disbelief bordering on horrified nausea, I said, 'Grant's Camps.'

As if she herself had revealed Buck's destination, Gabrielle said, 'It's a whole group of them, and one person dropped out at the last minute, and your father jumped at the chance, so here I am, a fishing widow!'

Perhaps it was Quinn Youngman's example that inspired me, or maybe it was the scorn for spinelessness evident in Kimi's gaze. Or maybe I had no choice. For whatever reason, I told Gabrielle the truth.

She responded with apparent understanding. 'Well,' she said, 'of course Steve didn't mention the trip. He wouldn't have wanted your father to feel left out, would he?'

Although it was true that I always felt happy to hear Gabrielle's voice, I ended the call quickly and immediately dialed Steve's cell number.

We'd been warned that the cell phone service was a little iffy, but I managed to reach him. With no preamble, I blurted out the news and said, 'Steve, there's a lot of water there! Where he fishes, you don't. And it's not as if he'd decided to follow you. He's been there before, it's a Maine institution, and he's crazy about it, and he unexpectedly got this chance to go, and I am so sorry.'

Silence followed.

I said, 'Rita would tell you that you are entitled to express your feelings.' I waited and then realized that by saying nothing, Steve *was* expressing his feelings. 'I take it that you haven't run into him yet,' I said. 'I'm not sure what time he left, so I don't know when he'll get there, but at least you're forewarned. Steve, could you at least say something? Swear? Holler?' It occurred to me that Steve wasn't the one given to hollering. 'If you haven't heard him yet, he probably hasn't arrived.'

At last, Steve broke his silence. Rita'd have been pleased to hear how forcefully and color-fully he expressed his feelings. Having done so, he apologized and said that we don't get to choose our parents.

'We don't get to choose where they go, either,' I pointed out. 'Or where they don't go. But damn it! Your fishing trip! Steve, you work so hard! You deserve a vacation!' I should've known better. A fishing trip is not a vacation; it is a pilgrimage.

Sounding freakishly – and unintentionally –

like my father, he growled, 'This isn't a vacation. It's a fishing trip.'

'I understand the distinction. I really do.'

I couldn't tell whether he'd heard me or not.
We began to lose the connection and then lost it
altogether. Symbolic, huh?

When the phone rang a minute later, I thought
that Steve must be calling back on a landline,
but the caller was Rita. Willie was asking to go
out. Was my offer still open? It was.

'I've cancelled our reservation,' Rita said.
'We'll reschedule. But that leaves you with no
dinner. Do you—'

'I have tons of food. Don't worry about it. I'll
be up for Willie in five minutes. Unless he's
frantic?'

He wasn't. Consequently, I took the time to
change out of my good clothes and into jeans, a
T-shirt, and a raincoat before going up to Rita's
apartment. When she opened the door, I could
see that she and Quinn had both been crying. He
stood behind her with a hand resting on her
shoulder. Interestingly, he was in his stocking
feet. His controversial hiking boots lay on the
floor near the door. Willie was on his best behavior, either because he was responding to the
emotional atmosphere, which was almost
visible and palpable, or because he saw me as
his welcome means to the outdoors.

'Just a quick trip out,' Rita said. 'Thank you.'

For all of Willie's high spirits, he was capable
of great seriousness. As he and I trotted down
the stairs, he wore an expression of the utmost

gravity, and he moved in a purposeful, determined manner. Although I'm supposed to know a bit about dogs, I couldn't interpret his mood. As someone who truly does know a bit about dogs, I'll venture a guess, however, that in the heart and mind of the dog, the perception of a beloved person's strong emotions may not differ all that radically from the sense of an urgent bodily need and the simultaneous wish to control that need before reaching the proper place to satisfy it. In other words, if I understand anything about dogs, what I grasp is their oneness with themselves, a canine unity that we human beings are doomed to lack.

THIRTY-FOUR

Walking Willie around the block did nothing to enhance my power to fathom the mysteries of his species, nor did Willie enlighten me about himself as an individual except to prove that he had, in fact, needed to go out. Accustomed to Rita's high-heeled pace, he moved his short legs much more slowly than my own dogs moved their long ones, but he kept his leash loose, didn't keep stopping to sniff or mark everything, and showed no sign of objecting to the rain. Also, he was such a handsome fellow that he was a pleasure to watch. We took Concord Avenue to Walden Street, followed Vassal Lane to Huron, and turned onto our block of Appleton Street. As we were heading down Appleton toward home, Vanessa hailed me.

'That's a funny-looking malamute you've got there,' she called.

'Very.' Although I kept moving, she caught up with me, and I came to a halt.

'Steve got off OK?'

'Yes. He's there. At Grant's Camps. I talked to him.' My father's unexpected presence there was none of her business, I decided.

'Any chance that you're free for dinner? I'm on my own. Hatch is at the hospital, and Avery's out, and Tom's with Elizabeth. I've got a chicken in the oven.'

'Thanks, but I've already eaten.' In case she issued an invitation to have dessert or watch a movie, I said, 'I'm in a mood for dog walking. I'm going to trade in this funny-looking malamute for the real thing and get some exercise.'

I'd lied about having eaten, but as soon as I said that I felt like walking dogs, I realized that it was true. Perhaps because of the chicken in the oven, Vanessa did not invite herself along.

Eager to get my own dogs and get going, I hurriedly returned Willie to the still-tearful Rita, ate a quick sandwich, and forced my water-hating Rowdy to endure a brief trip out to the muddy yard. As if expressing his sentiments about the rain, he limited himself to lifting his leg on the high ladder, which lay on the ground

286

next to foundation. My usual rule about where my dogs are allowed to relieve themselves is that man-made objects are verboten. I make an exception in the case of fire hydrants, which by tradition belong to dogs. Tonight, I decided to forget the rule. The ladder was preferable to the picnic table, and in any case, the rain would wash everything off. As I put on my rain gear and snapped on Sammy's and Kimi's leashes, I moved as quickly as possible, mainly because I didn't want to deal with phone calls. Or people! Even Steve. If he called, I'd feel obliged to answer, and I had no desire to listen to him complain about Buck and less desire to hear a report of how Buck had responded to the discovery that Steve was at Grant's Camps. I deliberately left my cell phone at home.

It must have been about quarter of eight when Sammy, Kimi, and I set off. The sky was still somewhat light, and the rain was a mere drizzle. A tremendous advantage of having big dogs is that if you have a powerful, furry brute at your side, there are no bad neighborhoods; you can safely choose any route you please. If the big dogs happen to be malamutes, however, the same takes-your-breath-away appearance that deters would-be assailants also attracts friendly admirers, so unless I'm in a mood to linger and to answer questions, I avoid crowds. If the dogs chose our destinations, we'd never go anywhere except Harvard Square, where students homesick for their own dogs fall all over mine; where the dogs have to be prevented from gobbling up heaven-knows-what dropped in the streets and on the sidewalks; and where in spite of million-dollar educations, the ill-informed brightest and best persist in telling me, 'Beautiful huskies!' So, I headed down Concord Avenue toward the square, but when we reached Garden Street and then the Cambridge Common, we turned left and ended up wandering through Harvard Law School and along Oxford Street and Kirkland Street as far as Divinity Avenue, where, because of the e.e. cummings poem, 'she being Brand', I always enjoy turning the corner. After that, we went back to the Cambridge Common, cut across, and took Appian Way past the Ed. School to Brattle, where we turned right. By then, it was dark, and the drizzle had become hard rain. My hands were cold, my jeans were wet between the tops of my boots and the bottom of my raincoat, and in spite of their water-repellent guard coats, the dogs were drenched. Consequently, we picked up our pace, sped along Brattle, turned onto Sparks Street, ran to Huron, and almost sprinted along Huron to Appleton.

As we turned onto Appleton, I slowed way down, in part because I suddenly realized that I'd stupidly picked a route that would take us past Vanessa's house and in part because I found myself dreading our return. Yes, home would be dry and cozy, but there'd probably be messages or calls from Steve and maybe from Buck. Worse, Rita might be alone and in great distress about a failure to reconcile with Quinn, who wasn't the man I'd have chosen for her – Max was – but who was her choice. Preoccupied though I was with imagining what I'd say to Steve, Buck, and Rita, I nonetheless avoided Vanessa's side of the street. By now, I told myself, her chicken was out of the oven, and she dining on it while reading Jane Austen or watching Emma Thompson in *Sense and Sensibility*. With her big fenced yard, she had no need to walk Ulla on this increasingly nasty night.

The thought had barely crossed my mind when Vanessa came dashing across the street almost as if she'd been waiting for me. Sammy, who was always happy to see almost anyone, shook himself all over, thus sending the water retained by his coat flying all over Kimi, Vanessa, and me. It was then that I realized that Vanessa might, in fact, have been waiting for me: she wore a long, dark waterproof poncho and Wellies.

'I've just talked to Pippy Neff,' she said with no preamble. 'I called her about getting Ulla's papers, and she told me about your inquiries.'

'About Buster?'

'Who?'

'Buster. The puppy she sold to some people named Snell. They called me, and I called Pippy. She told me that the Snells were going to give it another week and that if things still weren't working, she'd take Buster back. Did she tell you otherwise?' Knowing Pippy as I did, I considered it entirely possible that in her conversation with me, she'd totally misrepresented what she'd said to the Snells. In any case, it seemed likely that Pippy had offered Buster to Vanessa if the Snells decided not to keep him. The arrangement sounded reasonable. Vanessa already had one malamute of Pippy's breeding, and Pippy might well have asked whether Vanessa wanted the young male. Reflecting on my experience with Pippy, I asked, 'Does Pippy want to sell him to you? How much does she want for him?'

'I have no idea what you're talking about.'

'I called Pippy because she's Buster's breeder. The Snells said that she'd refused to take him back, and they wanted rescue to take him. That's why I called her. I asked her about the Snells and Buster.'

'You asked her about Olympia. About Ulla's first owner. On top of your sudden refusal to eat with me? And your jumpiness. Holly, I am so sorry. I thought we were friends.' She paused. 'All I am is an opportunist, you know. Really, I'm just what you are – half malamute.'

After an artificial little laugh, I said, 'Of course we're friends.' I couldn't tell whether my false assurance had fooled Vanessa, but it hadn't fooled my brilliant Kimi, who was now standing at my left side, her head tilted slightly upward, her body pressing against my knee and thigh so firmly that I felt the tension in her muscles. 'Look, could we discuss this some other time?' My tone was light. 'There's been some misunderstanding, but right now, the dogs and I are soaked. I need to get home and get us dried off.'

'Oh, you *are* going home. You are going to walk quietly home. But not into the house. Into the yard.'

I played dumb. 'It isn't exactly a great evening for sitting out in the yard, but you're welcome to come back and have a drink.'

'That's not quite what I have in mind. Walk!'

'Vanessa, I have no idea what's up, but—'

'What's *up*, as you phrase it, is that I have a revolver in my pocket, and it is pointed at *you*. Now, walk!'

'There's been some misunderstanding,' I said again. But I obeyed. Dog obedience training, I should mention, has a paradoxical effect on the trainers: we are the least blindly obedient people I know. We're thoughtful, clever, and manipulative, always seeking new perspectives and fresh approaches. But that's when we don't have guns pointed at us. I started moving. Did Vanessa actually have a revolver? If so, would she fire it right here on this peaceful block of Appleton Street? As I walked, Kimi leaned into me. In obedience, the fault of heeling much too close to the handler is called 'crowding'. But Kimi wasn't crowding; at the moment, it would've been impossible for her to get too close for my comfort. And if Kimi took Vanessa's threat seriously, so did I.

When we reached my driveway, I saw Rita's car and mine, but Quinn's car was no longer there. In the futile hope that Kevin had decided to visit his mother, I scanned the driveway next to ours, but only Mrs Dennehy's car was parked in it and not Kevin's. Had Quinn left without Rita? Or was she at home? I couldn't tell. There were lights in the third-floor windows, but Rita paid her own electric bills and was sometimes careless about wasting energy. I wished that before setting out, I'd been profligate. Frugal and energy-conscious, I had turned on the light over the back door and had left all of the other outside lights off. My cell phone was, of course, inside the house, where I'd deliberately decided to leave it.

I automatically headed for the back steps, but Vanessa stopped me. 'Open the gate,' she said.

'It's locked.'

'You have the key,' she said. 'Use it.'

It seemed pointless to stall for time by lying. I'd lost track of the time, but it had to be at least nine o'clock, maybe later, too late for Kevin to pop in on his mother. I fished in my pocket, found the key ring, unlocked the gate, returned the keys to my pocket, and led the dogs in. Vanessa followed. What in God's name was she going to do? She couldn't intend to shoot me! Not here, anyway, not in my own yard in our thickly settled neighborhood. Yes, cars and trucks occasionally backfired on Concord Avenue. Even so, the sound of a gunshot would attract immediate attention. By now, it was all too obvious that she did, in fact, have a revolver, and there was enough light for me to see that she really was pointing it at me. Or trying, anyway. She held it awkwardly in one hand, as if her lessons in firearms had consisted of watching old movies.

'Pull the gate closed,' she said. 'Don't lock it.'

I complied.

'Take the leashes off the dogs.'

I obeyed. Since she'd given no orders about what to do with the leather leads, I clung to them; they were as close to a potential means of self-defense as I had. Sammy, innocence personified, sniffed around and then ambled to the steps to the house. Kimi remained where she'd been, glued to my left side.

'The ladder,' Vanessa said. 'Those gutters and downspouts need work, don't they? It's just like you to climb up and play do-it-yourselfer in heavy rain.'

'No, it is not like me. I am fanatical about ladder safety.'

'Good. Put the ladder up. Make it go as high as it can. All the way.'

As I dragged the ladder away from the foundation, raised it, positioned it, and used the ropes to extend it, I pondered its potential as a weapon. But what could I do with it? It was big and unwieldy. I'd have been much better off with a two-by-four.

'Hurry up,' she said.

'With all this mud, I'd never use a high ladder. It could slip.'

Vanessa laughed. 'Yes, it could, couldn't it? Up you go!'

'At a minimum, I'd use shims.'

'Up!'

I took my first step upward. The combination

of the rubber soles of my Wellies and the wet aluminum rungs made for slippery, treacherous footing. Reluctantly, I let the leather leads drop to the ground. Although my hands were freezing, I gripped the ladder firmly. Remembering to keep my knees and shoulders relaxed, I slowly ascended another four or fives rungs. My balance felt good, and the ladder seemed less precarious than I'd expected. Glancing down, I saw Kimi standing where she'd been, at the foot of the ladder. Was there no way for her to help me? She was so accomplished and so intelligent! Was there nothing in her great repertoire that could be put to use? She could heel like an angel, clear broad jumps and high jumps, zip through tunnels, retrieve dumb-bells and gloves, drop on command, and make her way neatly and speedily up, over, and down the obstacles in the sport aptly known as agility. As to her brains, I thought of how she'd play-bowed to Sammy to get him to vacate the prime spot at my side. It was some consolation to realize that Kimi was too bright to climb the ladder after me.

'Get going!' Vanessa ordered.

I complied. Focusing on every little move, I made my way upward until I was just above the second-floor windows.

'Move!' Vanessa said impatiently.

It may have been the nervousness in her voice that made me look down. It was certainly Vanessa's nerves that made her raise the arm that held the revolver. With her hand outstretched above her head, she pointed the revolver

294

more or less at me, as if she were pointing a finger, but she couldn't possibly have aimed, fired, and hit her target. No one who knew anything about firearms would've done such a stupid thing. In fact, it seemed to me that she might even discharge the weapon by mistake.

Kimi leaped. The fastest of our dogs at stealing food, she was speed itself as she soared upward and hurled herself against Vanessa's upraised arm, catching her completely off guard. The revolver flew from Vanessa's hand. And fired.

Kimi yelped. And fell to the ground.

THIRTY-FIVE

Except for a fragmentary recollection of slipping and regaining my balance, I barely remember descending the ladder, but I know that the second my boots touched the ground, I brushed past Sammy, hurled myself at Vanessa, and delivered a body slam that knocked her off her feet. Even at the time, when I was out of my mind with fury and fear, her response struck me as peculiar and inexplicable. I knew every inch of that yard and knew that she'd landed on muddy earth and definitely not on some hard object. Nonetheless, she began to scream in

295

what sounded like excruciating pain, and instead of rising, she remained curled up on her side.

I felt no sympathy. Cursing the softness of the rubber boots, I was about to kick her hard in the head when I spotted the revolver, snatched it up, and shouted, 'I am going to kill you! My dogs are my life, and I am going to kill you!'

Vanessa's screams turned to moans.

From where she lay in the mud, Kimi, my fearless, brave Kimi, made a soft whimper. It is probably what saved Vanessa's life.

'Help!' I shouted. 'Help!' And again, in desperation, 'Help!'

'I didn't mean to!' Vanessa pleaded. 'I didn't mean to! It was supposed to be an accident. And I'm hurt! Something is broken!' Squirming toward my wounded Kimi, she reached out a hand.

'Don't you touch her! Get away from her!' I ordered. 'Help!' I screamed again. 'Someone help me!' Softly, I said, 'Kimi, I'm here. Kimi? Kimi, I'm right here, and I'm not going away. Kimi, stay with me! Stay with me!' Frightened beyond reason, I somehow knew that I faced a choice between saving Kimi and venting my rage on Vanessa. 'Kimi, stay with me! Don't leave! Sammy?'

My heart almost broke as I watched our overgrown puppy bend his great head down over his beloved Kimi, who had always bossed him around, manipulated him, mothered him, and adored him, and who now lay at his feet bleeding to death. Kimi had to come first! All that

296

mattered was running for my cell phone and for blankets and towels for Kimi, anything to keep her stable until help arrived.

As it suddenly did. The gate to the driveway burst open, and in marched a heavily shrouded figure with tremendous amounts of long, streaming white hair. Overwhelmed with fear for Kimi and with rage at Vanessa, I had the fleeting and entirely mad thought that our improbable savior was none other than Gandalf the Grey, miraculously sprung from the pages of Tolkien. In one hand, however, the startling personage bore an exceptionally long flashlight with a powerful beam, a device that was clearly of this earth rather than of Middle Earth and, moreover, one that I recognized as belonging to Kevin Dennehy.

'What's all this about?' asked his mother, who, I now realized, was wearing a long waterproof coat of Kevin's over her own floor-length nightgown.

'Mrs Dennehy! Kimi has been shot. Get an ambulance! Get help!'

'I've called,' she said without bothering to specify whom. 'I know a gunshot when I hear one. "Thou shalt not kill!" Holly, put that terrible thing down, and take care of your dog.'

She trained the light on Kimi, and for the first time, I saw the nature of Kimi's injury: she had taken a bullet in her thigh. Worse, I saw the copious flow of blood. Oblivious to almost everything except Kimi, I nonetheless called to Sammy, who followed me up the steps to the side door, where, with frozen hands, I fumbled with the keys, found the right one, and let us in. Rowdy, who was loose in the house, came dashing to me, but I hollered, 'Rowdy, move! Sammy, crate!' In no time, I had Sammy crated in the kitchen and Rowdy crated upstairs in our bedroom. Frantic, I ripped the king-size down comforter off our bed, flew to the bathroom, seized as many towels as I could carry, and ran back downstairs. In the kitchen, I snatched up my purse, tossed my cell phone into it, and took a second to turn on all of the many outside lights that Steve had installed. Steve! Dear God, if only he were here! He would know exactly what to do. Calmly and capably, he'd ... how would he stop the bleeding? I felt desperate and helpless. I had to get Kimi to ... I suddenly knew that Steve would get Kimi to Boston's legendary Angell Animal Medical Center. And I'd get her there, too. Plans flashed through my mind: use the down comforter as a stretcher, lift Kimi onto it, drag her to my car, and...

I couldn't have been in the house for more than two minutes, but I opened the door to the yard to discover a small crowd: Rita, Kevin Dennehy, four uniformed officers, and two EMTs who were ministering to Vanessa. Kneeling in the mud at Kimi's side was the heretofore none-too-dog-friendly Quinn Youngman, who spotted me and said, 'Let's get her to my car. Tell me where to drive. Rita, get my keys out of my pocket and start the car. Holly, give me those towels.'

Kevin Dennehy intervened. In the bright light, I was stunned to see tears in his eyes. 'I got a second emergency medical vehicle on the way.'

'They won't take a dog,' I said. 'Quinn—'

'This one will,' Kevin said. 'Angell?'

'Yes. Kevin, call them! Call Angell! Tell them I'm Steve's wife.'

Having grown up in Cambridge and having served on the police force his entire adult life, Kevin had a proprietary attitude toward the city: he viewed all of Cambridge as his personal responsibility and saw all of the city's resources as his to commandeer. As far as I could tell, he got away with his tsarist assumptions mainly because he was on a first-name basis with half the population and was good at making people happy to do him personal favors. As it turned out, the second pair of EMTs might've helped anyway, since one of them was a guy named Hal Gurevich whom I knew slightly because he bred and showed Siberian huskies and did some recreational mushing. For whatever reason – compassion? – it took almost no time for Hal, his partner, and Quinn Youngman to get Kimi on a proper stretcher and into one of those gigantic medical vans. Quinn, who was pressing a towel to her wound, stayed with her. I had the impression that he considered her to be his patient and that it never occurred to him to leave her side. Anyway, we were no sooner in the gigantic vehicle than it took off with its siren wailing.

'South Huntington Avenue,' I said.

'I know,' Hal told me. 'Angell.'

Then I turned all of my attention to Kimi. Weirdly, although everything I had done had been directed toward saving her, I had the sense of having neglected her, probably because I hadn't been right next to her. Now that I was, I rested one hand on her neck and used the other to stroke her face, and as I traced the bar down her nose, the cap on her head, and the goggles around her eyes, I looked into the dark depths of those eyes and whispered, 'I'm right here, Kimi. I'm right here with you, and you need to stay here, too.' She was hideously, terrifyingly still, so motionless, so completely unlike herself, that I could almost feel her spirit leaving and had the sickening sense that I was studying her face with my eyes and fingertips as a way to commit it forever to memory. As if I'd forget her! 'Kimi, I'm here,' I repeated. 'And so are you. We're in this together. Stay with me, good girl. Good, good girl.'

During the trip, I lost all sense of time. It seemed to take an eternity to get to Angell, but when we arrived, I felt as if we'd left home only minutes earlier. Once we pulled in, however, the action was non-stop. Kimi was immediately in the hands of the people known as Angell's angels, and I was saying, 'A gunshot wound. She has lost a lot of blood. Do you have enough? I have two big, healthy dogs at home, and I can get them here. Holly Winter. This is Kimi. She's in your computer. My husband is Steve Delaney.' Then I shamelessly dropped the names of veterinarian friends of Steve's who

300

worked at Angell, and everyone was incredibly kind and kept saying, 'Yes, we know,' and then all of a sudden, Kimi had been whisked away, and I was sitting on a bench in the big, beautiful waiting room with Quinn Youngman at my side. And without Kimi.

I fell completely to pieces. My sobs were violent and loud, and tears flowed down my face as if they were drops of Kimi's blood. Quinn said nothing, but he removed my raincoat, wrapped his arms around me, patted my back, and kept supplying tissues from a box that someone had given him, and the sight of all those tissues made everything worse than ever, proving as they did that this was a place where animals died and where people like me were expected to collapse in grief.

Eventually, I said, 'I have to call Leah. She'll want to come here, but she can't. She needs to look after my animals at home.'

As I was fishing in my purse for my cell phone and as Quinn was offering me his, Kevin Dennehy showed up. His bulk seemed to diminish the size of the big waiting area. 'Hey,' he said. 'How's my girl?' He meant Kimi, of course. 'Holding her own?'

'I don't know,' I said. 'She's in surgery. Kevin, she's lost so much blood! I thought that gunshot wounds were puncture wounds, but she's lost so much blood! The bullet must have hit a—'

Quinn interrupted me. 'We don't know. We don't know anything yet.'

Kevin added, 'Hey, keep the faith, Holly. You

301

know what you always say? In dogs we trust. Kimi's strong. And look at me. I got shot, and I'm OK. And if no one's been out here yet, she's gotta have a chance.'

Kevin took off his windbreaker and made me put it on. Only then did I realize that I was shaking with cold. Once all three of us were seated on a bench, with Kevin on one side of me and Quinn on the other, Kevin asked gently, 'You think you could tell me what happened?'

'Vanessa Jones tried to kill me,' I said. 'She had a revolver, not that she knew how to use it, but ... she wanted to make it look as if I'd tried to fix a gutter or a downspout and fallen off the ladder. No! I just ... she wanted to blame the dogs! She wanted to make it look as if the dogs had knocked me off the ladder. Kevin, she stages accidents. You remember Isaac McNamara? Down the street.'

Kevin nodded. 'My mother told me he died.'

'And her son's fiancée. And her dog's first owner. Maybe her husband. But ... I was so careful not eat or drink anything that she offered me! Or that anyone in her family did. Kevin, I can't ... I just can't ... not with Kimi...'

'It can wait,' he said.

'Your mother,' I said. 'If your mother hadn't ... and Quinn. Quinn, you did your ... I know that you tried to stop the bleeding. I haven't said thank you.' I was crying again. 'Vanessa,' I managed to say. 'Did she...?'

'She's got a broken hip,' Kevin said. 'She wasn't going anywhere on her own.'

302

I sighed heavily and wiped my nose. 'There's no proof of anything, you know. If there had been, I'd have told you, but there wasn't. There isn't. Except for the revolver. That's not mine. And for all I know, her father and her—'

Kevin and Quinn simultaneously put their arms around me. Feeling the tension in their bodies, I looked up to see that a startlingly beautiful young woman in blue scrubs was heading toward us. She was not smiling. More than anything else, I wanted to get up and run away, to get outside and run as fast as I could. I wanted to do anything to avoid hearing what she'd come to tell me. Rising to my feet, I found that running was out of the question. My legs were shaking, my heart was beating so hard and so fast that I could barely stand, and raw memories flooded me, vivid recollections of the deaths of all the dogs I'd ever loved. The hardest losses had been the sudden and unexpected ones, the ones that had hit me as grotesque mistakes and had made me want to scream, 'No, that's impossible! She was fine! No time ago, she was fine! Just yesterday, she—'

'Holly?' the woman asked.

I nodded.

'That's a strong dog you have,' she said. 'She's out of surgery. It'll take a while for the anesthesia to wear off, but she's looking good. She's just beautiful. She's—'

Out of nowhere, or so it seemed, Leah flew into the waiting room. Her masses of red curls were wild and wet, and her face was dead white.

303

'Kimi is out of surgery,' I said. 'She is—'

'She's alive?'

The surgeon replied for me. 'Oh, yes, Kimi is very much alive.'

THIRTY-SIX

Steve awoke me the next afternoon by letting Rowdy and Sammy bound into the room and jump onto the bed. 'It's three o'clock,' he said. 'I thought...'

'Kimi?'

'She's fine. Leah's there now.'

I smacked my lips at the dogs and got my face licked. Leah taught them that stupid kiss-kiss trick. They don't think it's stupid. They're crazy about it.

The air smelled of burning meat. 'My father is cooking,' I said.

Instead of complaining about Buck, Steve said, 'He wants to help.'

'Then let him go back to Grant's Camps.'

'Do you want to say that to him?'

'No, of course not. Let's hope that he'll make the decision on his own.'

'Dogs, off!' I said. 'I need coffee. And a shower. Off!'

I'd stayed at Angell until Steve arrived. In her

304

typical high-handed fashion, Leah had called Steve, who, remarkably, had alerted Buck. Even more remarkably, the two had driven to Boston together, accompanied, of course, by India and Lady and by Buck's golden retriever, Mandy. Once Steve had spoken with Angell and had been reassured about Kimi, he should've returned to Grant's Camps, but he'd wanted to be with me, as had my father. I still don't know everything the two of them talked about during the trip. What I do know is that my father regaled Steve with stories of cute things I'd said and done as a child. I will never live down having referred to the ocean as 'big bath'. If I'd been as bright a child as Buck claims, I'd have had the brains to keep my mouth shut.

My family rallies round in a crisis. Perhaps too much so. After my shower, I went down to the kitchen in search of coffee to discover that Gabrielle and Molly were there and that Steve had gone to Angell. Buck was hovering over the stove stirring what smelled like canned dog food. Seated on the floor next to my father was Sammy, who had a long stream of drool dripping from his mouth.

'Her children have turned against her!' Gabrielle announced. She sat at the kitchen table with Molly in her lap. Responding to Gabrielle's melodramatic tone, the little dog was all eyes.

'Vanessa's?' I asked as I put on the electric kettle.

'Hatch,' said Gabrielle in the low, confiding tone of hers, 'had always wondered about his father's death, but it was Avery who knew that her mother was thoroughly infatuated with your father!'

Buck issued an inarticulate bellow.

'And once the children compared notes,' Gabrielle continued, 'it all came out. Avery knew that her mother was determined to keep Hatch near Boston, so she wondered about poor Fiona, and all along, Hatch had been wondering about his father's death. What he thinks is that Vanessa just sat around and let his father die before she called an ambulance. And once Hatch said that to Avery, she said that she'd wondered, too, because the parents did *not* get along. And then Avery and Hatch saw the *convenience* of having Isaac out of the way. From their mother's point of view, it would've been ideal, having her father right next door but not actually living with her. And they perfectly well understood that their mother had wanted Ulla all along and couldn't get her hands on Ulla with the owner still alive.'

'How on earth do you know all of this?' I asked.

'Avery and I had a little chat.'

Buck said, 'People talk to Gabrielle. They tell her things.'

'I know,' I said, 'but how did you happen to have this little chat?'

'Kevin asked me to keep an eye on her.'

'You've talked to Kevin, too?' I made myself a cup of coffee, added milk and sugar, and took a swallow in the hope that caffeine would help me to make sense of Gabrielle's disjointed account.

'Yes,' said Buck, who was adding something to his concoction that made it stink worse than ever. Cat food?

'Kevin,' said Gabrielle, 'was there at the hospital when the children turned against their mother, and he didn't like the idea of Avery at home by herself.'

'Hatch could stay with her, couldn't he? And what about Tom?' It occurred to me that imbibing caffeine was insufficient; I needed an IV infusion. 'Gabrielle, would you like some coffee?'

She rejected the offer and said rather impatiently, 'Hatch was *with* Tom. He probably still is.'

'Well, where's Tom?'

'In the hospital.'

'With what?'

'A massive heart attack. He heard the sirens, and he went out to see what was going on, and he had a massive heart attack. He was a ... what do you call it? He was an unwitting accomplice.'

'Last night?'

'No. Before. With all his liquid medicines.'

'OK!' I felt pleased to have grasped a point. 'His supposed inability to take pills. Flavored syrups! Maybe cough syrup. Poor Fiona! Whatever it was must have been in the cherry crisp. A lot of those liquid antihistamines come in cherry flavor. Antihistamines really knock some people out. And some dogs.'

Because I wasn't sure that Gabrielle had told Buck about her own episode, I refrained from saying that she'd probably been dosed with the same thing, but when she caught my eye and nodded, I knew that she'd made the connection.

'And Isaac,' I continued. 'It would've been so easy to feed one thing to him and another to Elizabeth, because of her celiac disease. If something contained gluten, Elizabeth wouldn't eat it.' I remembered Avery telling me that Isaac had loved her cherry crisp. Since it contained flour, Vanessa could have spiked it with anything and been sure that Elizabeth wouldn't touch it. 'Acetaminophen, maybe. There are liquid versions of that. Large doses can cause liver and kidney damage. Steve won't even let me keep it in the house. It's very toxic to cats, and he doesn't want it given to dogs – or to us, either.'

'You do understand what her plan was, don't you, Holly?' Gabrielle asked the question and promptly answered it. 'Really, what she was up to was matchmaking. She wanted Elizabeth for Tom, of course, and Buck for herself – that's why she sent him that awful picture of me – and Leah for Hatch, and Steve for Avery, and—'

'Sammy for Ulla,' I finished. 'OK, something just fell into place. With me out of the way and Avery matched up with Steve, Sammy would be part of her family. I get it. She was an evil Emma.'

'Emma!' my father exclaimed. 'Now there

308

was a lovely bitch.' Emma was one of my mother's favorite golden retrievers.

'Not *our* Emma,' I said. 'Jane Austen's Emma. The novel is about matchmaking gone awry. But not this awry. I'm surprised that she didn't think that Steve was too old for Avery.'

'He had compensating virtues,' Gabrielle said. 'Notably, Sammy.'

'Steve,' I said. 'I need to call him.'

When I reached him on his cell, Quinn Youngman had just left Angell.

'He's decided that he wants to get a malamute,' Steve said.

'That's a terrible idea. He's never even owned a dog, has he?' Getting a malamute as your first dog is like taking your first flying lesson in a 747.

'He fell for Kimi.'

'Quinn really did save her life. I'd have known to apply pressure to the wound, but I'm not sure that I'd have done it right. And he was very kind to me. In fact, he was wonderful. He couldn't have been better. But that still doesn't mean that he should get a malamute. Well, maybe an old, mellow one.'

'He's also decided that he wants to marry Rita.'

'A much better idea. But he can't do both – get a malamute and marry Rita. She refuses to feed malamutes. You know that.'

'Max Crocker has a malamute,' Steve pointed out.

'Yes, but Mukluk is exceptional. He's easy.

309

And I hadn't quite worked out the Willie and Mukluk part of my plan. Or the cat part.'

'Or the Max and Rita part.'

'That does seem to be the hitch,' I conceded. Switching topics, I asked, 'So, when can Kimi come home?'

'Tomorrow, it looks like.'

'Tomorrow? Oh, Steve!'

'She's going to have to take it easy.'

'Is she putting any weight on that leg?'

'Not yet. But she will.'

When I'd hung up and reported the good news about Kimi, Buck said, 'Tough cookie.'

'Yes, she is. She's a heroine. She really is.'

'Kevin told us,' Gabrielle said. 'We are very proud of her. And of you, too.'

Buck grunted.

'I broke Vanessa's hip. That's what Kevin said, but I don't understand how it happened. I threw myself at her and knocked her down, but I'm not all that big. And I also don't understand what she was doing with a handgun. I could hardly believe my eyes. She never struck me as someone who'd even think about owning any kind of gun. But I obviously didn't know her at all.'

'The revolver belonged to her late husband, and her hip broke because she has osteoporosis,' Gabrielle said. 'Hatch knew, but no one else did because she didn't want her father to find out.'

'I can understand why. But she looks so fit.'

'She takes whatever that medicine is, and she walks. That's what she was advised to do.'

'A silent disease,' Buck said ominously.

'Very clever,' said Gabrielle. 'Exactly. That's exactly what that woman was. A silent disease.'

'I wanted to kill her,' I said.

'You're a tough cookie, too,' said my father. He dipped a spoon into the reeking mess, tasted it, and gave a sigh of delight. 'You ready to go?'

'Where?'

'To visit Kimi! What's the matter with you? You didn't think I was cooking for us, did you?'

THIRTY-SEVEN

So, it's mid June, and I'm out in the yard with Kimi and with Rowdy, who can be trusted not to slam into her. She's out of her E-collar, so she no longer has to listen to Kevin tease her about wearing a lampshade on her head, and although she still favors the wounded leg, Steve says that she'll end up without a limp. The hair may never grow back completely, but a heroine can't be faulted for a battle scar, can she? Speaking of scars, the yard bears no trace of the events that took place here, and now that the gutters and downspouts have been replaced and the north side of the house has been painted, I am perfectly comfortable here. I did not do the work myself. It may be a while before I climb a high ladder again. Also, the yard looks different from the way it did that rainy, muddy night. We've had it paved in stone that the dogs can't dig through. Or haven't managed to dig through yet, anyway.

Rita is engaged to Quinn Youngman. As it turned out, Max Crocker did call her. He was, however, asking for an appointment rather than a date. Rita respects patient confidentiality. It was Max who told me that he'd gone into therapy with her. He said that he needed to resolve his feelings about his break-up with his former partner, whose name was also Max. Oh, well, so Rita was right. She often is. Anyway, she and Quinn are thinking about buying Vanessa's house, which is vacant right now. Tom is in rehab, and when he gets out, he is moving to an assisted-living facility. Disillusioned with him and his whole family, Elizabeth McNamara has replaced him with a darling male puli puppy, who will be the perfect companion for Persimmon. Elizabeth holds the entire family responsible for Isaac's death. Her take on the Jones family is that every member has a propensity for betrayal. Maybe she's right. As Gabrielle kept emphasizing, Avery and Hatch turned on their mother. According to Kevin, it was Vanessa's sense that her children had ganged up against her that prompted her full confession. Avery has moved in with Hatch. More than that, I don't know. Rita has her theories, of course. I also don't know what the shocking proposition was that Hatch made to Leah. I do know, however, that neither Avery

312

nor Hatch showed any loyalty to Ulla, who, being a dog, betrayed no one. Pippy Neff grudgingly agreed to take Ulla back, but I told Pippy that I had the perfect home waiting, as I did. Ulla is doing beautifully with Max's Maine coon cat and with Mukluk and Max, too. The only surprise about Ulla was that Vanessa had lied to me: Ulla had actually not been spayed. Hence Vanessa's extreme interest in Sammy? Speaking of Ulla and Vanessa, Avery told me that her mother was furious that I'd given Ulla third place instead of first at the match. Honestly!

Surprises. This one is utterly weird. One day last week, Lucinda and Eldon Flood showed up here with four pies, two apple and two blueberry. The Flood Farm logo on their van had been painted over. In its place was a painting of a couple of sheep and Jesus holding a shepherd's crook. Eldon had found religion and had resolved to atone for the wrongs he had done. Hence the pies. Could Buck have knocked some sense into him? I hope so.

Leah has joined what her Harvard commencement ceremonies described as the 'company of educated men and women'. By implication, the rest of us don't work for the company, but I don't mind. By virtue of having attended a lot of classes with Leah, Kimi is at least an honorary employee, and after all, Vanessa Jones was an alumna, and where did it get her? She couldn't even handle a revolver, and she raised children who turned against her. It seems to me that

Avery and Hatch's disloyalty demonstrates why some people have dogs instead of children and, in some cases, instead of spouses or even human friends. If I murdered a hundred people, my dogs would put their paws on a Bible and swear to my innocence. So would the human members of my family, all of whom are half canine. And the better for it.